KINDRED

XANDER'S STORY

ROBBI RENEE

LOVE NOTES
BY ROBBI RENEE

SYNOPSIS

Kindred spirits are said to be individuals with the same beliefs, attitudes, and feelings. Similar souls who mutually experience an instant heart connection of love, peace, and understanding. But when that connection is threatened, can kindred souls fall deeply, dangerously in love?

Xander ~ warrior, protector, the defender of people. But the awkward, gangly teenager Xander Kindred contradicts the valor and strength of the Greek name. He covets a simple life away from the hustle and madness of the inner-city streets. The oldest of the Kindred boys, Xander denies his family's murderous legacy until an innocent walk home from school quickly transforms Xander from a boy to a man. Forcing Xander to protect his family and territory at all cost - even if it means sacrificing his kindred soul mate, the love of his life.

DEDICATION

My Life's Trinity ~ Grace. Grind. Gratitude.

*This book is dedicated to my first hero, protector, and the original Robby -
my daddy.
Thank you for simply being you. A man of few words, but your love,
support and encouragement is heartfelt with every beaming smile and
unique laugh.
I love you, Daddy.*

#alwaysyoursugarlump

Note from the Publisher: This is a work of fiction. Any resemblance to actual persons living or dead or references to locations, persons, events, or locations is purely coincidental. The characters, circumstances and events are imaginative and not intended to reflect real events.

LOVE NOTES
BY ROBBI RENEE

PROLOGUE

"Daij, why are you still sitting out here? Is Ms. Mimi or your Uncle Bean picking you up?" Fifteen year old Xander, with his severely lanky and tall frame dressed in khaki pants and a white polo shirt with the Penn-White Academy High School logo, asked his friend and neighbor Daijah. He darted towards her as she perched on the stoop in front of her school, Penn-White Middle School. Daijah was a few weeks into her eighth grade school year. Aggressively wiping tears staining her face, she shifted her body to conceal the tears before he could get any closer. Daijah and Xander lived on the same block in the Pleasant Pines community on the southside of St. Louis.

"Leave me alone, big head. I'm waiting for my momma to pick me up." Daijah whispered.

Daijah's green and blue plaid uniform stained with the Tahitian Treat drink she sipped for the past two hours, while frustratingly swinging her brown penny loafers. It was after 5 o'clock and her mother Daivaughna was supposed to pick her up from school at 3:30. It was no surprise that she was late but Daijah really hoped for the best this time.

"Vaughn ain't coming Daij. She's probably at Castlerock." Xander shook his head. "Come on. I'll walk with you."

"Xan, we gotta cross Franklin Street to get home. My grandma don't want me on Franklin by myself...ever." Daijah stressed.

"So, what you gonna do, Daij? Wait here? You don't wanna be in front of Penn-White either when it gets dark. And besides, you're not by yourself. I got you."

Daijah peered around her school building, noticing the empty parking lot and darkened buildings. After dark, the middle school building was a ghost town since the surrounding areas were occupied by vacant lots and abandoned dwellings.

"Are you sure I shouldn't wait a few minutes longer?" Daijah debated.

"Daij...you and me both know that she's not coming." Xander sympathetically uttered. "Let's go. I'm hungry." Xander nudged with his shoulder, encouraging Daijah to start walking. He'd observed his friend sadly waiting on her mother one too many times since they were little kids. Deep down Daijah knew he was right...Vaughn wasn't coming.

"I got you, babydoll."

"Don't call me that, big head." She gave him a deep eye roll only perfected by teenage girls. Daijah had a crush on Xander and despised when he called her babydoll. She wanted him to see her as more than just the little girl from down the street.

Pleasant Pines was a low-income community with generations of struggling families. Cannon Street was one of the few streets in Pleasant that was not overcome by abandoned buildings, addicts, and drug dealers. The families on Cannon worked mostly blue-collar jobs, collected social security, or some type of government assistance. The street was always filled with kids playing, running through the fire hydrant water and riding bikes. The elders of the neighborhood looked out for everybody. It was the kind of hood where the neighbor could beat your ass for something, then your momma would beat your ass again when she got home from work. Daijah's grandmother,

Geneva Marie Duvall, or Ms. Mimi as she was affectionately known, was exactly that neighbor.

Fourteen year old Daijah lived with her grandmother in a two family flat at 1420 Cannon Street. Her great uncle, Renaldo, nicknamed Bean, lived upstairs. Mimi and Bean grew up in the housing projects near Pleasant Pines and moved on Cannon Street almost 30 years ago. Daijah's thirty year old mother, Daivaughna Duvall or 'Vaughn', gave birth to Daijah just days after her sixteenth birthday. The same age as Mimi when she had Daivaughna. The generational curse ran deep in the Duvall family. Most of the women became mothers before they were able to legally drive.

Daijah's father, Jabari Blue, lived in a different neighborhood but rode the same school bus as Vaughn to Whitley High School in the suburbs as a part of the desegregation program. Jabari was over six feet as a freshman and quickly became a basketball star by his senior year. He was two years ahead of Vaughn so by the time he was headed to the University of Memphis on an athletic scholarship, Daijah Blu Duvall was born. Jabari and Vaughn thought they were in love. But the challenges of the distance, coupled with impoverished conditions, troubled the relationship.

He and his family supported the best they could but they were struggling financially too. Jabari had dreams of a career in the NBA, promising to marry Vaughn and take care of their family. Three injury plagued college seasons destroyed his hoop dreams. Jabari played overseas, vowing to continue to support Vaughn and Daijah, but that was a lie. A few weeks, then months, then ultimately years depleted with minimal contact or financial support from him. Vaughn was helplessly in love and believed in her heart that he would return to get her and Daijah. Three years after his departure, Jabari married a woman he met in Europe and remained there with his wife and two children. During occasional trips to the states, he would visit her, but Daijah hadn't seen or heard from her father since she was six years old.

After the devastating break-up, Vaughn found solace in sex,

prescription drugs, and alcohol. Temporarily soothing her pain but increasing the disdain for her daughter. Vaughn began dating the biggest drug dealer in south city, Malcolm Kindred. He already had three sons by his late wife when Vaughn became pregnant with his youngest child. Malcolm was known around the hood as Mack because the man was humongous like a big ass mack truck. Towering at 6'6" and easily 300 pounds with the most beautiful coal black curly hair that he wore slicked back into a ponytail at his nape. Mesmerizing umber eyes and olive skin made him simply beautiful in Vaughn and plenty of other women's eyes.

Mack was raising all four of his sons that were birthed from two different mothers. His deceased wife and Vaughn. Daijah's friend, Xander, was the oldest of the Kindred boys. Then Simeon and Hiram, all less than two years apart. Their mother died giving birth to a baby girl that perished days later. Xander was just six years old. A year later, Vaughn gave birth to Daijah's little brother, Adonis Kindred. Mack gained full custody before Adonis turned a year old because of Vaughn's drug addiction. She had already lost custody of Daijah to Ms. Mimi years ago.

Thankfully the Kindred family lived only five houses down from Daijah on Cannon Street so she was able to build a relationship with her little brother. She and the Kindred boys were inseparable. Although Adonis was her only blood brother of the Kindred crew, the rest of the boys were like her little brothers too. Except for Xander. He was her crush and best friend.

"You always seem to forget that you are not my brother, Xander. You don't have to protect me all the time." Daijah snatched her book bag, slinging it across one shoulder as they began walking the four blocks to their homes on Cannon Street.

"My pops said I'm the oldest and it's my responsibility to look after my brothers and you."

"But I'm not your sister. I'm not a Kindred." She rolled her eyes.

Sometimes jealousy reared its ugly head when she saw how her little brother lived compared to her. Mack stayed in the hood but he had money - straight up bank. Adonis had new Jordan's before he could even walk and the other brothers stayed in the flyest gear.

"Ah, Daij, you lose. You stepped on a crack." Xander cackled, pointing to her foot invading the cracked pavement.

"What?" Daijah rolled her eyes, breaking from her hopeless reverie. She was irritated and confused by Xander's ranting.

"Remember when we were kids? Step on a crack, break yo momma's back." He narrowed his eyes in confusion and mouthed, 'duh.'

"Well let me step on all the cracks then." Daijah laughed, jumping on each crack as they innocently meandered down the sidewalk.

The disappointment and hurt experienced at the hands of her mother were the only constant in their relationship. Vaughn was supposed to be getting clean and promised that she would pick up her daughter and have dinner together at Ms. Mimi's house. Daijah and Vaughn were more like sisters than mother and daughter, including the bickering, fights, and jealousy. Daijah had just celebrated her fourteenth birthday and physically, she possessed the body of a grown woman. Vaughn despised that her teenage daughter filled out her clothes better than she did, gaining unwanted attention from grown men.

Daijah was beautiful. The splitting image of Jabari to Vaughn's dismay. Tall, athletic frame with smooth brown sugar skin, and dark chocolate curly hair that fell just below her shoulders. Girls in the neighborhood teased her, calling her Ashley Banks from the *Fresh Prince of Bel Air* because she favored the young star actress Tatiana Ali. Naturally arched thick brows, smoky quartz almond shaped orbs that sparkled like crystal when she smiled, displaying a deep right dimple and gleaming smile.

They teased and played aimlessly until Xander noticed a group of young guys walking in the street coming towards them. They were absentmindedly vandalizing abandoned cars as they strolled down the street wreaking havoc. Xander instinctively moved Daijah away from the curb to the opposite side of the sidewalk in the middle of an extremely aggressive jump on a crack in the pavement. She was secretly hoping that her actions would bring significant harm to her mother.

"Walk faster Daijah." Xander urged her.

His teenage voice was laced with hints of pubescent bass. He firmly gripped her elbow nudging her further down the street.

"Don't look at them, just keep walking." Xander demanded. She nodded.

He recognized the guys from the worst block in the hood, Franklin Street. They were in their twenties and caused all types of shit in the hood. They'd recently had some beef with some of the guys that worked for his father.

"What's up Daijah? When you gone show me what's under that uniform? Can't nothing hide all that ass on you." One of the men taunted.

"Damn, you cannot be in middle school. Somebody is lying. Let me check some ID. With all that pretty ass hair, pretty girl." Another one lustfully grinned, grabbing the crotch of his dusty denim shorts.

Daijah didn't recognize these two men from the normal taunters she would encounter. She thoroughly examined the features of their faces. The third dude she recognized as Mishawn Carr who lived on Franklin Street. His little brother, Marshawn, was in Xander's class. Mishawn was downright scary. Shit, the entire Carr family were demonous humans - robbing, abusing, vandalizing throughout the neighborhood. Mishawn's dark, lifeless eyes surveyed Daijah from her green ponytail holder all the way down to the shiny penny in her shoes.

"Just leave her alone, dawg." Xander's voice cracked but he wasn't going to back down. He could hear his father's voice echoing in his head. *Don't back down to no man. He bleeds red just like you do.* Mack was raising his sons to be survivors.

"What you say lil nigga?" The taller man with the Beastie Boy t-shirt and khaki shorts moved closer to them.

"I - I said leave her alone. Just let us go home."

Daijah was pulling Xander as she glanced around praying that someone was witnessing this unfold. The street was eerily placid. No movement. No motion. No escape. Unfortunately, they were walking past the old, abandoned car wash and other dilapidated buildings. Just a block away from Cannon Street once they crossed the concrete barricade that blocked off the street.

"Oh, this nigga got some heart, huh?" Mishawn devilishly laughed.

"Come on y'all. You know that's Mack's lil nigga." The short darker boy with blonde tipped hair said. Usually, being the son of Malcolm 'Mack' Kindred provided a high level of security for his sons. Not this time.

"I don't give a fuck. Ain't nobody scared of Mack's big ass." Mishawn shouted.

"Yo, Daijah. Are you as good as your moms? Huh? You know Vaughn will do anything for a hit. You got it like your mom, baby-girl?" He tormented her, pulling Daijah's ponytail and toyed with the pleats of her uniform skirt.

While Daijah was fairly quiet, she was a fighter and wore a fiery attitude when pressed.

"Stop!" She screamed while the other men grabbed Xander, locking his arms behind him.

"What are y'all brother and sister...boyfriend, girlfriend? Is Mack yo daddy too, Daijah?" They sniggered.

"No!" Xander and Daijah shouted. "Just leave us alone." They continued to tussle and the men continued to taunt and instigate.

"Answer me, Daijah. You gone do me like your moms?" Mishawn snarled, his murky eyes now unnervingly expressionless.

Daijah momentarily was able to withdraw from his stern hold and swung her book bag before kicking him in the balls with the tip of her shiny penny loafer.

"Fuck you, Mishawn. Your trifling ass is always fucking with somebody." She shouted.

"Daijah, go! Run!" Xander demanded, tousling until he was able to break loose. He and Daijah fled but their escape wasn't fast enough. One of the men caught up to Daijah, aggressively clutching her in his arms. Xander felt her hand slip from his grasp as he peered to the side watching her drift further away. He paused his escape, never once did he consider leaving Daijah. His cease allowed the second guy to punch him in the face, causing Xander to fall to the ground. He quickly retreated, wildly swinging at the dude, landing a gut punch.

"This lil muthafucka is strong." The men's eyes bloomed in surprise.

Xander was screaming Daijah's name as she struggled with Mishawn. Her thrashing limbs flailed until her body disappeared into the darkness of the deserted building.

"Daij! Daijah! Let her go. Take me. Please let her go. Daijah!" Xander shouted until a final punch to his chest silenced him.

When he awakened, he clutched his ribs, sighing in pain. Lip busted and eyes swollen, Xander could taste the saltiness of his tears commingling with his blood. He leered around the blackened room, gasping at the sight of the glistening moon. Xander had no clue what time it was or how long he'd been passed out. Dirt, dust, peeling paint, animal feces among other things filled the gloomy hollow space. The horrific smell was overwhelming. He recognized the room as the back office of Terry's, the old car wash that closed about three years ago.

Xander tried to move but the pain and bound hands prevented any maneuvering. While he'd already shed tears, Xander understood that crying was not an option. *Are you a man? Well men don't cry. We get the job done.* He pondered his father's words, immediately considering his friend.

"Daij. Daijah." Xander coughed from the stench, wincing in excruciating pain.

"Daijah, can you hear me?" His voice echoed in the distance and then he heard movement.

"This lil nigga don't back down I see." Mishawn's frame parted the dusk like a thief in the night.

He gathered his loose pants, belt buckle scraping the floor. Mishawn kneeled down to Xander's level. "I respect your heart, lil man. You need to come run with me and my crew. We have beat your ass to a pulp and you still standing." He punched Xander in the chest, but he held his head high with one single tear like Denzel Washington in *Glory*, refusing to be defeated. Daijah's screams echoed from the black cloud across the room.

"You want a piece of her, lil nigga? I know you like her. Yo ass probably wouldn't know what to do with the pussy." Mishawn licked his lips.

Xander vigorously shook his head no. "Please. Just let Daijah go home. Please." He hopelessly, internally cried.

"Xan! Help me!" Daijah weakly screamed through her wails. He couldn't see her but he heard the strain and fear etched in her voice.

"Bring her pretty ass over here." Mishawn instructed, untying the robe from Xander's wrists.

The other two men appeared from the darkness, sweating and disheveled with their pants unzipped. They all had scratches and bite marks on their faces and arms. Daijah put up a valiant fight. The boy with the Tommy Hilfiger shirt pulled her by the ankles across the dingy floor.

Daijah's beautiful face was barely recognizable. Her wrists were bloody and bruised. Plaid school uniform ripped, white bra hanging from her right arm, Wonder Woman panties stretched between her ankles. She laid lifeless in white babydoll socks and one penny loafer. Her bloodshot eyes were unable to produce anymore tears.

"Xander." Daijah whimpered. Her poor body was exhausted.

"Oh, y'all see this shit. She calling for her lil boyfriend. Come on lil nigga. Come get yo girl." Mishawn taunted as the other men laughed.

He positioned Xander's battered body next to Daijah. Their glossy, painfully reddened orbs connected as they cried muted, dry, torturous tears. Xander used every ounce of energy he had left in his motionless, violated frame to slide his hand to meet hers. They locked fingers before everything faded to black.

The blazing sun aggressively beamed through the small window. It was morning. Daijah and Xander's mutilated blood stained clothes could not conceal their severely damaged and blemished bodies. They laid unconscious while their innocence was on display. Subtle movement in the hazy background roused Xander but his body was immobile. He heard noises, saw glimpses of flashing red and blue lights. Xander desperately wanted to scream; prepared to fight if his offenders were returning to finish the job. He figured they had left them for dead. For a moment, he wished he was dead rather than endure any more abuse. Images slowly emerged from the smoky haze.

"Come on. They're over here. Hurry up." Xander recognized the voice of Teddy. He was a homeless man that did odd jobs for people around the neighborhood. "It's the two missing kids, X and Daijah. They're back here. I think the girl is dead."

"Daijah!" Xander's thunderous bellow reverberated throughout the abandoned building before his world turned pitch-black...again.

1

TEN YEARS LATER

Te screeching sound of sirens stirred Xander from his unconscious state.

"Daijah? Where is she? Daij! Can you hear me?" He glanced around seeing only medical equipment and tubes in his blurred vision.

"Son, please calm down. We have to get you to the hospital. What is your name, son?" A low-pitched male voice whispered against Xander's ear as he began to lose consciousness again.

His heavy eyelids slowly fluttered, bloodshot pupils making it difficult to gain clarity. Glimpses of chocolate curls, a ripped plaid skirt, and blood-stained white shirt flashed before him. He extended his hand to her but she drifted further and further into the abyss.

"Xan." She croaked.

"Daijah. It's me. I'm here." Xander painfully lamented.

"Xander. Help me." The distressed cadence of her tone barely at a whisper.

Chaos ensued. Nurses and doctors crowded her battered and comatose body as the heartbeat monitor sound slowed to a sloth's pace.

"Daijah!" Xander jolted. Ragged, straining breaths awakened him from the torturous horror he'd suffered almost nightly since waking up in the hospital ten years ago. Rising from the dampened bed, his shirtless muscled chest was drenched in sweat. Xander sat at the edge of his king size mattress in the master bedroom of his new home. The illumination of the digital clock read 3:07am. He audibly sighed, peering around the empty room feeling an overwhelming sense of loneliness.

At twenty-five years old, Xander Kindred was a far cry from the gangly teenager of the past. Several inches taller and over a hundred pounds heavier, his milk chocolate Herculean frame stood at six feet four inches and 240 pounds of muscle and mass. Familial coal black silky hair was faded on the sides with thick curly coils on top. All of the Kindred boys had glistening umber eyes framed by tightly curled lashes. Xander was the darkest of his brothers with skin smooth like polished steel. The cutest baby face that once highlighted his innocence was no more. Xander's features were constructed to perfection. Bowed lips, chiseled chin, and narrowed eyes bearing the weight of childhood hurt and torment. He was painfully beautiful.

After the incident ten years ago, Xander became obsessed with building physical strength. He vowed to never allow another man to overpower him - to beat him. While neither his father nor Ms. Mimi ever placed blame, Xander carried an insurmountable level of guilt. Everyday he wished he could have traded places with Daijah. The mere thought of her transported unsettled commotion throughout his flesh.

Daijah was his best friend, his babydoll. He adored her for as long as he could remember. Xander vividly recalled the nights he'd sneak to Daijah's house at only ten or eleven years old, aimlessly navigating down the alley, through the back gate, two windows from the kitchen to her bedroom. Xander endured sleeplessness when the people who worked for his father would gather at their home devising a revenge plan on another crew that guaranteed blood shed. He was young but keenly aware that he wanted no parts of that lifestyle. Tapping against Daijah's window, she would sleepily unlock and crank it open for him to climb in. She always asked before returning to her bed, "we good, Xan?" and he'd lazily respond before settling at the foot of the bed, "we good, Daij." Those simple words were their friendship creed.

Xander crept across his oversized bedroom, navigating unpacked boxes before standing in front of the sliding doors. He stepped onto the balcony overlooking the lake behind his home. The humidity immediately snatched his breath away. It was going to be a scorching day in August if the current conditions were any indication. Xander rubbed a hand down his face staring into the darkness, trying to visualize her. With every nightmare, the curves of her gorgeous face vanished more and more.

The brilliance of the moon shimmered against the placid manmade lake. It was eerily still, no visibility into the other expensive homes that flanked the miniature stretch of water.

Xander was building his own wealth on the back of the empire his father produced. Drug money being the foundation of their wealth, but additional investments like real estate, night clubs, and stake in other legal businesses, creating generational wealth that Mack Kindred bestowed on his sons. Xander was Mack's right hand, overseeing the operations and investments arm of their fortune.

His latest endeavor was not for investment purposes this time. The new construction, five bedroom, five and a half bath house in the gated community was strictly for him. Fully loaded with a three car garage, media room, man cave, and personal gym. Xander desired a dwelling to call his own - a quiet place removed from his daily hustle and grind. It was outside of the city, not far from his father's mini-mansion but about a thirty minute drive from his childhood house on Cannon Street. After moving from the city almost five years ago, Mack maintained the Cannon property as one of several drug distribution sites in the city. As the Kindred boys got older, they would often reside in the home on the weekends instead of driving to the suburbs. But in actuality, the almost forty year old home was a borderline whore house for the brothers to act a fool with the neighborhood skanks.

Pacing the length of the balcony, Xander couldn't shake the treacherous nightmare from his psyche. Ten years elapsed and he could still see faded glimpses of her gorgeous honey-brown eyes flooded with terror and tears. Hear the revolting banter of the violators' duplicitous tone. The bellowing squawk of her screams chillingly echoed. He instinctively touched the scars against his abdomen, now concealed by tattoos, bearing his own wretched evidence of the life-changing traumatic event.

4:13am. Xander was wide awake, watching the moon clear a pathway for the rising sun. He transitioned from the balcony to the couch, the only other piece of furniture in his massive room aside from the nightstand and bed. He grabbed his phone, navigating to the news app and then riddled through stock market details, making mental notes of a few transactions he needed to execute. Xander was anxious, restless. Procrastinating for as long as he could, he contemplated dialing the number, hoping the phone call would liberate him from his disquietude. Laying his head against the back of the couch, still wearing nothing but grey boxers, he made the phone call. The blaring ring sounded two, then three times - Xander's leg bounced in anticipation. The ringing ended and the groggy voice resounded.

"We good, Xan?"

"We good, Daij."

"*Happy birthday to ya. Happy birthday to ya. Happy birthday.*" The crowd belted their best rendition of Stevie Wonder's happy birthday song.

The sun was unruly on the scorching hot August day. The courtyard at 1420 Cannon Street was at capacity with neighborhood friends and family perched in lawn chairs, on the grass and along the stoop in celebration of Daijah's twenty-fourth birthday and her second year of law school at St. Louis University. The celebration quickly transformed into a block party. The entire neighborhood's demonstration of how proud they were of Daijah. Everyone knew the story and were highly aware that it could have resulted in a deadly traumatic end. Random whispers often circulated Cannon Street and throughout Pleasant Pines, but no one ever openly spoke of the neighborhood terror again.

When Daijah's mother, Vaughn, walked into Ms. Mimi's house after 10pm that horrific night, high, drunk, and without Daijah, Ms. Mimi immediately called down the street to Mack's house. She was certain that Daijah had lost track of time while hanging out with Xander and her little brother and probably fell asleep like she'd done in the past. Concern hastily inundated Ms. Mimi when Mack said Xander wasn't home either. Daijah knew better than to go anywhere other than Xander's house after school. Ms. Mimi followed her intuition and called the police. Word spread throughout the neighborhood quickly and straightaway, a search began.

After all of these years even under the circumstances, Daijah was still stunningly beautiful although she wore evidence of her attack. The now faint scar snaked behind her ear to right below her jawline. Her chocolate curls were now bobbed at her neck and gorgeously framed her face. The pale yellow halter sundress kissed her curves perfectly, revealing the shoulder tattoo of a moon with an infinity symbol threaded through and surrounded by shooting stars. New Gucci thong sandals dressed her white painted toes. When Daijah smiled, her quartz eyes twinkled, temporarily eradicating the trauma and emotional suffering that was ever-present.

That night in September 2008 will forever be etched in Daijah's psyche. The day she didn't physically die, but her childhood and innocence completely perished. Suffering a ruptured spleen, broken ribs, fractured wrists and ankle, vaginal tearing, and extensive blood loss from the gash on her neck, Daijah was a survivor. She spent two weeks in intensive care and over two months in the hospital including rehabilitation. Over a year of her life was lost because she was too terrified to go back to school or even leave the house. Her memories of that night are sporadic and usually came in the form of horrific night terrors or triggered by darkened tight spaces.

"Happy birthday Daijah." A shaky voice stuttered behind her. It was Teddy. The man she considered her savior. Teddy didn't look like much and smelled like he'd been rummaging through the trash again, but she didn't care. Teddy's drug addiction likely saved Daijah's life.

Early Friday morning after Daijah and Xander were missing overnight, Teddy hauled his shopping cart, storing God only knows what, past Penn-White Middle School. He stumbled into the abandoned car wash to smoke his crack pipe in private that morning. Teddy was a picky addict. He didn't prefer to congregate with other addicts at the crack house on Franklin Street, also known as *Castlerock*. After one deep inhale, Teddy tossed his head back allowing the effects of the rock to take over. Slight movement and moaning in the background disrupted his high. He paused, intently listening, then he heard the faint sound again. Teddy went in search of the racket, confident he would find a stray animal or a homeless friend. The moan grew louder when he discovered two beaten and bloody bodies. He drunkenly limped out of the building screaming for help. Daijah was convinced that she and Xander would be dead if God didn't send an earthly angel.

"Thank you, Teddy. Are you hungry? Can I fix you a plate?" Daijah's eyes watered at the sight of him every time.

"If Ms. Mimi cooked, then hell yeah." Teddy slurred, having the nerve to also be picky about the preparation of his food. Daijah nodded, giggling as she strolled in the house to fix his plate. She piled on ribs, chicken, green beans, baked beans, corn on the cob, potato salad, and a separate container filled with different desserts. She took care of Teddy every time she laid eyes on him.

Daijah opened the screen door, carefully maneuvering the plastic bag packed with food when a familiar bass-filled timber immediately produced a glowing smile across her honey-bronzed face.

"Happy birthday, babydoll." Daijah turned to greet him as they immediately locked eyes. The corners of his mouth curled as he pulled her into a hug with one arm while holding a gift bag in the other.

He was magically delicious in plaid Polo shorts snuggled against his naturally athletic frame and baby blue Polo t-shirt exposing remnants of his tattoos that snaked the length of his biceps, across his chest and partially inked his neck. A fresh pair of Carolina blue and white Jordan's adorned his feet. Stud diamond earrings, a simple platinum link chain, and Rolex watch made him look like royalty. In Pleasant, that's exactly what the Kindred family represented. All eyes were on the sexy twenty-five year old who possessed more swag and confidence than a man twice his age. Women young and old wanted a taste of Xander Malcolm Kindred.

"Thank you, big head." She chortled, returning the embrace. "Here Teddy. This should be enough food to last a few days. I put some sodas in there too."

"Thank you, Daijah." Teddy whimpered, withdrawing in Xander's presence. "What's up, X?" He mumbled and swiftly walked away.

"What's up Teddy?" Xander withdrew too.

It was difficult for him to make eye contact with the man who rescued them that day. He appreciated and was thankful for Teddy showing up, but his mere presence was a trigger for Xander.

He suffered too. Broken nose, ribs, a few fingers, a concussion, and extensive bruising. Xander spent a significant amount of time in the hospital as well. Partly for his own treatment, but he also refused to leave Daijah's side. Especially when she was unconscious.

Xander watched Teddy until he disappeared down the street before extending the yellow gift bag to Daijah.

"Xan, what is this? You already gave me my birthday gift. I'm wearing it. See?" Daijah spun around showing off her new clothes and shoes.

Xander took care of Daijah. Protected her at all costs. Whatever she needed or wanted, he provided, although she never asked him for anything. Daijah and Xander shared an unbreakable bond, unfortunately rooted in pain and trauma. But over the years, they'd created stability and safety for one another. They needed the other's presence to survive triggering episodes. Shared memories of that day were kept locked away in an unattainable vault. Some recollections they chose not to recount even with each other.

"I see you, Daij. You look gorgeous, babydoll." He slightly smiled, admiring her. Xander didn't smile much other than when he was in Daijah's presence. "I had to give you something on your actual birthday. Open your gift, Daij."

Daijah giddily scrambled across the grass to an empty table. Her only other trusted friend, Zaria, joined her at the table squealing in excitement too. Xander shook his head at their schoolgirl giddiness. Sifting through the colorful tissue paper, two boxes with Apple logos were revealed. Daijah's mouth dropped.

"Oh, my goodness! An iPhone and Macbook? Xander!" She fussed.

"Wait a minute bitch. A rose gold iPhone and MacBook! That shit is unique. Everybody can't get that, girl." Zaria clarified, expression laced with seriousness.

"Xan! I can't accept this." Daijah muttered, pushing him in his shoulder. "No. It's too much. My phone works just fine and I already have a computer gifted by you, unless you forgot." She shook her head, shoving the boxes into his chest.

"X, you do too much for me. You don't owe me anything. I should be repaying you - showering you with gifts."

Xander ushered her into his arms to pause her ranting. Daijah buried her face in the fold of his bergamot scented neck to conceal the brewing tears.

They both carried so much guilt about what happened to them. Daijah often wished Xander would have just run when he had the opportunity to get away. But he stopped his escape to attempt to rescue her. Clearly it was understood that they did nothing to deserve that level of abuse and violation, but often argued about different *what if* scenarios - what if they went a different direction, what if they ran back to the school, what if they screamed louder.

"It ain't nothing, Daij. Don't cry. I do things for you because I want to and I can. You need a new phone because your shit is whack." He smirked. "And you killed your first year of law school with that old ass computer. This second year ain't gonna be easy. You needed an upgrade, so I got you the best. I'm proud of you, Daij. You killing it at that bougie ass school. I just want you to continue to show them what a lil Black girl from the projects on Cannon Street can accomplish."

Xander placed a firm hand at her nape, stroking his thumb across her scar. He was the only person beside a medical professional to touch the scar. Somehow, it was an unspoken message between Xander and Daijah. The affectionate stimulation gave her solace, reassurance.

The other three Kindred brothers entered the courtyard like they owned the place. They all grew up to become dangerously fine young men. Simeon, or Sim, was twenty-three and considered the muscle of the crew. That nigga was his father's clone in size and personality. Some considered him Mack 2.0. Hiram, or Ram, was twenty-one and he was the silent assassin. He was quiet but never opposed to defend his family or his crew. And Adonis, D or Doni, was the baby boy at eighteen years old. He was the pretty boy of the crew and the ladies loved him. Borderline genius like Xander, but more into technology than finances. Adonis was headed to St. Louis University with a full academic scholarship - future software engineer. Grown adult ass women showed no shame when ogling the mature manly physiques of these young men.

"Happy birthday, sis-" Doni yelled before noticing Daijah's disturbed demeanor. "What happened? What's wrong with her?" He directed his questions to Xander.

Adonis didn't play around when it came to his big sister. He was almost more protective of Daijah than Xander if that was even possible. Plenty fights ensued if he thought someone was stepping to Daijah out of line - his brother included.

"Nothing, Bro. She's good." Xander lifted her chin searching her beautifully dewy eyes. His pinky finger unconsciously locked with hers. "Right, babydoll? It's all good?"

She nodded.

"I'm good, D." She affectionately addressed her baby brother, accepting his open arms for a hug. "Thank you for gracing me with your presence on my birthday." She teased.

"Well, you know I be busy on these hoes. But I thought I should give them a lil break to celebrate my one and only sister." Adonis joked.

"Boy bye!" Daijah and Zaria sang in unison.

The group roared in laughter. "You better be protecting your lil shit with these hoes." Daijah bantered. Adonis rolled his eyes.

"Ain't shit little about my shit." He raved.

"Eeeewwww!" Daijah squealed.

Although Daijah and Adonis were siblings because they shared a mother, their lifestyles were distinctively different. Their mother was still struggling with drugs, seemingly homeless roaming from house to house and bed to bed. It broke her heart, but Ms. Mimi did not allow her daughter to dwell at her home. She held Vaughn completely responsible for what happened to Daijah. Often reminding her that if she would've done as she said she would, Daijah would've been safe. But instead, Vaughn was getting high.

Daijah still lived with her grandmother and they continued to struggle - often living paycheck to paycheck. Ms. Mimi was diabetic and had a heart condition so she was no longer able to work. They survived off of her minimal retirement and social security check. Daijah made money braiding hair and tutoring on campus. Thankfully she received a full scholarship for her undergraduate studies, otherwise her life path and future potential would've been starkly different. Student loans and a partial scholarship would pay for law school.

Xander tried to help but Daijah always refused. He opted to buy her things she needed for school, designer clothes and shoes and sneak money to Ms. Mimi instead of arguing with Daijah. Although Mack wasn't her father, he actually loved Vaughn and thought of Daijah like one of his own. Anytime Adonis requested help for his sister and grandmother, Mack never said no. He even helped out with some repairs and disability accommodations for the house once Ms. Mimi became ill.

"Come on, sis. It's your muthafucking birthday. We 'bout to kick it tonight." Adonis started doing a silly dance.

To her chagrin, Daijah was having two parties for her birthday. The neighborhood barbeque that was well underway, and then a party with a small group of friends at a hotel suite downtown. Xander planned the second party all the way down to her outfit, so Daijah was instructed to just show up and have fun.

"First of all, stop cussing. Second, your young ass ain't doing nothing tonight, D." Simeon chimed in.

"Nah Sim! Pops said me and my boy Rel can stay in the adjoining room as long as you and X don't let us get in no shit." Adonis stuck out his tongue, exemplifying the baby of the family behavior.

Xander and Daijah shook their heads, laughing at their brother. The party was live until well after five o'clock. There was not another rib or piece of chicken left. Ms. Mimi always fussed about these *'hungry ass niggas'* as she and her sister Germaine cleaned up.

"Ok, ok listen up. What's the saying, Maine?" Ms. Mimi sipped her clear liquor before turning to her sister. They were both drunk and laughing.

"Y'all ain't gotta go home, but you gotta get the hell outta here." The sisters barked in unison. The crowd ignited in laughter as they began shifting the party into the street.

"Daij, I'm about to head out. Are you going to be ready by eight?" Xander stood from the blanket in the grass that they were resting on. He helped Daijah to her feet.

"Yes, I'll be ready. I just need to decide what to wear?" She yawned and stretched her arms above her head.

The glare from the sun accentuated her honey-brown orbs. Xander trailed a finger down her face before stroking her neck. He leaned in, pressing his lips against her forehead.

"Wear the black dress, babydoll." The lustful timber of his tone made her belly tremble.

2

"Grandma, I'm leaving in about 20 minutes. Do you need anything before I go?"

Daijah was scrambling through her room making sure she had everything she needed to spend the night at the hotel. Xander bought her four new outfits for her birthday, in addition to the phone and laptop. As he suggested, she wore the black spaghetti strap tank dress that he paired with blinged out Converse but she opted for a strappy black wedge sandal instead. Her curly tresses were pulled into a partial high ponytail with fringes sweeping across her shoulders. Gold bangles, hoop earrings, and red lipstick completed the look.

"No Daijah Blu. I don't need anything. Your Uncle Bean is coming down here to watch this movie with me and Germaine." Ms. Mimi's voice echoed down the hall as she approached her granddaughter's room. "Oh, my word. Daijah, you look beautiful. Lord, my baby girl is all grown up."

Her beautiful brown dewy eyes lovingly surveyed the granddaughter she'd raised since a baby. Mimi didn't have much but she made sure Daijah focused on school, stayed physically active, mentally sound, and spiritually grounded. Even after the incident, Ms. Mimi didn't allow Daijah to wallow too long in fear. After long days of physical and mental therapy, PTSD episodes, and uncontrollable sobbing, Mimi whispered her favorite Bible scripture in Daijah's ear until she fell asleep. *"God is our refuge and strength, a very present help in trouble. So fear not, for I am with you; be not dismayed, for I am your God; I will strengthen you, I will help you."* Daijah carried this mantra with her daily.

"Awww, Grandma, why are you crying?" Daijah pouted her lips at the sight of her grandma's tears.

"I'm just so proud of you, Daijah Blu. Under horrendous circumstances, you have achieved everything you set out to accomplish. So much more than I was ever able to do in my lifetime. I'm just so thankful that you are happy and whole and fulfilled in your life. I thank God for Xander because I don't know if either of you would've survived the past ten years without each other. You know that boy loves you, Daijah Blu." Mimi stared at her granddaughter's reflection in the mirror fixing the straps on her dress.

"I know Xan loves me. But, I don't think he *loves me, loves* me, Mimi. Xan has love for me like he has for his brothers. So -"

"No baby, that boy loves you, loves you." Her grandmother teased, mocking Daijah's soft voice. "I know you two have an unbreakable bond rooted in your childhood pain that cannot be severed. But when Xander looks at you, honey, it's all love. Just like the innocent little boy who sat right out there on my front porch for hours when you had chicken pox. *I just need to see her face, Ms. Mimi.*" She mocked his dejected voice.

"Girl, he was unwavering. I had to reason with an eight year old and explain to him that the chickenpox was contagious and he could catch it. But that lil hard headed child didn't care." Mimi laughed. "That boy was willing to get chicken pox just to be near you. I ain't had much love in my life, but that sounds like love to me, baby girl." They both smiled. The one resemblance of her grandma she shared.

A knock at the bedroom window disrupted their moment. *'Xander,'* they mouthed in unison.

Since they were kids, Xander never knocked on the front door like a normal person. He journeyed down the alleyway, through the gate, and straight to Daijah's window most nights.

"Babydoll, you ready?" Xander called through the bedroom window.

"Xander Malcolm Kindred, please come through the back door and stop knocking on my window, boy." Mimi shouted, unsuccessfully controlling her laughter.

"Yes ma'am." He said, walking up the back steps and into the house entering the kitchen. Daijah was standing in the threshold of her bedroom chuckling at the exchange. Xander eyed her and swallowed hard. She was gorgeous. The black dress was perfectly painted on her body like a priceless canvas.

"I'm ready Xan. Zaria should be coming up the street." She paused, trying to decipher the look on his face. "Xan, what's wrong? Xander!" She sang, shaking him from his reverie. Ms. Mimi blushed as she observed the blossoming of an inevitable love connection.

"Um, yeah. Nothing. I'm good. Let's be out." Xander regained his composure.

Daijah kissed her grandma goodbye as they walked to the front of the house. Sounds of flirtatious chatter could be heard from outside when the doorbell sounded. Daijah opened the door and was greeted by Zaria, Simeon, Hiram, Adonis, and his friend Rel. Moments later, a pink and black Escalade limousine with Around Town Limo & Party Bus inscripted on the side pulled in front of the house. Daijah's mouth practically hit the floor and she turned to Xander. He smiled, fully prepared to show her the best birthday.

"You are too much." She nestled against his face and whispered in his ear.

"Anything for you, babydoll." He rested his hand slightly above her rotund ass, before softly kissing her forehead.

Before arriving at the hotel, the limo ushered the rowdy group around downtown, taking pictures in front of some of the city's most historic landmarks. After that, Xander arranged a scavenger hunt. Daijah's cheeks were rosy and aching from smiling and laughing so much. She caught glimpses of Xander staring at her. He periodically lifted his eyebrows to confirm that she was having a good time. A few of Daijah's college friends met the group at the Arch to join the scavenger hunt. Although Xander knew the two girls and the guy from some school events he attended with Daijah, he was not necessarily a fan of new people. And he definitely wasn't cool with the way ole boy was gawking at Daijah.

The limo pulled in front of the W Hotel a little after ten. In true Adonis fashion, he wore aviator sunglasses and had to let the world know he'd arrived, yelling those words through the sunroof of the limo. Simeon quickly popped him in the back of his head, giving his first, *do I need to call Mack?* warning.

The valet loaded the luggage on the cart and Daijah grabbed her book bag.

"Let me help you with that, Daijah." The guy, Tristan, said then winked.

Xander quickly stepped in front of Daijah before she could consider responding.

"Nah. She's good, dawg." He retrieved her bag then extended his hand, signaling Daijah to walk ahead of him.

The group piled into the elevator seemingly violating the weight capacity as the car inched to the 25th floor - the penthouse.

"Damn Daijah! The fuckin' penthouse!" Zaria whisper-yelled. She wiggled around more excited than the birthday girl.

Xander parted the small crowd formed at the double doors, ensuring Daijah was the first to enter the suite. As soon as she crossed the threshold, one of their neighborhood wannabe DJ friends played 50 Cents "Go Shawty It's Ya Birthday." Daijah strolled into the room dancing to the bass-filled beat.

"Aye. Aye. Aye." Her friends cheered, encouraging her to continue dancing.

But Daijah paused for a moment to digest the beauty of the room. Floor to ceiling windows offered the most magical backdrop of the city. The suite was massive. The living room, kitchenette, and bar were positioned in the center, with a master bedroom at each corner of the room. A yellow and silver balloon arch framed the entryway, with a second one positioned against the wall with *Happy Birthday Daijah* in gold letters acting as the background for the photos. A long table positioned on the opposite side of the suite overflowed with her favorite food - Mexican. Xander ordered enchiladas, nachos, and a taco bar with all of the fixings. And a two tier marble cake with her name written in yellow and white icing. He took care of every major and minor detail all the way down to the party favors because he knew Daijah was still a kid at heart.

Daijah's drink of choice was pineapple flavored rum. One of the guys that worked for Xander acted as the bartender and he kept the alcohol flowing all night. Daijah was so footloose and fancy free. After four grueling years of college, she was ecstatic to have her dual degree in business and psychology. Now off to her second year of law school, Daijah desired to open a center in her neighborhood that would offer legal assistance, job training, entrepreneurship development, and wellness classes. Daijah simply wanted to create a haven to elevate the greatness that resided in her hood.

Dancing, singing, eating, drinking, and heartily laughing with her friends, she was having the time of her life. Daijah twerked through all of her favorite 90's hits - Jermaine Dupri's *Money Ain't a Thang*, Snoop Dogg's *Drop it Like it's Hot,* Jay-Z's *Money-Cash-Hoes,* and Salt-n-Pepa *Push It* until sweat beaded her rosy cheeks.

She was good and tipsy when Usher's "There Goes My Baby" blasted through the speakers. Xander slouched on the plush couch with a glass of dark liquor in his hand lustfully assessing her. The room was dim but his spotlight beamed on her as she leisurely swayed to the music with her eyes closed. That damn dress magnified the curve, dip, and arc of her body. Loose strands of curly hair stuck to her glistening damp skin. She released the ponytail allowing the wild mane to kiss her shoulders. Drawing her hands behind her head, she momentarily pushed the hair up exposing her neck. That damn neck was so gooey butter deliciously smooth, Xander unconsciously licked his lips. He knew she was feeling herself because Daijah made no effort to conceal her scar. While she was self-conscious about the scar, he, on the other hand, thought it was beautiful - a symbol of survival.

Xander focused on her plump, delectable lips as she aimlessly sang the words.

"There goes my baby (ooh girl look at you). You don't know how good it feels to call you my girl. There goes my baby. Loving everything you do. Ooh girl, look at you"

He'd had the pleasure of kissing those lips and tasting that tongue once at her twenty-first birthday and he desperately desired another chance. But...

His thought trailed off when Daijah stood before him shyly indicating she wanted to dance. Xander would dance with her in the confines of her bedroom but never in public. She pressed her praying hands together and pouted her glossy, irresistible lips.

"Please Xan."

It took him less than a second to acquiesce.

Xander's glorious frame loomed over her, placing firm sizable hands at the small of her back. Daijah wrapped her arms around his neck, still maintaining some distance, but Xander demanded that she come closer. He caressed his hands up her spine urging, begging her to erase the gap keeping her from him. She willingly obliged. Tossing her head back between her shoulder blades, capturing his umber eyes to absorb everything that was *him*. They glared at each other for a long minute exchanging inhales and exhales. She desired to taste the spicy Hennessy against his tongue. The vibrance of whiskey entangled with his sandalwood aroma made her puss tingle. If they were any closer, one wouldn't be able to breath without the other.

Xander was drunk but not from Hennessey. Daijah had the audacity to stand before him, so gloriously woman, so goddamn sexy with the hypnotizing scent of her essence penetrating his soul. *Shit!* Normally, he was able to control his wanton desires in her presence, often training his dick to behave. But tonight, the way she was swaying her hips and ass, Daijah was a grown ass, voluptuous ass woman.

"Are you enjoying your birthday, Daij?" His hooded eyes were lustfully alluring.

"I am. Thank you, Xan, for everything." She kissed the tip of his nose.

"I forgot to give you one thing though." He said.

"What more could you give?" She playfully giggled.

"Your birthday licks."

Xander trailed kisses from her temple to the tip of her nose, then her cheek before nibbling on her ear. She gasped, but he wasn't finished, steadily gliding his hands down her back cupping her pillowy ass. He gently smacked, causing her bare ass to jiggle.

Fuck! She's wearing a thong. He mused, fruitlessly attempting to control his growing manhood. He planted soft kisses against her lips before ushering his lengthy tongue into her mouth. Xander made love to her mouth with languid, deliberate, loving kisses. Admittingly, drunkenness minimized his inhibitions but his intoxication - his vice was her.

The song switched to Tony Toni Tone's "Ask of You." Daijah blushed because she knew how much Xander loved this song. Lost in the music, he caressed, kneaded, and tapped her ass to the beat, journeying his tongue down her neck. Her body slightly froze when he kissed the scar. Xander matter-of-factly whispered, "Babydoll," and all uneasiness immediately ceased.

Shit! Daijah was dripping wet. She could smell her saccharine juices penetrating through the cotton fabric of the fitted dress. Xander's senses were heightened as well as he delighted in her appetizing zest. Daijah was ready to accidentally on purpose slip and fall on his dick.

Twirling her around, he admired the voluptuous curves of her body, mouthing *damn babydoll*. Daijah's ass was now pressed against his still present, still growing erection. Touching, rubbing, squeezing, groping - they were spellbound, captivated, completely immersed in the moment. Daijah damn near had an orgasm standing on her four inch wedges.

The whole room was lost in the song because it was quiet with sexed-crazed, drunk and horny partygoers. Xander smoothly sang in her ear.

"Just give me all your lovin', girl, after all the rubbin'
That's all I ask of you
I'll kiss you anywhere, yes, love, even there
That's all I ask of you"

Daijah wanted this. Shit, she wanted *him* - bad, but Xander never displayed this much intent and affection...ever. The two opportunities they'd had to seal the deal were prom night and her twenty-first birthday, but Xander denied her. In a loving way but denial, nonetheless. Daijah practically begged him to be her first. To rid of the unruly virginity. Fear of sex and any physical intimacy plagued Daijah since being violated. But not with Xander. He was the one and only man that Daijah truly trusted with her...*everything*. She was confident that Xander would understand her desire to take things slow. He would revel in the blemished parts of her body. But he couldn't bring himself to take it to another level. Desiring not to taint her world - change their friendship. Xander was afraid of the potential traumatic memories it could summon. But tonight, it appears all of those concerns disintegrated.

Xander slithered fingers up the length of her body, encouraging her arms to wrap around his neck as he firmly rested his hands around her waist. Kissing the moon tattoo on her exposed shoulder before singing, in his opinion, the most important verse of the song.

"I really love you. I love you, Daijah."

Xander and Daijah were so connected that she almost cried at the thought of being relinquished from his embrace. Breaths infrequent and shallow, she ventured to breathe but her lungs were temporarily unavailable. Daijah slammed her eyes shut tight holding on to him and he to her. Collective heartbeats resounding in sync - harmonized.

Daijah's back was still firmly pressed into Xander. Both of his colossal arms enfolded her waist while he nestled in the folds of her neck. They were enraptured and didn't give a damn who noticed. The tempo changed but they didn't surrender.

"Xan." Daijah's sweet voice was barely a whisper. Softly encouraging him to hold on.

"Daij, the song is over. We have to-"

"No." She whined, as he repositioned her body to face him.

Xander cupped her cheek, gazing at her in a familiar way that made Daijah believe that all the goodness in the universe originated in the depths of her eyes.

"To be continued. I promise. No bullshit." He breathily uttered and she understood exactly what that meant.

――――――――――

1:07AM. Daijah stared at the large clock on the wall watching the seconds tick by. She'd been pretty quiet since her and Xander's entanglement and his promise. *To be continued. I promise. No bullshit.* That was almost two hours ago and he hadn't paid much attention to her since then. This was Xander's mode of operation though - ignore, disengage, and shut down when he was in his head and doesn't want to talk.

The suite was now hushed. Only Zaria, Simeon, Xander, and Daijah remained. Zaria was sprawled across the couch drunk while Simeon rubbed her feet. *Weird.* Xander sat at the bar on his phone. As the seconds ticked by, Daijah's pissy mood and attitude elevated. Being ignored by Xander while her kitty was drenched and pulsating and ready was torture.

"Zaria! Get up!" Daijah shouted. "Let's go to our room. Looks like this party is over."

Xander spun around in the bar stool staring at her. She unsuccessfully endeavored not to make eye contact, but he was simply irresistible. Strangely enough, the attraction to him was heightened when she was angry. Xander shook his head, internally laughing at her bratty behavior.

"Sim." Xander's voice was calm but commanding and his brother moved swiftly to address him.

Xander mouthed some words to his brother that Daijah couldn't comprehend in the midst of her annoyance. Zaria stumbled from the couch to settle next to her friend. She drunkenly slurred unidentifiable words as Daijah rolled her eyes. The way Simeon was massaging Zaria's feet was a clear indication that her kitty would be satisfied tonight. *At least somebody is going to get a taste.* She irritably mused.

Daijah's tipsiness was an afterthought, but her puss was still throbbing and saturated.

"Zaria. Come take a walk with me." Simeon's gruff, yet slow rumbling tone filled the room.

Zaria blushed and mysteriously sobered, immediately closing the distance between her and Simeon. Daijah felt raw, exposed, stupid. She'd put herself out there again with Xander and again he was rejecting her.

Daijah and Xander stood alone in the hazy room. She could feel his brown eyes on her as she leaned against the couch, but he didn't move. They held the blemished gaze for a long minute. Xander remained motionless. She swiftly turned on her heels to walk towards the master bedroom of the suite, hoping he would follow but he didn't. Daijah tried her best not to stomp away like a child. She composed her emotions until she entered the bedroom, slamming the door behind her.

Daijah kicked off her wedges while peering around the beautiful suite. The king size bed was the focal point second to the floor to ceiling windows that offered a panoramic view of the skyline and cityscape. The visual was stunning but Daijah's eyes focused on the crescent moon that appeared to be so close, she tried to reach out and touch it. The moon always gave her solace. Daijah contemplated every sane and insane reason why she shouldn't get her shit and storm out of the suite to catch a cab home. Deeply inhaling, she closed her eyes to quell the sadness and embarrassment before silently exhaling.

"I see the moon and the moon sees me." The thunderous boom of his voice transmitted a reverberating sensation through her body.

Eyes still closed, Daijah shyly blushed but remained silent. Xander softly closed the door, suavely depleting the air between them that he required to breathe. Trailing a finger down her arm, he repeated the words, sheathing her in his embrace.

"I see the moon and the moon sees me." He echoed.

Daijah relinquished the breath she was holding, resting her head against his shoulder.

"God bless the moon and God bless me." Daijah sweetly sang, completing the rhyme, recalling the first time she'd heard the words.

"Daijah, can you hear me? Wake up Daij. I can see the moon." During moments of consciousness, Xander tried talking to Daijah to get her to stay awake. The three men who attacked them were gone for now but it was too painful for Xander to move. Daijah had only opened her eyes once. Xander kept staring at the moon, praying that someone would find them. He recalled the nursery rhyme his mother sang to him and his brothers before she died. "I see the moon and the moon sees me. God bless the moon and God bless me." He quietly recited.

"Daijah, say it with me. Please." He cried. "Daijah, please wake up."

Xander continued to repeat the rhyme over and over again for God only knows how long. His voice weakened as sleepiness invaded his broken body.

"I see the moon and the moon sees me." He yawned through a whimper. "God bless-"

Daijah's brittle, fragile tone cracked, harmonizing, "- God bless the moon and God bless me." They linked hands and drifted back to blackness.

Xander gazed at Daijah, while she admired the moon. He lightly fingered a loose tendril of hair that grazed her cheek, stirring her from the memory. Their eyes were passionately affixed. Trauma-ridden minds telling them to pause, resist the temptation, but their bodies were woefully cooperative and ready to explore. The moon was no longer satisfying their collective greed, the sexual desire was critical, fucking lethal.

"Daij, are you sure? Is this what you want?" Xander nervously questioned, firmly encasing her nape while trailing his thumb across her scar.

Daijah anxiously fisted the fabric of his t-shirt. Unwavering conviction punctuated her beautiful quartz eyes. Tone resolute and confident.

"Yes, Xander. I want this. I want you. You're the only person I trust with -" Daijah paused, then swallowed hard before catching the tear that salted the corner of her mouth.

"I'm the only one you trust with what, babydoll?"

"With...me."

Xander momentarily misplaced his breath before capturing the full of her lips, trading sweet kisses as he guided her to the bed. He'd dreamed about this day, shit, fantasized about inhabiting the warmth of her essence. Envisioned every single curve and swell of her innocently sexy body. He would be the first with her consent, and Xander was honored, emotional, and scared as shit. But all the more reason to be gentle and delicate.

Xander didn't know what it meant to make love to a woman. The chicks he fucked with in the streets were for a good time but definitely not a long time. Sex was just sex - dispassionate, emotionless, rough, get his nut off, and then he'd send their asses home. But Xander was anxiously ready to learn - decode the riddle, decrypt the sensitive, yet complicated layers of Daijah Blu Duvall.

Xander kneeled before her, positioning himself between her legs. Buttery brown sugar thighs were exposed as her dress slowly crept up the arc of her hips. He rested his head in her lap, stroking and caressing her smooth skin, as if he was praying to make the right decision. Daijah gasped, unsure of what to do, but did what was natural. Love him and surrender. Fondling his silky thick coils, she leaned down, inhaling his delectable scent, kissing and nestling the back of his neck. Xander's sensual touch alone was climatic.

"Xan." She whimpered.

"Stop me, Daij. Please just tell me no." Xander pleaded.

"Why?" Daijah whined.

"Because... baby. Your mind or body is not ready for what you're requesting of me. I will possess your soul, Daijah, snatch it from your grasp and you will never be the same." Xander practically growled against her lips.

She panted, a welcomed fear invaded her flesh as he continued.

"You don't know what you're getting yourself into. The things I want to do to your body. I don't want to hurt you, Daij." His voice trembled, his stare was laced with so much love, lust, and concern.

She saw traces of the teenage boy that sat next to her hospital bed petitioning the most innocent prayers.

Dear God, it's Xander. I really don't know how to talk to you but I promise I will learn if you let Daijah be alright. I really tried to save her but those dudes were just too strong. I promise to get bigger and stronger and I promise to always protect Daijah if you just help her this one time.

The recollection caused Daijah to blush.

"Xander, look at me." She cupped his face. His misty umber eyes transmitted a sensual surge through her belly. "You're not capable of causing me any pain."

He nodded, irises still locked in a lovingly unyielding gaze.

"I love you, Xander. And I'm willing to risk it all only for you." Daijah confessed.

Seeking no further confirmation, Xander devoured Daijah's lips with soft bites and nibbles before entering her mouth. He clasped their fingers, situating their joined hands at the small of her back while still knelt before her. Xander's warm tongue traveled down her neck, resting at the arc as he licked and sucked - passionately marking his territory. He released her hands before nudging her to lay on the bed. Daijah's breaths were unstable. She tightly shut her eyes then quickly opened them to make sure she wasn't dreaming. This was Xan...Xander Kindred. Her best friend, her savior, her protector. The only person in the world who understood the depths of her violation and trauma because he shared the same trepidation.

The cool sensation across her breast shook Daijah from her reverie. The spaghetti strap dress was settled at her waist and the hooks of the sheer black strapless bra were unhinged.

"Ahhh-sssh!" Daijah hissed, caught off guard when he inhaled one nipple, then two. His warm, thick tongue continued to journey down the center of her stomach. It was still. She wasn't breathing. Her lungs took a momentary hiatus.

"Daij, baby, breath." Xander's gruff, raspy tone extended permission for her to exhale. He kissed along the rising and falling waves of her stomach. Focused on her belly button, he gently kissed then tickled the dimpled folds with his tongue. She arched her back. Xander committed that reaction to his mental rolodex. His mission was to explore, consume, and master the nuances of her anatomy. The anterior, posterior, ventral, dorsal - Xander was about to ace Anatomy of Daijah 101.

He lifted her body removing the dress and panties simultaneously. Daijah laid on the bed shivering. Not from the cold breeze circulating the room but being unveiled, bare. She'd surveyed her body a million times. Some scars have since dissipated while others bore a reminder of the anguish. Daijah recoiled, vainly striving to conceal.

Xander's eyes darkened and he shook his head.

"Are you really hiding from me, babydoll? I don't ever want you to mask your fucking beauty. Especially not from me." He settled next to her, clutching her hands as he kissed her fingertips. "Daijah, you are perfect. I adore all of you. Every flaw, every scar. Do you understand me?"

She nodded. No words, only muted tears.

Xander continued his exploration, licking her blackberry areolas, nipples hard as priceless diamonds. He inhaled, smelling the sweltering nectar simmering between her legs. Xander adjusted quickly, hovering above her succulent core like an animal sniffing out his prey.

"Damn, Daijah." He whimpered, mesmerized by the candied glazed goodness residing amidst her buxom thighs.

"What? Did I do something wrong?" She roused, nervously opening her eyes seeking Xander's.

"No, babydoll. Nothing is wrong. You are so fucking right and smell so goddamn sweet." He breathily professed. "Daij, how are you this wet? Shit!" Xander desperately desired a closer glance of her portly puss.

"It's you, Xan. It happens at the mere thought of you." She muttered. Words barely comprehensible.

Xander was dumbfounded at the revelation, yet enormously in love - and turned the fuck on. His dick was heavy, balls aching for Daijah, but her pleasure was obligatory. Precedent over anything. Xander was excited, giddy as he nudged her legs open. Like a kid on Christmas morning unwrapping his favorite gift; a sacred treasure. At the apex of her thighs dwelled the perfect pussy. It was smooth, and glistening, and delicate - fucking flawless.

Without warning, Xander feasted, slowly licking her sweetness from top to bottom. Satisfying an uninhibited hunger as he searched, hunted, delved in the deepest corners of her puss. He'd waited a lifetime to have the savory flavors of his babydoll on his tongue. And damn, she tasted so fucking good. All of his most beloved things, meticulously coupled to create a masterpiece.

Daijah was his masterpiece. To anyone who was actually paying attention, it had always been Daijah. But Xander's demons haunted him in ways that he couldn't comprehend. As much as he loved and adored her, she didn't request a ride on his roller coaster of life. Xander refused to make her a part of his complication.

"Xan!" Daijah whisper-screamed as he inserted two blunt fingertips into her tight treasure, preparing her puss for his impending arrival.

Slow, deliberate strokes as he sucked in the plump bud of her clit. He massaged and caressed her sensitive breasts with his available hand, leaving no flesh neglected. There was a commotion bubbling in her core. The ability to hear, see, or smell vanished. She was drifting into untapped territory and needed to be rescued. Daijah peered around searching for something, anything to save her from this unbearably satisfying sensation. The moans grew louder, the titillation more intense.

Daijah fisted the sheets, pounding into the top of Xander's head, begging him to cease and continue at the same damn time. Her pussy was a traitor - throbbing and pulsing and squirting - doing unfamiliar shit. Heart ferociously pounded, drowning out all rational thoughts and common sense. Xander was relentless, slithering his blazing tongue into her dripping hole. He tightly gripped her thigh with one hand preventing escape. She was at her peak and he knew it. Daijah was no stranger to self-exploration with a vibrating toy while images of Xander floated through her psyche. But didn't shit compare to the actual touch and tongue of this warm-blooded, sexy-ass, fine- ass, mahogany-hued homosapien that she'd loved since she was thirteen. He tongue-kissed her pussy lips like they were dessert. His two fingers found a playground in her sodden treasure reaching Daijah's g-spot.

"You ready to rain on me, babydoll?" He asked but wasn't seeking a response.

Instantly, Xander's fingers deliciously occupied both of her drip-ping private openings.

"X!" Daijah screamed her pleasurable appreciation as her body lifted from the mattress as if her soul was possessed.

He sexily grinned because Daijah never called him 'X', and he kinda liked it. Heated honey-maple juices squirted from her essence, gleaming against his smooth skin.

Xander was gratifyingly satisfied, moaning as he licked the

evidence of her enjoyment from his fingers. Daijah, on the other hand, was dazed and delirious. That damn orgasm was exquisitely violent. She roughly gasped, body still uncontrollably quaking from the aftershock.

"Babydoll. We good?" Xander nestled against her quivering belly.

"Shit. I don't know. I wasn't - I didn't -" She audibly exhaled through swollen, puckered lips. Daijah covered her face with both hands, slightly embarrassed as her body was still quaking. Still cumming.

"It's all good, babydoll. Just let your body respond to the feeling. Enjoy it, Daij." Xander peppered her with treasure-flavored kisses as he admired her revel in the afterglow. He was fully prepared to follow her lead; if she was done for the night, so was he. Being in her presence was satisfying enough. He pulled her closer as she snuggled against his bare chest. Daijah trailed her finger, outlining the intricately detailed tattoo that stretched across the right side of his chest, shoulder, and down his arm. It was beautiful. He was beautiful.

"Xan?"

"Yeah?"

"Can I have more of you? *All* of you." Daijah shyly nestled in the nook of his neck, seemingly bracing for his response...rejection.

"As you wish, beautiful."

Xander softly kissed the top of her head before standing to remove his shorts. His dick distended against the zipper ready to pop. Daijah had a front row seat and she was ready for the show. He lustfully bit the corner of his bottom lip as he unbuckled the belt, then undid the button, then the zipper, and the beast was released. That thing hurriedly ejected from the hole of his boxers like it had been emancipated from a life sentence. Xander was a big man who possessed a big dick. Daijah swallowed hard. Part fear, part drool.

"Hey big man." She sexily grinned, voice just above a whisper. She embarrassingly covered her mouth with both hands, not intending to say that aloud.

"Daij, did you just say *hi* to my dick and call him...big man?" Only

Daijah could produce the massive grin spread across his face. He instinctively grabbed the glorious mahogany beast, chuckling at her innocence.

"Come here, babydoll." He ordered.

Xander was ready to beautifully breach her unblemished virtue. Stealthily, he climbed on top of her, protectively hovering over Daijah's shuddering flesh. He kissed her temple. She shivered in anticipation. Daijah desperately yearned for him to come closer. Tugging his nape, she initiated the sweetest, yet spiciest kiss. He moaned, delighting in the game of hide and seek she was playing with her tongue in the heat of his mouth. Xander glided his dick against the slick folds of her puss. She was still so damn wet. His breathing was labored as he nibbled against her lips and stroked her wild hair. They were so close that they relied on each other for every breath.

"Daijah. Look at me." She obeyed, then he continued. "Promise me this won't change me and you. I don't know what we can be. What our future holds. But one thing I'm certain of is that I fucking love you, babydoll."

Xander dismantled any chance for a rebuttal when he rawly, leisurely entered her sodden oasis. Drifting deeper into her taut pussy, he settled for a few minutes allowing her to absorb the moment...and him. They locked eyes and adoringly smiled in unison. Substantial, veiny, girthy, heaviness crowded every available inch of Daijah's pussy.

Xander whispered, "Daijah. Breathe, babydoll. It's ok. I won't hurt you. But you have to breathe."

His cup runneth over with adoration and respect as his umber orbs examined the curves of her face for any signs of distress or regret.

Daijah deeply inhaled with her eyes sealed tight, digesting him inch by loving inch by salacious inch. She cried as her soft places became acquainted with his hard places. This was it. Her dream was now reality. Her friend and protector was now her lover. Xander had no idea how his mere presence healed her all of those years ago. His voice and gentle touch were the motivation she needed to fight when she was ready to throw in the towel. Xander was her soulmate, a kindred, connected spirit. The manifestation of a dream she never imagined would come to fruition.

"Thank you for this honor, babydoll. Is this what you want? How you want it?" He breathily probed.

"Ahh, babe...this is what I needed! Xan, I love you so much. I would've waited a lifetime for you."

Daijah adjusted her hips, grinding into him. Determined not to miss an inch. The pain was an insignificant afterthought when Xander's baritone whispered loving sentiments of *'I love you Daij,' 'you are so fucking amazing,'* as he massaged through her hair. He panted at the realization that he was in fact making love to Daijah Blu Duvall.

"Fuck, Daijah. What are you doing to me?" He grunted, intently grinding and sweetly thrashing. He was lost in the cavernous depths of her essence.

"X!" She suddenly moaned, an indication of her impending climax.

Xander's strokes were meticulous, careful, and calculated. Pleasantly pounding, her melodious moans were like a Shakespearean sonnet - poetry in motion.

"I can't. I don't understand. Why does this feel so damn good? Oh, shit." She groaned, welcoming every beautiful blow preparing her gooey goodness to satiate the immeasurable circumference of his dick.

"You feel it building? Hmm, babydoll? That rumbling, tingling sensation in your belly? That's me, baby. You feel me, Daij? Hmm? Just keep accepting me, baby." He raspily, sexily instructed as he anchored her legs over his forearms, leaning heavier into her wetness.

She moaned through gritted teeth, slightly arching her back to receive more of him.

"That's my babydoll. Good job, gorgeous." Kissing her dewy neck, he rewarded her good behavior with a delicious combination of sucks and thrust that catapulted Daijah beyond the crescent moon and glistening stars.

"Xandeeerrr! Too much. Too much. X!" Daijah screamed, unconcerned if the entire city heard her scream his name.

Moments later, Xander experienced an intensely salacious release of his own.

"Daijah. Baby. You feel so good... shiiiittt." He gritted. "Babydoll!"

They momentarily remained immovable, eyes hooded, temples kissing as they exchanged lovingly labored breaths. Xander gently lifted from her frame, quickly retrieving a blanket, sheathing her from the cold air. He handled her like a precious gem - with the utmost care, enfolding Daijah as she began to drift off to sleep. Planting gentle kisses on every bead of sweat and hushed quiver, he placed a final kiss on her pouty lips and whispered, "Happy birthday, babydoll. I love you and I'm sorry."

3

T he sullen melodies of Toni Braxton's "Seven Whole Days" blasted through the speakers as Daijah conducted her early Saturday morning cleaning. It had been three whole weeks since her birthday and no word from Xander. She called and texted nonstop, and even walked down the street at times she thought he would be at the Cannon house. After a week, she stopped calling but would send a random text referencing things that reminded her of him or news she wanted to share with only him.

Babydoll: Hey Xan. I started my classes this week. You were right. This shit ain't gone be easy. Can we talk?

Babydoll: That damn bird was at my window again. I think it misses you.

Babydoll: I miss you.

Babydoll: Shit! I had another nightmare last night. This time they were chasing me but I couldn't find you. I hate this. Can you call me please? I really needed you.

Babydoll: Wow. I can't believe this is us, Xan. I can't believe this is you. Don't worry about me. Fuck you and I'm done.

The final message was a week ago and she still hadn't spoken to him. Messages remained on read with no response, no explanation. Daijah mopped the laminate tile kitchen floor singing into the mop handle from her gut.

"*Deep in my heart, you were number one to start. But then you changed, you threw my heart away. Told your friends that you were runnin' thangs. Why'd it have to be that way?*

You're wrong. Dead wrong. Tell me how. How can we go wrong?"

"Daijah Blu?" Ms. Mimi timidly crept into the kitchen disturbing Daijah's soul-wrenching performance. Her grandmother knew not to press too hard when she was in a mood.

"I don't want to talk about it." She paused her movement without even making eye contact, still holding on to the mop.

"I was just going to say that your Uncle Bean is going to have somebody try to get the car started today. I really don't want you on the bus anymore. You are coming in later and later and it's just not safe, baby girl."

"Ok, grandma. Thank you." Daijah's dismissive and somber tone concerned Mimi.

"Daijah Blu, he'll come around. Maybe he has a lot on his mind. Not sure what he should say or do."

"Don't make excuses for him, Mimi. He knew exactly what he was doing." Daijah angrily blurted.

"Babygirl, mixing sex with a friendship as passionate and intimate as yours can be fulfilling in the moment but confusing and terrifying when you contemplate what's next." Daijah and her grandma never kept secrets. Aside from Zaria, Ms. Mimi was the first person to know she lost her virginity to Xander on her birthday.

Daijah dropped the mop and slouched in a kitchen chair. Ms. Mimi carefully tiptoed across the damp floor and pulled a chair next to her granddaughter, embracing her.

"But he made love to me, Mimi. How could he just walk away after that?" Daijah blinked back tears.

"How do you know it was making love, Daijah, if you've never done it?" Ms. Mimi inquired. "At almost 60 years old, I can say that I don't believe I've ever made love."

Daijah heaved, saddened by her grandma's disclosure. The night she experienced couldn't have been anything but the glory of love-making with Xander. She gazed at her grandma, mulling over the inquiry, then her gaze was transfixed seeing only images of *him.*

"Xan was so soft, gentle, and careful with me. He sought permission to love me. I felt every part of him from the crown of my head to the soles of my feet. He was embedded into every fabric, every strand. Transmitted through every vessel in my body. My satisfaction was his honor. It was mandatory over his own. I saw Xan lose himself in me and I disappeared too. Whispering, '*I love you, I won't hurt you.*' But -" Daijah blinked, biting the fleshiness of her lips to quell the cry, she shrugged. "But I guess he lied. So maybe I'm wrong. Maybe it wasn't making love after all, Mimi."

"Daijah Blu, don't say that. I know Xander loves you. I believe he's just scared, baby girl." Daijah nestled her head against her grandma's bosom and wept.

"Today's his birthday, Mimi. I just want to see him. The last time I didn't spend his birthday with him was -" She paused, rejecting the recollection of rehab preventing her from celebrating Xander's sixteenth birthday.

"Baby, the Bible tells us love is patient and kind but it don't tell us anything about love being a damn heartbreaker when dealing with a man." She tsked. "But that thing called love feels damn good when it's right. Shit, and sometimes even better when it's all wrong." Ms. Mimi giggled then cupped Daijah's face, focused on her reddened irises.

"And you have to decide if Xander is worth these tears, the pang in your heart. If you're prepared to deal with all the shit that comes with loving a goddamn man, baby girl. Especially a commanding, Alpha man like Xander Kindred. His daddy practically drove your crazy ass momma insane." She chortled. "Now if he's worth the insatiable insanity then fuck it, show him what he's missing and go get your man. But if he's not, then move the hell on."

Ms. Mimi didn't have the most elegant delivery but her point was made transparently.

————————————

DAIJAH HAD two braiding appointments later in the afternoon. Cornrows and box-braids touch up. The small, enclosed porch at the back of the house was her makeshift studio once Xander had a new air conditioner put in the room. He actually replaced all of the units since the outdated ones were not cooling the house properly.

It was about four o'clock in the evening and Daijah was finishing her last client when Zaria called.

"Hey girl. I'm going to be over there at about six." Zaria blurted.

"For what?" Daijah held the phone against her shoulder to finish the braid pattern.

"To get ready for X's party."

"I'm not going." She huffed.

"What do you mean you're not going? It's Xander's birthday. Your number one best friend, or did you forget?" Zaria's tone was laced with irritation.

"More like he forgot that we are best friends." Daijah rolled her eyes.

"Daij, what the hell are you talking about-"

"I haven't talked to Xan since my birthday, ok!" She yelled, then quickly quieted realizing her client was ear hustling. "Hold on Z."

Daijah recommended a break for the client and showed her to the restroom. She stepped outside to finish the call.

"Okay Z, I'm back. But I haven't seen nor heard from Xander since the day after my birthday."

"Bitch, what? Why? Why didn't you tell me?" Zaria annoyingly questioned.

"I don't know why and I was embarrassed. Bragging about our

time together then he ghosts me. I thought we all had a good time at brunch that next day. He said he had some business to take care of but would come see me that night. He never showed. I called, no response. Even his brothers have been making excuses for him. I'm over it."

Daijah walked back onto the porch when she saw her client be seated.

"Z, let me finish this last section and I'll call you back. You can come over if you want to but I'm not going." They disconnected the call.

Thirty minutes later Daijah was collecting her money and thanking the client. As she cleaned up the tiny area, she thought about Xander's birthday. It was his twenty-sixth. She'd had his gift for several weeks but now she wasn't certain she wanted to give him shit. It took Daijah forever to decide on the perfect gift. What do you get the man who has everything?

Xander loved writing music and was very musically talented but never focused on his craft. In high school, he secretly wrote endless pages of music, beautiful songs and poetry. The creative outlet became a key component to Xander and Daijah's therapy as kids. That was how they both fell in love with 90's R&B and Hip Hop. In those moments when they could not erase the treacherous sound of each other's screams, they'd spend hours laying side by side listening to everything from NWA to Babyface. Both Daijah and Xander agreed that the 90's remained the best music era and they would argue anyone down who disagreed. Admittingly, the early 2000s was good too, but in Xander's words, anything after 2010 was trash other than a few sprinkles of greatness.

One day a couple months ago, Daijah was helping Xander pack his old room at the Cannon Street house before he moved. She found a box filled with his handwritten work. For his birthday, she had the sheets protected and bound into a beautiful leather book with *X-Factor* embossed on the front.

"Daij, what do you think about X-Factor for my producer's name?

That's the shit, huh?" She laughed just as heartily today as she did all those years ago.

"Daijah, come and see what this man is talking about." Ms. Mimi yelled from the living room and she didn't sound happy. Daijah trotted to the front room to understand the clamor.

"This man says he has a delivery for Daijah Duvall." Ms. Mimi pointed to the scrawny looking white man dressed in blue Dickie pants and shirt with *Ben* stitched above the pocket. Ms. Mimi didn't really trust white people.

"They always coming to collect something from black folk. Either our money or taking away our men."

"Um, ma'am, are you Daijah Duvall?" He mumbled.

"I am. How can I help you?"

"I have a delivery for you." Ben turned and pointed to the flatbed truck parked on the street carrying a midnight blue BMW X3.

"There must be a mistake. I didn't buy this car. I can't afford this car." Daija's brows furrowed.

"Ma'am, I was instructed to deliver this car to this address and pick up an old Saturn." He shifted again, pointing towards the driveway at the faded green, dilapidated Saturn sedan that wouldn't start for almost two weeks. It was Ms. Mimi's old car that she gave to Daijah during her senior year of high school. It had definitely seen better days.

"Who authorized this?" Daijah muttered. Extremely irritated at this point because she already knew the answer to her question.

"Ma'am, I am not at liberty to say." Ben nervously peered around periodically checking his surroundings. He probably didn't come on this side of town often.

"You know what, nevermind. I do not accept the delivery." She crossed her arms as if that would make a difference.

"Ma'am, unfortunately, I can't accept that response. I was instructed not to leave this house without swapping the cars. No matter how much you argue, ma'am." He cleared his throat.

"Can you wait a moment, please?" Daijah was furious.

This had Xander written all over this bullshit. There was no point in calling since he hadn't answered the phone in almost three weeks.

Daijah nudged Ben out of the way then angrily trekked the five doors down to the Kindred house. She knew he would be there because it was the location of his birthday gathering. And she knew Xander was watching to ensure his plan was executed.... he was always watching. She busted through the front door that was rarely locked during the day. Xander's brothers were perched on the couch playing a video game.

Daijah blocked the TV with her thick thighs prevalently displayed through the fitted biker shorts with hands on her ample hips.

"Where the hell is he?" She angrily questioned.

The brothers didn't play with a pissed off Daijah. They had no verbal response, simply pointed to the back of the house in unison. Xander was likely on the porch smoking. Daijah burst through the door leading to the screened in extended porch inhaling the ganga smell.

"Xander what the fuck?!" She yelped.

Perched on the outdoor lounge chair, his face was placid and eyes dilated when he peered at her landing on the belly button peeking from the half shirt. He was high.

"What's up Daij?" Xander drunkenly slurred.

"You know what's up. Why the fuck would you buy me a car?" She was making a scene and didn't care. A few of Xander's crew intensely watched the exchange...and her ass.

"Who said I bought you a car?" He remained unbothered.

"Xander, stop bullshittin'. You are the *only* person I know who can afford a damn BMW." She slightly closed the distance between them. Fearful that a close proximity would put her under his spell.

"Daijah, you been on the fuckin' bus for the past couple weeks. Getting in late and shit. You don't need to be walking from no goddamn bus stop at night." His voice was smooth, mellow...sexy.

"That's not your *goddamn* problem, Xander. And the bus stop is right at the corner, it's fine." She dismissively flailed her arms.

Xander's demeanor quickly transformed from serene to agitated.

"It's *not* fuckin' fine and it is my fuckin' problem, Daijah." That made her belly rumble and her traitorous ass puss tingle.

"Xan, the bus stop is only like five minutes from my house." She shrugged. "It's not a big deal."

Xander angrily stood from the chair, knocking it to the floor. He simply motioned his head to the door and his crew expeditiously exited the porch.

"We were just five minutes from the fucking house and look what happened, Daijah! So, it *is* a big mutherfucking deal." He shouted. She'd officially fucked up his high and pissed him off.

Adonis rushed to the porch peering around to assess the situation. He looked between Xander and Daijah saying nothing verbally but his flaring nostrils said enough. Daijah was the one and only person in the world that could make him question or defy his older brother. Xander didn't release his glare from her face - eyes wide and misty.

"She's good, D. We're done here anyway." Zander separated himself from her, walking to the other end of the patio.

"Xan, Uncle Bean is getting the car fixed. Problem solved. So tell them to take it back."

"No disrespect Daijah, but if you're waiting on your uncle, your ass will be on the bus forever. You got a new ride. The problem is already solved. Go sign the fucking papers because it's not going back." Xander commanded.

"So that's it, huh? Nobody can do anything for me but Xander the Great, right? I gotta play on your terms, by your rules. I guess you like telling everybody how you take care of your poor charity case of a friend." She sarcastically waved her arms.

"Oh, look y'all, you see them J's Daijah's rocking, I bought that shit. Them diamond earrings, that's all me. A damn BMW, yeah, X did that shit. Is that what you need Xan, a fucking hand clap? Well whoop-ditty-doo. I don't fucking need none of that material shit!" Daijah huffed, tear-stained face indignantly hollering.

Xander's fiery eyes bulged. That shit hurt him to his core. And pissed him the fuck off. Daijah didn't even believe the shit she was spewing. Xander never bragged about what he did for her. If anything, he kept that shit private not wanting people in his business. Being a provider of things was the only way Xander knew how to demonstrate love. But never for accolades, show, or reciprocity.

"I don't need you to take care of me or protect me, Xander. I'm good. We're not kids anymore. And you're not daddy, my brother or my man." She nastily muttered.

His scorching orbs leered at her before peering outside acknowledging the neighborhood DJ who had arrived to set up for the party. Xander walked toward the back door of the patio. His back was to Daijah and voice was low.

"I've never done anything for you to win a fucking prize. Whatever I do for you is because I choose to. No fucking gimmicks, but I believe you know that already. Honestly Daijah, I don't really care what you think my reasons are or even what you claim you don't need. Me protecting you, taking care of you is not up for negotiation. That shit is constant - engrained...forever." He walked out, slamming the screen door.

Daijah couldn't control the rise and fall of her chest; she was so angry and so in love. This must be the insanity her grandma referenced. The vicious cycle of love - right or wrong. She huffed, biting the corner of her mouth endeavoring to not burst into wails. But she knew it was not about the car at all. Daijah was hurt, brokenhearted.

"Did you know about this, Doni? The car?" She heatedly asked her brother who was still standing in the doorway. "It's his birthday and he buys me a car. I mentioned that my room is hot and the next day, new AC units are being installed. He can't keep doing this shit." Sighing, Daijah leaned against the wall tired and defeated.

"Nah, I didn't know. But let it go, Daij. The house needed AC. You needed a car for you and grandma. And you on the bus just ain't ok.

So just let it go. You already know how X is when it comes to you." Adonis started to walk away, his baby face was agitated.

Daijah stood in the doorway leering at Xander. She wanted to hate this sexy ass specimen, but it was impossible. Her heart adamantly disagreed. He looked up, momentarily making eye contact but remained muted.

"Yeah, I thought I knew how *X* felt about me." She whimpered under her breath. Daijah turned around, slowly departing the house.

The delivery guy was seated on the steps impatiently waiting. Clearly Ms. Mimi wouldn't let him in the house. Daijah defeatedly marched up the steps and snatched the clipboard from his grasp to sign the paperwork, accepting the delivery.

ZARIA ARRIVED at Daijah's house looking cute in a Run DMC cropped off-the-shoulder t-shirt, booty shorts, and high top Vans. Her shoulder length ombre bob was fresh from the beauty salon. Zaria's lil chocolate self was so pretty. She looked like the 90's actress Taral Hicks that starred in one of her and Daijah's favorite movies, *A Bronx Tale*.

"Z, I told you I'm not going." Daijah's muffled fussing sounded from under the pillow while sprawled across her twin bed.

"Uh bitch, yes you are. You and X will be mad at each other for a minute and then go back to your best friend, no second best friends allowed coveted circle shit."

"Whatever." Daijah chuckled.

"Watch what I say. Anyway...did Ms. Mimi get a new boo with a BMW?" Zaria started pulling Daijah off the bed, forcing her to get dressed.

"Nope."

"So, who's ride is that? It's bomb as shit." She proceeded to pull a denim skirt out of the closet.

"Um...I guess it's mine." Daijah said hesitantly.

"Bitch what!? Did you hit the lottery and failed to inform your second best friend?" Zaria clutched her imaginary pearls.

"You already know who's the cause of that car being outside." Daijah walked the mini skirt back to the closet.

"Un huh, I know. The First National Bank of Xander." She chuckled, slapping her hands but wasn't shit funny. " He's also the same person who's the cure for that stank ass attitude of yours. Maybe he needs to caress that kitty and snatch your damn soul again." Zaria howled. Daijah sucked her teeth.

"You know what I would do if I were you, Miss Daijah Blu? Ah shit. That rhymed." Zaria tickled herself.

"Anyway. I would put on a sexy lil outfit. Pull them bomb ass twists into a cute bun. Rock them expensive ass earrings and whatever other jewelry that nigga bought you and go down the street flaunting all them double Ds and ass in his face. X may not know what the fuck he wants, but one thing's for sure, he don't wanna see no other nigga with his babydoll."

Daijah pondered her grandma's words. *Show him what he's missing and go get your man.* She thought the shit was petty as hell but sounded like the perfect plan. She was more than ready to show Xander that he was not her brother nor her daddy, and she was not a little girl who needed protecting.

4

Daijah crept through the backyard gate for Xander's birthday party a little after nine o'clock. She did as Zaria instructed - twists swept into a high bun, Simone I. Smith platinum hoops, and matching Chanel necklace and bracelet. Daijah rocked a cropped Tupac t-shirt, denim mini skirt, and black and red Jordan's. Honey-bronzed shea butter soaked skin on full display. Too much makeup wasn't necessary, so eyeliner and red lipstick completed the look.

The backyard was murky from the night sky and ganja smoke. Niggas were drunk, high, and acting a fool. Twerking asses filled the makeshift dance floor with thirsty chicks on the prowl for a d-boy sugar daddy. It wouldn't be another day in the hood without spades, dominoes, and a bunch of trash talking. Xander was perched in a high back chair in the center of the patio overlooking the party like his ass was Nino Brown, treating the patio like it was the VIP section at the club.

Zaria was itching to get on that porch, however Daijah had no desire to be in Xander's presence. Especially with the enhanced-ass chick vying for his attention. Simeon quickly exited the patio, swiftly closing in on Zaria.

"What's up Z?" Zaria wore a similar grin on her face. "Y'all smoking?" Simeon asked.

"Come on Sim, what kind of question is that?" Zaria looked at him like he was crazy. "Of course, we're smoking. At least I know I am. Party pooper over here may not be in the mood." Zaria chortled.

Daijah nor Zaria would partake regularly but periodically enjoyed the soothing effects of the ganga.

"I'm good right now." Daijah said. "You got my drink though?"

"Yeah Daij. You know X got you that girly ass pineapple rum shit you like." Simeon chuckled. "Yo, Daij. You like your new ride? That shit hot, huh?"

"You knew about that and didn't say shit to me, Sim? You are usually my spy when Xan is up to something." Daijah playfully punched his rock-solid arm.

"Yeah, but dawg, I couldn't let you keep rolling in that trifling ass hooptie, man. You're just like a Kindred, Daij. You can't be riding around like that. Our family has a reputation." He popped the collar of his pink and white Polo.

"But I'm *not* a Kindred, Simeon. I don't have money flowing out my ass. Driving a Benz at eighteen like you, spoiled brat." She rolled her eyes.

"Yeah, but you know if X got it, you got it." Simeon confidently confirmed.

"Material things are not what I desire from Xander, Sim. You know that better than anybody."

Simeon was often Daijah's listening ear and voice of reason when it came to handling Xander. He helped her understand this new version of Xander she was experiencing. He had two very distinct personalities. Xan was Daijah's loving, adoring best friend. The person who watched old movies with her and occupied her dreams every night.

Then there was X. The street savvy heir to the Kindred throne.

The mastermind behind the legal expansion of the Kindred dynasty. Xander was smart as shit. His fascination with Warren Buffet and the stock exchange turned a $100,000 investment his father gifted him at eighteen into a million dollar payout. Mack couldn't deny his son's brilliance and trusted him with the family fortune. Xander wasn't built for hustling on the streets. He was perfectly constructed for the office of the CEO and that's exactly where he was headed. Don't get it twisted, while Xander was a chill, kinda nerdy brainiac, nobody fucked with X. That nigga was cold, cryptic, and calculated.

Daijah and Zaria were standing in the yard dancing, drinking, and looking cute. Xander's eyes were focused on her because there was no shortage of niggas checking for the smart, hella thick, introverted beauty. But most of the dudes in the neighborhood understood that Daijah was off limits. Xander surveyed her from the crown of her twisted bun to the red soles of her J's. A slight smile crept across his blunt-darkened lips as he enjoyed this confident, jovial, sexy version of his babydoll. He remembered a time when he had to bribe her with Neapolitan ice cream to convince her to leave the confines of her tiny bedroom. Oversized jogging pants and t-shirts were her attire of choice until Xander began gradually introducing her to different styles and new designer clothes. He simply encouraged his friend to flourish and grow into the fucking exquisite soul he adored.

Xander missed the shit out of her. Purposely avoiding and not communicating was killing him. He literally licked his lips repeatedly trying to find a leftover morsel, any remnants of her sweet pussy. The morning after Daijah's birthday, Xander laid in the bed of the hotel suite gazing at her beautiful face. So peaceful, serene. They'd made love two more times before he bathed her and feasted on her sweet molasses center one more time in the shower. Unable to take anymore of his goodness, Daijah practically passed out in the shower. Lasciviously satisfied. Xander carried her limp frame to the bed as she slept against his shoulder. He outlined the curves of her face with a fingertip and brushed across her luscious lips. Inhaled the raspberry scent of her hair while meditating to the melodic hum of her light snore. But with all of her sated innocence and beauty on display, he couldn't eliminate the traumatic visuals of their past from his head.

Xander recalled the slash of the brass belt buckle across her neck, causing the ever present scar. The blood that seeped from her ear after being repeatedly beaten. Even through the calm of her magnificently curvy frame, he remembered how they riotously touched her, defiled her. Daijah was a permanent resident in the four chambers of his heart. He loved her and was *in love* with her but after what they'd endured, Xander never envisioned being her boyfriend. Only her protector and provider. He was willing to graciously grant Daijah everything she didn't know she needed but from a distance. But the spirit of selfishness was powerful. Xander didn't believe he was good enough for her, but neither was anyone else. He knew that shit wasn't fair but he honestly didn't give a shit.

Nights like Daijah's birthday, he conceded to his self-doubt and let the genie out of the bottle. Allowing shit that couldn't be undone to beautifully, yet dangerously evolve. His head urged him to pause his pursuit of Daijah that night, but his unyielding desire to acquire her, to be her inaugural love, was resentfully accommodating. Being buried in the cavernous depths of her pristine pussy was the softest place on earth. And it scared the shit out of him. Xander had to escape her sorcery. He'd already been under Daijah's spell for years without even tasting a dollop of her mouthwatering puss. But now that he sampled her candied goodness, he was shackled, bondage by the thought of not being the protector she trusted him to be.

The asses bouncing in Xander's face brought him back to reality. Neighborhood females and unknown hoodrats were surrounding him, trying their best to be his birthday sex for the night. Daijah recognized one particular female from a party at the Kindred house several months ago, but at the time, it was unclear which brother piqued her interest. Tonight, this chick was clearly aiming for Xander. Charai was her name, but in the hood, she was known as Cherry. *No surprise.* Daijah wasn't jealous. Xander's sexual history was no secret. Being his best friend, she was privy to more information about his sexual escapades than she cared to share. Daijah remembered when he lost his virginity at sixteen to a twenty-three year old woman who worked for his father. This woman had the nerve to be sprung over a damn teenager and wanted to fight Daijah when Xander spent more time with his best friend and not the woman. Xander was ready to beat that chick's ass until his father intervened and fired her instead. Mack would curse a woman like she was a man but didn't tolerate abuse.

Charai was dancing on Xander's lap while his gaze was still following Daijah. Her ass and titties looked like they were produced on the Ford assembly line. That shit was just so...faux. Charai's eyes followed Xander's line of sight directly to Daijah. Cherry knew exactly who Daijah was and began twerking and dancing a little faster and harder against Xander. His eyes stayed focused on his babydoll.

I guess that bitch is going to be his birthday sex. Just look away Daijah. Fuck her and fuck him. She vainly attempted to convince herself. Daijah wasn't mad about Charai, Cherry, whatever her name was, because even through their storm, she honestly knew that if she wanted Xander for the evening, she only needed to say a word and he'd shut this shit down. Xander could have his fun with that...canine.

Daijah was pissed that she literally craved Xander. At every turn she could feel his tongue against her breast, warm whispers of love against her lips, his solid, veiny dick massaging her pussy walls. Daijah physically quaked at the thought. Her damn panties were useless now. *Shit!* She gulped down her rum to gain a little liquid courage to twerk on one of these fine ass professional thug niggas. Daijah glanced back up at Charai, momentarily comparing herself.

"That bitch ain't got shit on you, Daij." Zaria shouted over the music as she danced past Daijah. And Cherry really didn't compare. Daijah was effortlessly beautiful. The *Ashley Banks'* look as a teenager evolved over the years. Warm caramel macchiato skin, big brown eyes with long, fluttery lashes. Almond-shaped face with the faintest dimples. A mole above her lip that Xander swore was shaped like a heart. Daijah's damn lips were beautiful - plump, pouty, and always ready to kiss. Voluptuous was the only way to describe the thick curviness of her meticulously crafted body. Breasts, thighs, hips, ass - oh my. The one positive trait of her maternal family's lineage.

"What's up, Daijah Duvall?" A smooth bass-filled baritone voice echoed over her shoulder. Daijah turned around to identify the owner of that sexy ass voice. *Roman Strong. Damn!* Roman was the second oldest of the five siblings comprising the Strong family. Like the Kindred family, they acquired their wealth on the streets before broadening their reach legally.

The Kindreds were the family of the south side while the Strongs ran the north. The families maintained mutual respect and under-standing, but either stood ready to clear the block if some shit popped off. Roman was a lot like Xander; the intellectual of the family. After his namesake father's death a few years ago, he sat at the helm alongside his gorgeous and gangsta ass mother, Indigo Strong.

"Nothing much, Roman Strong." Daijah was a little tipsy...and blushing.

"It's been a minute. Look at you all grown up. How old are you now, Daijah?"

"What? You want to card me. Make sure I'm legal." She bit the corner of her lip. *Shit. Am I flirting? I think I'm flirting.*

"I'm freshly twenty-four. Totally legal." Daijah chortled. "You've *been* grown up though. What are you now, thirty?" She teased.

Daijah remembered Roman from around the block when his father would meet with Mack attempting to keep the peace and mini-mize bloodshed. Roman was at least a junior in high school when Daijah was in seventh grade. Back then he seemed like a grown man to her and she, a little girl to him. But now, Daijah was a fucking woman and Roman couldn't stop gawking as soon as she walked in the party. He thought his boy was bullshittin' when he said that the tall, bodacious beauty was none other than Daijah Blu Duvall.

"Damn... don't age me like that. I'm twenty-eight." His pearly white Colgate smile made her belly flip. "You still live in Pleasant?"

"Yep, my grandma still lives up the street. One more year of law school and I'll be getting a place of my own though." She proudly declared.

"Oh damn. Congratulations, baby girl. Second year law student. That's what's up." He trailed a finger down her forearm. "So, when can I take you out to celebrate? Dinner, a movie. Whatever you want. Your choice."

"Celebrate what?" Daijah inquired, brows furrowed.

"You, beautiful. Not too many people from where we come from can say they are in junior college, let alone law school. That's a major accomplishment." His pearly whites were mesmerizing.

Roman was a glorious specimen of manly human. A toffee-colored God in a simple black t-shirt, khaki shorts, and all black Jordan's - he was exquisite. The gold chain sinfully hugged his thick neck. And those damn tattoos that ran up the length of his arm to his neck and one lone ink on his calf - good Lord. Daijah was a sucker for a man with tattoos. *Xander has tattoos.*

"Um, I'm not sure if that's a good idea. What would the hood folk think? We would have a lot of explaining to do." Daijah channeled her best Ricky Ricardo's voice.

Roman pinched the bridge of his nose, flashing that damn perfect smile again. "I honestly don't give a fuck what either hood thinks." Roman darted his eyes to the primary VIP seated on the VIP porch.

To the naked eye, Xander appeared unphased. But Daijah knew him. That hateful scowl was present, and she would hear about it before the night was over.

"Just tell me if you have a man, Blu." He closed the distance between them, biting his lip, with his hands resting behind his back.

"Blu?" Daijah chuckled. "Real cute."

"Nah, not cute. You are absolutely beautiful." Roman slowly scraped his teeth across his bottom lip. "I remember you telling me with a whole lotta attitude that only your grandma could call you Daijah Blu." He continued, licking those damn lips.

Roman reached out clasping her hand pulling her deeper into the yard concealed by darkness. Daijah reluctantly followed, knowing that she would face the Kindred family fire later. She quickly glanced at the patio. Xander's eyes were heavy with his hand on Charai's manufactured ass. She whispered in his ear while grinding on his lap. Xander smirked at her then sipped the brown liquor shifting his flaming umber orbs to Daijah. Now she was jealous...and pissed.

"On second thought, I would love to go to dinner, Roman." Daijah's nose flared as she flashed a false smile.

"Does Sunday work for you, beauty?" He asked.

"Yes, Sunday should work." She truthfully smiled this time, accepting his phone to enter her number. He dialed it, making sure she had his.

"Lock me in, baby girl. Don't be trying to play me when I call." He sexily grinned.

"Nah, never that. Call me with the details and I'll see you Sunday."

"Alright, beautiful. I'm about to get outta here. We'll be talking real soon." Roman winked, then signaled for his boys to roll out.

She bit her bottom lip, watching him disappear behind the gate. Zaria closed in on Daijah. "Who the hell was that and where can I get one?"

"Roman Strong. You know the twins from Gemini Salons? Their older brother."

"Damn he's fine with his Reggie Bush looking ass." They cackled until Daijah was snatched up by Adonis and Hiram dragging her towards the house.

"What the fuck are you doing, Daij?" Adonis said.

"First of all, watch your damn mouth with me. You are still my *little* brother. And second, I'm minding my fucking business." She yanked away.

"Daijah, stop bullshittin' man. You know we don't fuck with no Strongs like that." Hiram enforced.

"*Whatever!*" She mouthed, waving them off. "I have to pee. Are we done here or do I need a chaperone?" Daijah ambled onto the porch when Simeon continued the interrogation.

"Stop playing, Daij. You heard what he said. We don't fuck with the Strongs."

"And who is *we*, Simeon? Hmm?" Her eyebrow raised, seeking clarity.

"Fucking Kindreds." Simeon shouted.

Daijah stared directly at Xander who remained a silent observer. Her leer was fiery as she screamed, "I am *not* a fucking Kindred! So, I can do what the fuck I want, with who the fuck I choose to do it with. Now...can you kindly let me go?" She gawked at Simeon's firm hand clutching her wrist. He didn't acquiesce, angrily leering at Daijah.

"Sim, let her go bro. Now." Xander impassively demanded. Simeon apologetically released her.

———————————

DAIJAH STORMED THROUGH THE HOUSE, shuffling upstairs to the restroom in Xander's room on the second floor of the house. The two family flat was converted to a two story home with two master suites upstairs and three bedrooms and two and a half baths down stairs.

Daijah had to get herself together. She was so damn irritated with this whole scene. While she didn't necessarily want to go on a date with Roman, it was clear that Xander was on some bullshit. In the few words they said to each other, not once had he explained why he played disappearing acts for the past three weeks. Wishing she followed her intuition by staying at home, she splashed water on her face, dabbed it dry, then retrieved her lip gloss from her Louis Vuitton fanny pack. Staring at her reflection in the mirror, Daijah painily exhaled before sauntering out of the ensuite bathroom into the bedroom to find Xander sitting on the footboard bench at the end of his bed. He was leisurely flipping through the leather bound engraved music book. Before she and Zaria joined the party, Daijah snuck upstairs to Xander's old room leaving his gift on the bed. She was certain he would be too drunk to drive home and would find it there later.

With matching narrowed eyes, they leered at one another for what seemed like a lifetime but only a minute ticked by.

"When did you do this?" Xander's eyes were still heavy, somber and indignant simultaneously.

"I don't know. I guess it was a while ago." Daijah shrugged dismissively. She was standing stationary in front of the bathroom door.

"Daijah come here." The raspiness of his voice was commanding.

"No." Her voice quivered, as did her puss. She shifted to lean against the wall.

"Daijah." He commanded again.

"I said no."

Xander slightly tilted his head glaring at her as if she'd grown five noses. Seemingly surprised by her lack of acquiescence. The crimson blaze flickering behind his umber eyes was different. Daijah suddenly realized that this was not her best friend Xan, this was that nigga X. He licked his lips before biting the bottom corner. Gently placing the gift on the footboard, he stood to his full, dominant height then put his hands in his pockets, giving her a second to rethink her stance. Her feet remained bolted to the worn carpet.

Daijah surveyed him for the first time tonight and Xander looked so fucking good. Just effortlessly sexy. Crisp white V-neck Lacoste t-shirt, gray shorts, and brand new gray and white Air Force One's. Fresh haircut, a new shadowed beard added to his deliciousness. Xander stealthily meandered towards her, so close, not even a gust of wind could traverse their meshed bodies. Daijah was heavily panting.... fucking hyperventilating and he had not made one move.

"You didn't tell me happy birthday, babydoll." Xander whispered in her ear.

The faint graze of his lips against her flesh caused a guttural tremble in her center. If she didn't know any better, Daijah was convinced she just had an orgasm standing on her two feet. *What the fuck?*

"I didn't hear you, Daij. We don't say happy birthday anymore?" Xander trailed a finger down the curve of her face, caressing her nape. He fully comprehended the level of control he possessed when fondling that scar.

"Hmm, can I at least get a birthday kiss?" Licking against the seam of her lips, his words set fire to places that remained North Pole chilly for weeks. Xander was teasing her. And the shit was working.

"Cherry ain't giving birthday kisses? Or maybe some birthday sex?" She brashly questioned.

"Nah. She's not what I want for my birthday. I want your birthday kisses." He softly tongue kissed her, then continued. "And your birthday sex, babydoll."

"X." Daijah breathily whimpered, then returned a heated lick against his lips, but refused to say what he wanted to hear.

Xander massaged her breast through the cotton shirt before journeying his fingers under it. Kneading, pinching, and driving her insane. His sizey imposing hands trailed down her belly and under the skirt. He rubbed her swollen clit through the sodden fabric.

"Tell me, babydoll."

"No." Daijah whined.

Xander pinched the fatty folds of her private lips.

"Ah, shit!" She cried with pleasure.

"Say it, Daijah."

Relentlessly, recklessly, roughly, Xander squeezed and palmed her pussy. Daijah was wantonly spent when she sang through a moan.

"Happy birthday, Xan. Ah - Fuck!"

"Good job, babydoll." He lustfully chortled. "Damn, I fucking missed you."

Xander lovingly stroked her cheek before rashly kissing her, devouring every crevice of her mouth. Lips tenaciously hungry and so damn tasty. Daijah was still clutching her purse with her back pressed against the wall. Xander cupped her ass, lifting her to straddle him. Daijah dropped that damn purse so fast when Xander used one hand to pin her wrists above her head. His other hand crept under her cropped shirt, unhooking her bra before suckling a swollen nipple into his mouth.

"Ah, shit. Xan. I missed you too, big head." She moaned. The pleasure and pain marvelously commingled - genuine, unrelenting and welcomed.

They exchanged juicy, sloppy, messy kisses - lips, neck, breast, no surface was overlooked. Xander's strong body was cut like steel, welded to perfection as he maintained the strength to restrain her arms while securing both their bodies against the wall. He made quick work of his shorts, pooling at his feet in seconds. He slid her soaked panties to the side, blunt fingertips invading her waterlogged pussy.

"Mmm. Xander. Baby, that feels so good." Daijah acknowledged that she was about to be fucked by Xan. Correction, she was about to be fucked by that nigga X. And she delighted in the cringe of terror that arrested her flesh. Xander plunged his fingers into her core at an unabated, merciless pace until she screamed.

"X! XAN! SHIT!" Daijah didn't give a damn if every partygoer knew that she was being properly screwed by the birthday boy.

He swallowed her moans while simultaneously driving that *hey big man* dick into her taut oasis. He was so big. She gasped, the initial pressure of his heaviness snatched her breath away. Damn he was deep. So deep Daijah feared becoming a permanent fixture of his bedroom wall. Xander's eyes were pinched tight, biting his lips as he slithered in and out of her hole at a steady briskness, simultaneously manipulating her clit with his thumb. Xander released her hands and

Daijah tightly, hurriedly caressed his neck, so close their hearts drummed a corresponding beat.

"Fuck! Daijah. Shit. Look what the fuck you do to me." Xander gritted, repeatedly banging a palm against the wall, as he beautifully banged her puss.

Daijah was confused. What was she doing to him when she was the exposed victim? Thick thighs suspended midair, J's dangling from her feet, titties bouncing while his enormous penis encroached all of her guts. He stroked, and pounded, and drummed, and stroked some more at an uncompromising velocity against her contracting dampened walls. Her pussy was still perfect and tight but steadily conforming to the contours of his dick. Welcoming him home.

"X. X. X!" Daijah climaxed with a force so strong, she broke skin when biting into his shoulder. Plump scratches blistered his neck from her death grip. He looked like he'd been in a brawl and lost.

"Babydoollll!" Xander groaned into her chest, hammering towards the pinnacle. The stinge of her assault and that tight ass pussy was gratifyingly succulent.

Xander rested inside her folds, shivering every time her essence quaked around his manhood.

"Daij, fuck. Quit playing." He huffed.

"I'm not playing." She shuddered through the aftershock.

After several minutes of strained breathing, he gently settled her wobbly legs on the floor, clasping her waist until she balanced on her feet. Daijah licked her lips, the weed and bourbon deliciously unified on her tongue. She adjusted her wet panties and skirt, palms pressed to smooth the wrinkled t-shirt. Somehow her phone was still clutched in her hand. Completely disheveled, her bun even had the gangsta lean. Xander stepped back, giving both of them some room to get their shit in order. Daijah's phone chimed a few times and illuminated. She didn't look at the screen before sliding it into her back pocket. He ran a hand down his face before clasping both hands at his nape. Tossing his head back eyeing the ceiling fan, Daijah sensed irritation, apprehension...regret. She swallowed hard.

"Xan." Her sweet voice narrowly above a whisper.

"Roman is not an option for you, Daijah." Xander blurted without flinching.

Shocked that they were back to that topic, Daijah shook her head, bending to pick up her purse.

"I don't believe Roman is any of your business, Xander."

"Daijah, please don't fuck with me about this. I'm only going to say it one more time. Roman Strong *is not* an option. Find somebody else."

That hurt. That shit cut like a fucking machete because Daijah thought she found her somebody. After what they shared on her birthday, shit...just ten minutes ago...their entire lives.

Wow! She mouthed, eyes engorged with tears but she refused to let them fall. She stared at him for extended moments.

"Xander, you said you loved me. Actually, your exact words were, *I fucking love you, babydoll.*" Daijah was trembling. Rage, panic, and heartache ripped through her core. She felt sick.

"I also said I didn't know what this could be or what the future held for us." He placidly rebutted.

"You just told me you missed me. Was that a lie?"

Xander savagely glared at her as if her question was inappropriate.

"I see. So, there is no love, you just wanted to fuck me? Like I'm that manufactured fucking canine, Cherry? I was just another chick to add to your harem of bitches."

Xander was hushed, face expressionless as he settled back on the footboard.

Daijah chuckled but wasn't shit funny. She briefly considered throwing her phone against his big ass head.

"I guess this is the 'X' I keep hearing about, huh? Cold, callous, and a fucking asshole. I don't know this person. I don't *want* to know this person. The man I know delicately liberated me from my virginity. Making sweet love to me just three weeks ago. Confessed his love for me and I believed him. The man I know taps on my window at night and climbs in the bed to comfort me when I have nightmares." Daijah stood right in front of him. Previous proximity concerns eliminated.

"You know, I've always wondered, how did you know? How did you know that I was having a bad night? How did you know that I needed you? But I quickly realized that this strong, unemotional man has nightmares too. He needs comforting too. And although right now he won't admit it...he needs *me* too." She poked against his firm chest with every word.

Freeing the tears, she sobbed at the realization that she was losing more than a lover, but her best friend.

"So, when *my* Xan, my best friend, is ready to resurface, come holla at me. But until then...stay the fuck away from me!"

Daijah stormed out of the room, running down the steps and out the front door. That was her last time at the Kindred house on Cannon Street.

5

The afternoon sun disrespectfully beamed through the collapsible sliding balcony door of Xander's master bedroom. It was almost one o'clock in the afternoon and Xander had no desire to face the day. He was so fucking drunk and high last night that he barely remembered how he made it home. Confident that one of his brothers drove him home, Xander peeled out of the bed feeling every ounce of the Hennessy White banging in his head. His birthday was the one day he let his guard down. Treading into the modern white and charcoal grey bathroom, he retrieved the bottle of Tylenol, gulping down two pills with little to no water.

The whole night was a blur, except for Daijah. Xander licked his lips, still tasting remnants of the spicy pineapple rum he seized from her tongue. He remembered that she looked good as hell last night in that little ass skirt and Jordan's. Crawling back into the bed, his manly parts began to expand at the recollection of how her perfect pussy contracted around the swell of his dick. *Shit Daij!* He honestly didn't go upstairs intending to have sex with her. Xander followed Daijah upstairs to check on her after the argument with his brothers. He knew Simeon went too far, forcibly grabbing Daijah's wrist like that. Xander reminded himself to beat Simeon's ass before the day was over.

Drunkenly walking into his old bedroom last night, Xander knew Daijah was going to be on some bullshit because he'd been on some bullshit the last few weeks. So he was prepared for an argument until he noticed the gold-foil wrapped box on the bed. Opening the box, his steely exterior softened at the gesture. Xander didn't need to talk to Daijah to know that she was heartbroken by his vanishing act. Even through the hurt, Daijah didn't forget his birthday. *Shit! You're a fucking asshole, man.* Xander mused, when he emptied the box and read the engraved front cover and the handwritten inscription inside.

'Xan, my protector, my savior, my best friend. Your beautiful words saved my life. They gave me hope, encouragement, and the will to fight another day. Your poetry and lyrics were my therapy, my cure. I hope this reminds you of your gift and encourages you to continue to make magic. No matter what happens, we will forever be good, Xan. I love you.
~ Your Babydoll, Daijah

After reading her words, Daijah's pretty ass appeared in the doorway and all restraints disappeared. Daijah had to be a connoisseur of witchery because he was in a trance - under her salacious spell. When he requested her presence and she said no, her forceful, yet unconvincing response caused an impulsively carnal stir in his belly. His dick was aching for Daijah. Her sweet Xan had officially left the building, and X hastily emerged.

Xander adjusted himself to alleviate the pressure building in his balls at the thought. The swelling quickly deflated when he recalled the way she blushed and flirted with Roman Strong. Xander had no beef with Roman...until last night. The niggas in his hood understood that Daijah was a no-fly zone. He believed Roman was aware as well, he just didn't give a fuck. After sexing the shit out of her, Xander had no intentions of mentioning her exchange with Roman. He wanted to continue his birthday celebration with love making until the sun kissed against their satiated flesh. But her phone chimed, indicating a text message, and he knew it had to be that nigga. And Xander was pissed. While he meant the shit he said about Roman Strong not being an option for her, he wasn't proposing that she find someone else other than him. Xander fucked up and he knew. But he also understood that he may never be able to mend the broken pieces.

"X! Is your ass still sleeping?" Hiram's voice boomed on the other side of the door. "Nigga, I'm coming in. Daijah, if you're naked say something?" He chuckled, peeking around the bedroom door.

"Ram, what the fuck are you doing here? Why the hell would Daijah be in my bedroom? And naked, nonetheless." Xander stood from the bed, pulling on his grey sweatpants.

"After y'all went upstairs last night and then disappeared, I figured you brought her home with you. I knew Cherry's ass wasn't here because you don't want her to know where you live." Hiram plopped down on the bed.

Xander aggressively pushed his brother's legs. "Get your damn feet off of my bed. I'll ask again, what the hell are you doing here?"

"Your dumb ass brothers are downstairs." Hiram continued.

"Oh, so now they're just my brothers." Xander chuckled. "What do y'all niggas want?"

"Sim came to get his ass whooping like a man. He knows you are mad as fuck about what he did to Daijah. He called her but she ain't answering for him. Shit, she ain't answering for Doni. She big mad." Hiram guffawed.

"Yeah, Sim's ass already know. Let me hop in the shower real quick." Xander ambled towards the bathroom. "Aye, see what Miriam left in the refrigerator to warm. I'm hungry as shit." Simeon nodded as Xander closed the bathroom door.

Twenty minutes later Xander came downstairs wearing a fitted t-shirt, black sweatpants, and black Nike slides. Hiram laughed, shaking his head. *This nigga really thinks he's Nino Brown.* He pondered. Simeon and Adonis kept their heads hung low avoiding eye contact with their big brother.

"What did y'all find to eat?" Xander's tone hinted at irritation, bothered.

"Man, Miriam is the shit. You know she got your food organized in aluminum containers. All you gotta do is pop them in the oven. I'm getting that kinda housekeeper when I move out. Ricki's lazy ass don't cook shit but daddy keeps her around." Hiram rambled.

"You said all that shit but still didn't tell me what we are eating?" Xander shook his head.

"Some chicken with black bean shit she made. It looks good as hell. I just put it in the oven since your ass refuses to use a microwave."

"Shit tastes like rubber in the microwave. I like my food fresh." Xander stressed.

"Yo ass is bougie, X." Hiram laughed and so did Xander because he couldn't deny it.

Simeon and Adonis were still muted and afraid.

"Why the fuck y'all sitting here like two dumb ass bumps on a log?" Xander finally was seated at the head of the table in the eat-in kitchen. He loved to cook when he had time so a chef's kitchen was the first priority when he had the house constructed.

"I'm sorry X. I fucked up. I was just pissed when I saw Daij with that nigga Roman." Simeon blurted.

"Me too, X. I don't know what the hell she was doing but I'll talk to her." Adonis concurred.

"Don't nobody talk to Daijah about Roman except for me." Xander commanded. "Sim, if you ever put your fucking hands on her again, I will bring you a world of fucking hurt, bro. I keep telling your big ass that you don't know your own damn strength and it's going to get your ass killed or in jail one day over some stupid shit."

Simeon nodded his understanding.

"Doni, your sister is a grown ass woman. Like she said, she can do whatever the fuck she wanna do, with whoever she wants to do it with." Xander mocked Daijah's voice.

"But, X -" Adonis attempted to interject but Xander put his hand up, not wanting to hear whatever his little brother had to say.

"You heard what I said. Just leave it alone, D." Xander got up to check on his food.

"Maybe if you stop bullshittin' and treat my sister right, she wouldn't be fucking with no Strong." Adonis mumbled under his breath but Xander digested every word. He closed the oven, adding more cooking time before he slowly turned around, glaring at his brother.

"What did you say, D? Huh? I didn't hear you. Say it again." Xander lifted a brow as he cupped his ear, motioning for Adonis to repeat himself. He remained hushless.

"Nah, say that shit it again. But say it from your chest this time since you wanna be a fucking man in my goddamn house." Xander was standing over Adonis who was still seated at the table. The room was silent.

"Real talk, X. If you would just stop bullshittin' about your feelings for Daij, she wouldn't even be considering no damn date with Roman Strong. She would be right here with you. Like she's always been. Y'all in love - *been* in love. So, what's the problem?" Adonis quickly quieted, waiting for the fire, but none came.

"Alright. Since we getting shit off of our chest, does anybody else got something to say?" Xander leaned against the kitchen island expectantly, arms folded across his chest. A few hushed moments ticked by.

"Daijah loves you, man. I mean - I don't even know what else to say. I ain't never seen no shit like y'all's bond. You are her everything, and I believe she's yours. Shit, Daijah is a fucking beast. Beautiful, smart, body for days...she's not threatened by yo hustle. Daij is ride or die. What more could you ask for? But -" Simeon paused, collecting his thoughts. "The shit you doing to her...it ain't right. Can't nobody fuck with her, but you ain't trying to fuck with her. That's selfish as fuck, X. You know Daij is like blood, bro. You know me and her are tight. So, while you buying her cars and shit, all she really wants, nigga, is *you*." All the brothers nodded concurrently.

Xander angrily glowered at them, deadpan, motionless. He believed every word his brothers uttered to be true. But they didn't know the real history with Daijah. They were too young to truly conceive what he and Daijah endured those twelve or more hours in the abandoned car wash. No one would ever comprehend the demons he wrestled daily. Xander had his reasons why he couldn't love Daijah the way she deserved and he was settled with the decision.

"I said what the fuck I said. Leave Daijah to me and only me." He paused, not offering a response to his brothers' inquiries. "Enjoy your food and lock my door when you leave." And with that, Xander escaped to the confines of his media room, slamming the door behind him.

Roman: Hey beauty. Does tomorrow at 6 work for you?

Daijah: Aren't you the charmer? LOL! Yes, that works.

Roman: I just call it like I see it. You are a beautiful woman Daijah.

Daijah: #blushing

Roman: Ha. You are something else.

Daijah: Just casual right?

Roman: If that's your preference. Yes. Casual it is. I'll see you tomorrow. Have a good night beautiful.

After the fight with Xander a week ago, Daijah walked away properly fucked, pissed, and heartbroken, but it gave her the motivation she needed to go to dinner with Roman. He texted her that night shortly after Xander disrupted her entire womb with that monstrous dick. Briskly taking the walk of shame home, Daijah checked the message.

Roman: I still smell your sweet ass perfume, beauty.

Damn I'm in trouble.

But that's cool.

Sweet dreams.

Daijah successfully and purposely played phone tag with him all week using school and her grandma's doctor's appointments as excuses. Partially true. Honestly, she didn't know if she was capable of visualizing another man beyond Xander. He was literally her everything - best friend, fake boyfriend, virginity bandit, soul snatcher, and very real love. Her muse. As fine as Roman was, Daijah needed more than just his luscious lips, tatted up muscles, and athletic thighs to get a second date. She desired mental stimulation, thought-provoking conversation and merriment.

Daijah: It's a date. Goodnight.

Holy Shit! I have a date! Daijah's pondering shook her from the reverie. Her blush quickly transformed to fear. Technically she'd never been on a date before. *Pathetic! Twenty-four damn years old and not one date.* Irritably musing, she rolled her eyes. If Daijah was keeping it one hundred with herself, no other boy or man had ever made it past hello. Honestly, Daijah and Xander's relationship was borderline dependent. The three weeks he ghosted her, she felt physically sickened, feeble. The past week since their fucking and fighting fiasco in his room, her mood instantaneously shifted from jovial to downright wretched. Some ole bipolar'ish shit. Ms. Mimi even escaped to Uncle Bean's apartment upstairs to avoid Daijah's wrath.

There was definitely no shortage of suitors for her - hood niggas, d-boys, professional thugs, and sophisticated college men. But none by the name of Xander Malcolm Kindred. He was how she spent her time outside of school and work. It was her norm since middle school. The only outing she could think of with a guy who wasn't Xander was prom. But was that classified as a date? His name was Keith Sullivan. *Poor guy.* Keith admired Daijah from afar since their freshman year in high school. He was certain that she would go to prom with Xander. Everybody knew they would be prom King and Queen. But when Xander dropped out of school their junior year to get his GED because he was *"over this mediocre bullshit,"* Keith was ready to shoot his shot....and Daijah said yes. Partly because Keith was kinda fine, but mostly to piss off Xander.

But Xander had other plans for Daijah on prom night. He allowed Keith to do all the formal bullshit - Poindexter suit, corsages, pictures in the park, and the boring ass dance. Daijah and Keith arrived at the Hyatt Hotel to meet a group of classmates who were having an after party in one of the suites, when the familiar baritone timbre ricochet through her floor-length yellow taffeta gown.

"Daijah." Xander glared at her. She was beautiful with her spiral curled hair swept to the side draping her shoulder. The sweetheart neckline strapless gown hugged her bodice and belled from the cinched waist.

"Xan. No! You are not about to do this." She scoffed to his unspoken demand. Daijah knew Xander didn't give a damn that she was at prom and he definitely didn't give a damn about her date.

Xander confidently exited his white Escalade dressed in navy slacks, a blue and yellow striped dress shirt - no tie, and peanut butter Ferragamo loafers. This nigga was wearing Ferragamos at eighteen. It never crossed his mind that it was inappropriate to disrupt her prom night. Nor was he concerned about her denying him. Xander was holding a bouquet of yellow and red roses as he minimally smiled, crooking his finger requesting her presence. Daijah swallowed hard, but her nipples were harder. He looked so fucking good. Daijah wanted to resist, but she would follow him to hell if that's where he was headed.

"Yo, Keith, thanks for taking care of my girl. I can take it from here." Xander shook Keith's hand before coupling his hand with hers. "Come on, babydoll."

Daijah's damn panties were soaked and halfway down her legs in her mind. She clasped his hand, while still holding Keith's. It took about a millisecond for her to make a decision. Daijah released Keith's hand, then apologetically whispered, "I'm sorry."

Xander pulled her into his solid frame before kissing against her temple. He was such a fucking man - a boss, at only eighteen. Opening the passenger door, Xander gathered the short train of her dress, helping her into the truck. People stared as Keith stood embarrassed and alone. A white box with a red bow rested on the dashboard.

"I figured you would want a snack. Open it." Xander motioned to the box.

Daijah squealed, lightly clapping her hands as she recognized the logo. Carefully opening the box, it revealed chocolate covered strawberries and pineapples. Her smile beamed brighter than the full moon. Poor Keith was still dumbfounded. Xander chucked him the deuces and sped off.

"Xan. You are so bad. Why would you do this?" Daijah fruitlessly tried to mask her chortle.

"Because you promised me in seventh grade that you'd go to prom with me. You checked the yes box and I still have the note to prove it. I'm just making you keep your word, Daij." He smiled, biting into a strawberry.

Ten minutes later they pulled into the W Hotel greeted by the valet. The bellman retrieved the luggage and informed Xander that everything was in order. Daijah had no clue what was going on so she sauntered towards the automatic double doors when Xander clutched her waist to pause her pursuit. He shook his head then signaled to the street. A gorgeous white horse with braided hair in yellow ribbons pulled and even more glorious white carriage with red velvet seats for two. Xander lived for every moment that he was responsible for her smile.

"You wanna take a ride with me, babydoll?"

"Absolutely." Daijah beamed, extending her hand ready to follow his lead.

Sparkling cider and two champagne flutes sat perched in an ice bucket to accompany the dipped fruit. Daijah felt like a princess being enchanted by her prince. They reached the Landing on the River where a late night candlelit dinner awaited them at the Boathouse.

Returning to the hotel, Daijah actually prayed to God that she would lose her virginity tonight at the hands of Xander. Understanding that's not really the way God worked, she crossed her fingers all the way to the twentieth floor.

"Xan, if I forget to tell you later, thank you for kidnapping me. This has been the prom night of my dreams." Daijah leaned over and extended the

softest, sweetest kiss on his cheek. She was spellbound and he was mesmerized.

The blaring ring of the phone disrupted her daze. Daijah deeply exhaled, reminiscing on the Xander she fell in love with and saddened by what he had become.

"What's up, Zaria?" Daijah answered.

"Hey Daij. What are you doing?"

"Trying to figure out what one does on a date." Daijah giggled as she organized her desk.

"So, you're really going out with Roman, huh? Damn, did X piss you off that bad?"

"This is not about X, Zaria." She partially lied. "This is about the fact that I'm twenty four years old and the only real dates I've ever had were with my best friend who fucked me then tossed me aside like a pair of scuffed J's."

"Daij, I think you're overreacting." Zaria chuckled. "But I guess he did disrupt all your peace and happiness with that big man dick he put on you...well, in you."

"Zaria!" Daijah shouted. "Don't ever repeat that. I told you that in confidence."

"Sorry, boo, but that shit is funny as hell." Zaria continued to howl.

"Z, it's not that damn funny. And I'm not overreacting. Xan had the nerve to tell me Roman was not an option for me so I should find somebody else. Somebody else Z! Who? Who am I gonna find? That shit hurt my feelings. Broke my fucking heart." Daijah's voice cracked into a whisper.

"I can't keep allowing him to control every aspect of my life. Especially if he doesn't want to play the role I need him to play. I want a boyfriend who takes me on dates, cupcakes with me on the phone until we both fall asleep. I want long walks in the park and explore new restaurants where he feeds me random food I've never had. I want the prospect of a family in the future - husband, babies - all that shit we see in Lifetime movies." Daijah audibly exhaled, motoring through her pouty lips.

"Then go get it, Daij, because you deserve that shit. I love X, but fuck fine ass, sexy ass, rich ass Xander Kindred." Zaria was always going to find a way to make Daijah laugh.

"If he can't realize that a gem - his entire fucking world is staring him right in the face then that's his loss. Now go on dates and long walks and shit with fine ass, sexy ass, rich ass Roman Strong."

"You are a complete fool, Z!" Daijah cracked up laughing. "Now get over here and help me find something to wear."

Seven outfits later, Daijah found the right one. In Zaria's words, it's heaux-classy; whatever the hell that means. Red strapless crop top with matching fitted skirt that accentuated her curves and a racer-back denim waist vest. Since Roman said casual, she opted for simple gold t-strap sandals. Her curly braids pulled into a high ponytail and thin hoop earrings.

"Daijah Blu. You have company." Ms. Mimi sang. She offered Roman a seat and iced tea that he declined. Daijah peeked down the hall to see her grandma surveying him. Ms. Mimi knew fine when she saw it and Roman was exceptional.

"Does she have the nerve to be flirting?" Daijah whispered to no one but herself. She sauntered down the long hallway leading to the modest living room.

"Well, hello, sir." She bashfully smiled.

"Well, hello, beautiful. Your grandmother and I were just getting acquainted." He flashed that Colgate smile.

Ms. Mimi was standing there with a toothy grin holding a bouquet of flowers. Roman held a second bouquet of red roses that he extended to Daijah.

"You're so sweet. Thank you." "

"My pleasure, beauty." Roman winked.

"Roman, please call me Ms. Mimi, sweetheart. I'm still too young and too fine to be called *grandmother*." She interrupted the moment before rolling her eyes.

"Well *Grandmother...*" Daijah teased, mimicking Ms. Mimi. "I won't be too late. Call Doni if you need anything. Love you." She kissed her grandma's cheek.

"It was nice to meet you Ms. Mimi." Roman shook her hand, but she returned with a hug.

"You as well, Roman. Be careful with my baby. I know people." Ms. Mimi warned with a smile.

Daijah stood on her porch as her grandma continued bantering with Roman. She peered around the neighborhood knowing that Xander had eyes on her, even if they weren't his. The details of her attire, Roman's car, the length of the chat with her grandma were certain to get back to him. Roman settled his hand on the small of her back slightly above her ass and leaned in to whisper, "you ready beauty?" Daijah lightly chuckled, thrilled that Xander would get that intel as well.

6

"Here's to six more months, six more years, maybe even six more decades." Roman lifted his champagne glass, gazing at Daijah as she did the same. His beautiful smile glistened before taking a sip. They were enjoying dinner at Milano's, an upscale Italian restaurant downtown.

Hours earlier, Daijah ambled into Roman's condo after her last class before spring break. Two white boxes with red velvet bows perched on the charcoal grey leather couch in the living room. Roman was in his office when she arrived.

Not disturbing the boxes, she peered around the freestanding decorative brick wall that divided his office from the rest of the living space. He was a sexy shirtless specimen with dark rimmed glasses and grey sweatpants. Daijah ogled him for a moment too long. She was ready to swipe all that shit off of the desk and allow him to fill her to capacity.

"Hey." She shyly uttered instead.

Roman blushed, lifting his head from the computer to greet her. He always took an extra heartbeat to study her. Daijah's beauty was free, uncomplicated, and easy.

"Hey." He warmly returned.

"Is it somebody's birthday?" She sexily blushed, biting her bottom lip.

"Nah. But it is a celebration." He stood, removing his glasses and revealed more of his deliciously muscly abdomen. "Come on." Roman kissed her temple, then ushered her to the living room.

Daijah was confused. It wasn't her birthday and she prayed that she didn't forget his birthday. So, what were they celebrating?

"Blu, get out of your head and open the boxes." He instructed.

"Roman, what is this? What are we celebrating?"

"Us, baby girl. We are celebrating six months of me and you." He curled the corners of his lips as he often did when he was nervous.

Roman was eerily similar to Xander. Both intellectuals, a little hood, fine as hell... and a mystery. Roman had two distinct personalities - well, actually three. There was Roman - the sweet, smart, loving man that she'd fallen in *like* with. Then there was RJ - the adored momma's boy and paragon of the Strong family. Finally, there's Rome - the street savvy, not to be fucked with nigga from the north side. Daijah only had experience with Roman and a little of RJ when she met his mother. Unlike with X, she hadn't encountered the Rome version of her friend or boyfriend. She wasn't exactly certain about their title.

"Roman!" Daijah happily squealed before she even opened the boxes. "You are so thoughtful. Thank you." She melted into his brawny arms when he opened them to embrace her. Unpacking the first box, Daijah pulled out a stunning pair of black, silver studded Louboutin's. Her eyes widened as he motioned for her to open the second box. It revealed a deep wine toned strapless jumpsuit. Daijah was speechless.

"And the last thing..." Roman's rich baritone calmed her ardently beating heart. He pulled a smaller box from his sweatpants pockets. Daijah began to hurriedly back away, heart furiously pounding against her chest. She shook her head.

"Baby, it's not what you think." He chuckled, gently grabbing her arm to pause her impending departure.

"Oh, thank God. Whew." Daijah loudly exhaled.

He opened the box since her jittery hands wouldn't allow it.

"What did that chick call it in that silly ass movie you made me watch...how to lose a nigga in ten days? It's just a little frosting." His Colgate smile beamed, gifting her an exquisite pair of sparkling diamond and platinum hoop earrings.

"Now before you find a reason to reject the gifts, go get dressed. We have reservations in two hours." Roman commanded, smacking against her ass.

Daijah quickly scrambled to get ready for her anniversary date with Roman. She surveyed the beautiful gifts, surprised by the sentiment. No stranger to lavish things, Daijah was only accustomed to these acts from Xander. In the past six months, Roman had wined and dined her in some of the most extravagant restaurants in the city but he'd never given gifts of this nature. He did, however, offer her monetary support for school and she abruptly declined.

The current juxtaposition of Daijah's life was mind blowing - poor struggling law student from the hood with maybe one hundred dollars in the bank, driving a new BMW, material possessions like Gucci, Louboutin, and diamonds gifted from her wealthy ex-best friend and her current boyfriend, or whatever. *What a life!* Daijah shook her head, as she straightened her hair.

Dinner was marvelous. Roman considered every detail from the limousine to the roses, a walk along the Promenade, and the VIP table at The Cabaret Club where they enjoyed live music. It was perfect.

Daijah rested her head against Roman's shoulder as they meandered to the door of his condo. She immediately removed her fancy, painfully beautiful shoes. They rested at separate ends of the couch when he captured her feet. Roman rubbed, kneaded, caressed, and massaged her into oblivion. Daijah slightly moaned, crossing her legs to conceal the poignant fragrancy of her sizzling arousal.

"Blu, can you come closer?" Roman sexily smiled, summoning Daijah nearer to him. Roman was everything Daijah said she desired in a man - fun, romantic, and stimulating. But she couldn't comprehend why Xander's handsome face flashed before her eyes. She missed him. Roman had been everything she didn't know she needed. Patiently penetrating her mind, he never forced the issue of physical intimacy. But tonight, if Daijah's brain wasn't amendable, her awashed palpitating puss was voluntarily willing to escalate the relationship to a heightened level.

He whispered again, "I promise I won't bite. Can you come to me please?"

Daijah obliged, extending her body over to straddle him. Roman caressed his fingers through her silk-pressed tresses, licking gently against the seam of her lips before he kissed. Humming, he delighted in the taste of sweet champagne lingering on her pillowy lips. What was once a gentle soft kiss escalated into a deep passionate tongue lashing. The roughness of his hands felt like the most tender touch as he kissed, licked, and nestled in the folds of her neck. He played there for a minute, inhaling the sweet strawberry scented aroma of her perfume.

Roman unzipped her jumpsuit, unveiling the beauty of her naked sun-kissed skin. He softly kneaded her sizable breasts, pinching diamond hard nipples that distended against the sheer black bra. She moaned, tantalizing goosebumps invaded her entire body. Roman's fiery tongue traveled down her neck. He grazed the scar and she froze. His touch didn't transmit the same calming effects as Xander's. Lifting her hand to cover his, she encouraged him to travel in another direction. He obeyed, engulfing her right breast with his warm silky smooth lips.

"Mmmmm, Roman!" She muttered as he offered the same treatment to the left breast. He quickly repositioned her to stand on her feet, completely disrobing the jumpsuit to reveal more of her voluptuous flesh. Daijah hadn't had sex since Xander's birthday six months ago and her body was feigning that level of climax again. The kindred connection with Xander wouldn't allow her to believe that another man was capable of lifting her body to the loftiest of heights. Just as the thought of Xander penetrated her mind, Roman introduced the tip of one, then two fingers into her sodden pussy. Gliding slowly, softly, against her private lips to the rhythm of Anita Baker's "Good Love."

Daijah was so damn scared and so damn wet, saying no in one breath, while begging him to continue in the other.

"No, baby, wait! Oh shit, Roman, don't stop." She contradicted.

Daijah trusted only one person with her body, so this endeavor was a major step. Roman was privy to some pieces of her traumatic story, but he could never penetrate the depths of her pain. To his dismay, Roman was fully aware that she reserved those intimate disclosures for someone else. Daijah recoiled, trembling as she nervously anticipated his analysis of her unclothed frame.

"Blu. Baby. You're beautiful." He whispered.

Roman was being extremely patient as he caressed every quiver, massaged every chill, and kissed every looming tear, uttering, "Daijah, it's ok. We can stop if you're not ready."

But she was so fucking ready and reluctant all at the same time. Roman made her feel special, coveted, and it - he, felt so damn good. While Xander would never be an afterthought, Roman occupied spaces that she never allowed another man to reside. With no further hesitation or opposition, Daijah fully relinquished herself to him.

"Roman, yes." She simply whimpered.

Roman lifted her with ease then ambled to the bedroom, her legs draped around his waist, passionately kissing. He gently settled her on the bed, hovering with his mocha orbs meeting her honey quartz eyes for what seemed like forever. Roman kissed her temple, nose, lips, and continued to travel the length of her quivering body until his mouth met the crown of her essence. Still gazing, he whispered, "relax, beauty."

Seconds later, his warm lips were kissing her treasure while his hands caressed against the apex of her thighs. Roman tongue kissed her pussy lips at a measured, languid pace. Licking and slurping to the rhythm of the music piping throughout the room. Daijah moaned with pleasure. She tried her best to pull away because death was upon her. Anything that transmitted shockwaves through your entire being had to be murderous.

As brilliant as she was, Daijah couldn't identify coherence. Unable to form a rational sentence, "Rrrr!" "Ro!" "Rome!" "Shit!" "Baby!"

He firmly gripped her thighs, not allowing her to get away. Roman lifted her ass, massaging and kneading the juicy bodacious flesh. The new position gave him direct access to lick her pussy from beginning to end before darting his tongue into her saturated ocean.

"Oh shit, oh shit, oh shit!" Daijah screamed again.

This time she was so loud, she scared her damn self. She couldn't breathe - hyperventilating. Her lungs sprinted away faster than Alison Felix, leisurely returning moments later.

"Roman, please." She whimpered, her arms crossed over her face.

"Please what, Blu? Baby talk to me." He pleaded.

"Don't hurt me." She breathily requested.

Roman paused his pursuit to remove her hands from concealing her face. Kissing against her forehead, he muttered, "Do you trust me?"

Breathlessly, she responded, "yes."

"I'll never hurt you, Daijah. I promise."

And in an instant, Roman's monumental girth entered her treasure with soft, heedful, cadenced, strokes. His eyes never strayed from hers as he mumbled, through his groans.

"Damn, beauty. You feel so fucking good."

The pleasure and the pain were overwhelming as Daijah's puss reluctantly stretched to meet his weighty demand. She lustfully observed as the countless inches traversed in and out and in and out of her swollen jewel. It was a sight to see. Roman was lost in the moment too, his muscles tensed, biting against his bottom lip as he meticulously, deeply grinded into her pussy. He devoured the fullness of her treasure, capturing her essence with so much passion and rapture, a single tear escaped her eye.

"Ah, Roman." She hissed.

"Blu, baby. Shit, you are perfect." He moaned.

Beautifully battering her pulsating puss with merciful yet unyielding strokes until her entire body jerked uncontrollably. Daijah was blinded and deafened with ecstasy as the muted tears became vehement sobs of bliss. Roman wiped her tears as he freed a delectably violent release of his own.

"You are so fucking beautiful, Daijah, shit!" He boisterously groaned.

Their breathing was ragged and labored. Daijah lethargically drifted asleep solaced in the rapture of Roman's tender arms. He gazed at her, fearful because he was plummeting into the abyss as *I love you* capered on his lips. But Daijah wasn't ready for what he desired. Roman admired her for a moment longer before placing an adoringly gentle kiss against her forehead, then coasted into a satiated slumber.

"PLEASE! Please stop. I can't take any more. I don't - Please." Daijah lightly scuffled against the silken white sheets. Her groans of pain and agony evident in the furrow of her face. Her naked body jolted, but she was sound asleep. *"I see the moon and God bless me."* Daijah's voice gruffly quivered, but her words were clear and coherent as if she was awake. Her breathing labored, beads of sweat pooling on the bridge of her nose. She violently quaked.

"Daijah. Baby, wake up." Roman gently shook her from the hypnotic state. "Daijah!" His voice was noticeably elevated and distressed.

Daijah's eyes popped open, frightened, as she examined her

surroundings. Recognizing the dark painted walls and contrasting soft hues of the furniture, she was in Roman's master bedroom.

"Roman?"

"Baby, are you alright? You had another nightmare. They seem to be getting worse, Daijah." He cupped her chin, angling her head towards him. "What's going on, Blu? Talk to me."

Daijah deeply exhaled, still endeavoring to gain her bearings.

"It's fine, Roman. They happen more often when I'm stressed and overwhelmed. I have a lot going on at school and with Mimi, so -"

"So, I'm just supposed to watch you fight and be tortured in your fucking sleep? And I can't do shit about it?" Roman was concerned and irritated.

Daijah had been plagued with lucid nightmares for the past ten years, but they'd become more frequent in the past few months. The second year of law school was brutal with work, managing Ms. Mimi's health, navigating the relationship with Roman, and the absence of Xander. Although Daijah and Roman spent every available moment together, he asked that they become officially exclusive after making love for the first time a few weeks ago. Daijah was happy with Roman, but she still was hesitant to fully share the depths of her nightmares. Disclosing the painful horror would expose too many details about Xander and his privacy and protection were non-negotiable.

"Daijah, I'm serious. Tell me what I can do. How have you managed these in the past?" He pulled her to snuggle against his chest.

Daijah's mind immediately transitioned to Xander. He was how she managed her nightmares because they managed them together. She often wondered how Xander was sleeping or if he was sleeping at all.

Xander had been absent from Cannon Street lately. It had been months since she'd seen his truck parked in front of the house. Daijah would discreetly question her brother about Xander but refused to contact him. This time around, he needed to grow the hell up, apologize, and communicate what he wanted. *But does that matter anymore?* She pondered, as she peered at Roman's beautifully structured face. I guess the saying, 'be careful what you ask for' was true. Roman was exactly the man Daijah described to Zaria. He enjoyed long walks, didn't scoff at midnight phone calls, and was just as much a foodie as Daijah, so exotic dinners became a norm on date nights. Would it matter if Xander suddenly had a change of heart and wanted to openly love her as much as she always desired him? *It absolutely would.*

"Bae, I've just been overdoing it. I need a little down time, some rest, that's all."

"Baby, you were reciting something about the moon and praying you wouldn't die. That's more than just needing some rest." Seriousness covered his face. "Daijah, are you ever going to tell me what happened to you?"

"Roman! No! It's been almost eleven years. It's the past. I don't want to talk about it. Please, Roman, let me focus on my future. Just let it go. Let me handle it." Daijah climbed her naked body out of the bed, irritably ambling to the bathroom.

Daijah used the restroom then tried to adjust the water temperature, confused by the multiple knobs in his massive shower. She settled, placid, just staring at the water pounding against the sparkling white tile. Roman heard the shower start at least ten minutes ago but no movement from Daijah. He rubbed a hand down his face before knocking on the door while simultaneously opening it.

"Blu? Baby?" He peered around the door. Daijah was wrapped in a towel seated on the bench next to the shower opening. She looked up at him, quartz irises pooled with tears.

"Daijah, baby, I'm sorry. I didn't mean to push you. I just...I'm worried." Roman kneeled in front of her.

"There were three men. After raping and beating me for hours, they basically waited for me to die. Meandering around me, shooting the shit like nothing happened. Just a normal day. I believe they thought I was already dead, but I still tried my best not to move." She tightly closed her eyes and stiffened her body as if she was teleported back to September 2008.

"I don't remember much after that, but I'll always remember the glow from the moon. Right down to the faint shades of bluish grey in the center. How it slouthly drifted away as if refusing to make a path for the sun. I could've sworn I counted at least ten shooting stars, like they were fighting for my attention."

"It makes sense now...your fascination with the moon." He smiled, stroking her moon-shaped tattoo.

She nodded, a miniature smile slithered her lips. "It was my only indication that I was alive. The moon was my saving grace." *And Xander.* Daijah mused.

"Where can I find those mutherfuckas? Do you know what happened to them?" Roman carefully inquired. This was the first time she'd disclosed this level of detail.

"Once I regained consciousness, the streets had already taken care of two of them. One was killed in a drive-by shooting and the other accidentally overdosed." She motioned air quotes. "And the only one I recognized, Mishawn, I don't know if he's dead or alive. The police searched for weeks but he fled probably hours after he heard we weren't dead. No one has seen him."

The mention of the three violators was disturbing but Mishawn's demonous name dispelled an eerily petrifying chill down her spine. While they all were guilty, every slash, bruise, and broken bone were delivered by him alone. She could still smell him, feel the sticky sliminess of his rough hands, the sting of his belt buckle against her flesh. She recoiled, caressing the hallucinated pain from his punch to her face.

"How were the others identified if you were unconscious for weeks?" He intensely probed.

"Xander." She whispered.

"Ah, I see." He paused questioningly. "X couldn't do anything to those niggas...I mean...something." Roman's brow furrowed, indignant, angry.

The blaze in Daijah's quartz orbs ignited instantly. She tossed up one hand while warily shaking her head.

"Uh uhn, no - pause. Let me stop you before you even consider allowing anymore hateful words to fall out of your face about what Xander could or should have done that night. Nobody was in that room but us, so you have no fucking right passing judgement. Trust me, this is not a bridge you wanna cross, nor a cross you're capable of bearing."

Her nose flared, body shaking, visibly infuriated. Xander was off limits and she would correct anyone that needed a better understanding. Refusing to tolerate any ill words against him. Period.

Daijah mentally sequestered, becoming muted, hushed. Her vulnerability and willingness to expose any more wounds was exterminated. She needed Xander.

Her phone rang, momentarily diminishing the haze that plagued her. Roman was still positioned in front of her but remained voiceless. He knew he'd fucked up. Daijah stood, snatching the phone from the bathroom countertop. Roman reached for her, fruitlessly attempting to cease her exit when she defensively threw her hands up and mouthed, '*don't touch me.*' Daijah speedily fled the bathroom while answering the phone.

"Sim. What's up?"

"Daij, we need you."

7

Daijah pulled her BMW into the emergency room parking lot at St. Gabriel Hospital. A place she despised after spending three miserable months of her life behind four sterile white walls. She struggled to get out of the car. Her feet were bolted to the plush interior carpeted mat. Daijah audibly exhaled. After the tumultuous nightmare last night, arguing with Roman, and the vulnerable breakdown, this was not the day for another point of contention.

"God please give me strength." She whispered.

The hospital's automatic double doors jolted open on que. The ER entrance was eerily quiet. In Daijah's nightmares, the emergency room was always chaotic - patients screaming while the nurses and doctors strangely sauntered at a snail's pace not offering any assistance. Life support machines and heart monitors deafeningly blared; systems going haywire while Daijah screamed for Xander to help her but he couldn't penetrate the hospital window that divided them.

"Daij." Simeon's thundering tone rocked her into the present.

"Sim. Um, hey. What's going on?"

Before he could respond, shouting ensued in the close distance.

"Somebody needs to tell me how the fuck my pops is right now. Where is he? I don't give a fuck about the goddamn doctors and your bullshit ass protocol." The petite desk clerk was visibly shaking as Adonis's threatening six plus feet loomed over her tiny frame shouting. "Bitch, call the police. I don't give a fuck. Just tell me if my pops is dead, man. Just fucking tell me." He began to break.

"Doni." Daijah gently whispered. Her calming voice immediately broke him from his tantrum. Adonis heavily stalked towards his sister, collapsing into her arms, sobbing.

"Sim, what's going on? What happened to Mack?" She continued to caress Adonis's back, kissing against the satiny coils of his coal black hair.

"Heart attack. We don't know shit yet." They walked to the seats near Hiram and Mack's longtime girlfriend Ricki. Hiram rocked uncontrollably while Ricki's eyes were fixed on nothing. Daijah peered around searching for...*him.*

"X is back in that room." Simeon motioned to a door off of an empty hallway. He knew exactly who she was looking for. Daijah could see a sizey figure pacing behind the slightly cracked blinds in the room.

Adonis lifted his head, "I need to get some fucking air." He somberly ambled outside. She watched his monstrous frame disappear behind the doors.

"How are you holding up?" She turned, addressing Simeon. He shook his head, unable to articulate. Daijah gently placed her hand on his shoulder. "You want me to see if I can find out anything?"

He nodded.

Daijah walked to the same petite woman pleading for her forgiveness before she even reached the desk.

"I'm so sorry." Daijah glanced at her badge. "Sheila, please accept my apology. My little brother gets crazy emotional in these types of situations as you can imagine." Sheila nodded but was still a bit stirred. "Anything you can offer about the condition of Malcolm

Kindred would really give my family some semblance of calm right now." Daijah's face was authentically laced with concern.

She loved Mack like a father. Aside from her Uncle Bean, Mack was the only father figure she'd known. She recalled the time Mack was at the school with Simeon for donuts with dad. When he realized her uncle couldn't make it because he was sick, Mack asked Daijah to join him and his son. Her eyes flooded at the thought. Mack had to survive this...for everybody's sanity.

Sheila nodded her understanding before clicking a few areas on the computer screen. "And you are family, correct? His daughter?" She asked and Daijah nodded expectantly.

"Mr. Kindred is being prepped for surgery. An exploratory procedure to determine the location of the blockage in his heart. The doctor will be out shortly to brief the family."

"Thank you so much. I really appreciate it and my apologies again."

Daijah returned to where the family was seated and provided the update from the nurse. The brothers remained fairly calm, while Ricki finally shook from her reverie.

"What the fuck do you mean surgery? What kind of damn surgery? We need to see Mack before he goes into any damn surgery." She howled.

"Ricki, like I said, the doctor will come and talk to you before he goes into surgery. I'm sure you'll be able to see him." Daijah's voice was calm and soothing.

"Nobody asked you, Daijah. I know how to go talk to these people about my mutherfucking husband." Ricki scoffed, rolling her eyes.

She'd never been a fan of Daijah. Honestly, Ricki was jealous of the relationship Daijah had with the Kindred men. They didn't realize Adonis had returned until his thunderous shout resumed.

"Ricki, shut the fuck up talking to my sister like that, man. And you ain't nobody's damn wife. Your ass has been here the whole damn time and they ain't tell us shit until Daijah got here. So gone somewhere with that bullshit." Adonis thundered.

Daijah glanced towards the consult room to see Xander's silhouette paused, standing at the blinds observing his family's commotion.

"I was only trying to help, Ricki." Daijah lifted her hands in surrender as she hesitantly trekked down the empty hallway.

She settled in front of the door, deeply inhaling. This was the first time she saw Xander in months. Gently knocking while slowly opening the door, she watched Xander perched at the window, arms crossed, glaring out into the waiting area.

"Hi." She swallowed hard, unable to gather her words.

Xander looked good. Correction - he was a fucking sexy ass beast. The beard that he started growing months ago had fully bloomed. The tattoos on his neck appeared more vivid, alluring. Navy Polo sweatpants with a coordinated hooded jacket and crisp white t-shirt nestled his Herculean frame flawlessly. White Polo hat pulled low on his brow.

"Um, hey, Xan. How are you?"

He shifted, gazing at her for a long moment before turning back to the window.

Damn what a gorgeous specimen. He thought. Xander didn't hide his appreciation of the visual, intimately admiring her canvas. Chocolate curls now straightened into a chin-length bobbed haircut. Simple university branded hoodie and tight ass jeans that hugged the newly developed, *I'm being duly fucked* curves. And Xander noticed because he couldn't desist his eyes from gawking.

"What's up, Daij? I'm..." His somber baritone trailed off.

Instinctively, she closed the distance between them, tenderly resting her hands at his waist.

"The doctor should be out soon. Mack needs to have an exploratory surgery to determine the extent of the blockage in his heart." She explained.

Xander was inaudible. He simply peered down at her. Umber eyes transfixed, sad, and bloody red.

"He's going to be ok, Xan. You have to believe that. Ok?"

"Fuck, Daij. He was just laughing and talking shit on the phone with me. Making bets on the damn Lakers game then nothing. The next thing I heard was Ricki screaming in the background, then silence again." Xander blurted.

"He can't die. We - I can't lose him, babydoll." The sound of him calling her babydoll made all things right in her universe. Daijah internally scolded herself for still being so impacted by this arousing human.

Xander lifted one hand and reached for her, drawing her closer into him by her nape. He grazed his thumb against her scar before extending the other arm for a full embrace. Xander discharged his suppressed emotions, collapsing against her frame, he mutedly wept. Reaching with one hand to close the blinds, Daijah tightly, affectionately enveloped him until a soft knock on the door halted the endearment.

"X, the doctor is ready to talk to us." Hiram uttered through the cracked door.

"Give me a minute." He muttered, needing to gather himself to be strong for his brothers.

Xander clutched Daijah's hand before they exited the small room. He paused, connecting their temples with his eyes closed tight.

"Stay with me. Please." His voice cracked through a whimper.

"There's no other place I would rather be." Unlike his, Daijah's tone was strong, convicted.

The doctor began to approach before he was interrupted by a nurse. The family gathered, silently praying and supporting one another. Adonis positioned himself next to Daijah, leaning against his big sister for comfort while Xander still held her hand. He nervously grazed his thumb across her palm. The ER doors abruptly opened behind them.

"X! Baby. Are you ok? Ricki called me." A woman shorter than Daijah but just as thick with cinnamon skin, dark narrowed eyes, and a decently installed weave pulled into a ponytail trotted to console Xander.

Daijah stared at this woman, trying to determine who the hell she was. No woman had ever referred to Xander as 'baby' in her presence. She knew her thinking was crazy, but those other hoes knew their place, this bitch clearly didn't.

"Aleah, what the fuck are you doing here?" Xander angrily inquired, not releasing Daijah's hand. "Ricki's ass shouldn't have called you. This is a family situation."

"Damn, X. Really? I'm looking around and it don't seem to me like everybody is family." Aleah leered, surveying Daijah from head to toe. Paying close attention to her fingers coupled with Xander.

"Um, I'm Aleah, X's girl. And you are?" She abruptly stepped to Daijah.

"Man, please. X's girlfriend? Shiiiit! That's the funniest shit I've heard all day." Adonis quipped. Simeon and Hiram couldn't help but cackle too.

"And watch your mouth, Aleah. You've been here for what, a hot ass second. Don't get it twisted, my fucking sister is family." Adonis continued.

"Fuck you, Doni." Aleah shouted, causing yet another scene.

Daijah relinquished Xander's hand, ready to remove herself from the bullshit. For the most part, Daijah appeared timidly quiet but she wasn't a punk and would mop the floor with this bitch if necessary. Xander hooked his finger through her belt loop, pausing her exit, drawing Daijah back into his solid frame. He positioned his hand at the small of her back, a commanding gaze made her unruffle instantly. Lips curled taut in frustration, she lifted an eyebrow, silently signaling that he needed to handle his bitch.

"Aleah, you showing up real fucking disrespectful right now. My mutherfucking father had a heart attack and you bring your trifling ass in here on some bullshit. Get the fuck up outta here, man."

She didn't budge.

"Now!" Xander gritted. "Trust. You don't want me to escort your ass out."

"She's here for me, X. I need her to stay. You have your support, I need mine." Ricki chimed.

Aleah pouted, harshly slamming her body into a chair in the waiting area. She remained quiet other than the ludicrous eye-daggers she randomly shot at Daijah.

The four brothers and Daijah spoke to the doctor. Mack didn't have a massive heart attack, thankfully, so the damage to his heart was not extensive. He would, however, require a stent to keep the blocked artery open and a nutritional program to lose weight.

Ricki watched the family bonding in isolation. She irritably settled next to Aleah.

"Who the hell is she?" Aleah whispered.

"Daijah Duvall." Ricki sarcastically sang.

"And? Who the fuck is that?"

"Adonis's sister and the love of Xander's life." Ricki shook her head as Aleah's fire orbs burned towards Daijah.

"Cousin, there are a few things you must tolerate if you want to be a part of the Kindred family. Especially if you desire, X." Ricki bitterly scowled at Daijah.

"And *she* is one of them. When it comes to her, X is inflexible so don't even question him. Daijah is a constant. A *non-negotiable*, as he calls her." Both women enviously stared. "Her ass is always going to be a factor."

―――――――――

DAIJAH WAS EXHAUSTED. Between classes, work, Ms. Mimi, and avoiding Roman, she was constantly bustling. Evoking old harms caused Daijah to retreat to her protective corner at her grandma's house. She hadn't returned to Roman's condo, requiring some time to process their conversation. Still reeling from his comments about Xander, she was also concerned about his perception of her now that he carried a portion of her truth. Daijah had no interest in pity or being handled with kid gloves. Roman extended her grace, affording the space she requested. But he wouldn't wait too long. He'd already decided that another weekend would not pass without him laying eyes on her.

Daijah slowly sauntered to her car after a grueling exam in Commercial, Business, and Labor Law class. The never-ending day wasn't complete. She glanced at her watch, noticing she had a few hours to spare before her Equality and Human Rights study group. Instead of driving home, she decided to stop by the hospital to visit Mack since it was only a few blocks away from the coffee shop where her group was meeting.

Thankfully, Mack's surgery went well and he was recovering in the hospital for a couple more days. Adonis was keeping her updated on his father's progress. Surprisingly, Xander even briefed her via text. They'd exchanged a few quick 'hellos' and 'you good' but no substantial conversation. Daijah was working her own nerves; giddy and enraptured when text notifications attached to the name 'Xan' illuminated the screen. Her belly fluttered and puss tingled - and she hated it. Just as she quaked at the thought, her phone chimed.

Roman: I want to see you, Blu. Can we talk?

Daijah rolled her eyes, resting against the headrest as she pulled into the hospital parking garage. Audibly sighing, she replied.

Blu: We will talk Roman. Let me get through this last exam and I promise we will talk. Ok?

Roman: I miss you Daijah.

And honestly, Daijah missed him too. He'd been her constant for the past six months and she cared about Roman...alot. But seeing Xander had her mind and body topsy-turvy. With little hesitation, she continued.

Daijah: I miss you too.

6:06pm. Daijah silently prayed that the family had already dispersed from the hospital, especially Ricki and her cousin Aleah. Stopping in the gift shop, she picked up a card, a get well balloon, and a bottle of water. Again, the hospital was eerily noiseless. She navigated the long narrow hallways to find the elevator. Anxiously riding to the seventh floor, Daijah inhaled and exhaled deeply as the elevator stopped on the floor she dreaded - intensive care. Her eyes remained tightly shut until the elevator resumed to the cardiac unit on the seventh floor. Daijah nodded at one of Mack's security guards camped outside of the room before lightly tapping against the door of room 704.

"Knock, knock." She whispered, peeking around the large door.

"Daijah Blu. Come on in here, babygirl." Mack's naturally gritty voice resounded through the empty room. He was a mammoth of a man, his large feet dangled off of the miniature hospital bed.

"Hey Big Mack." Daijah's smile was bright and genuine, thankful to see that his condition had improved.

'Big Mack,' he mouthed, laughing. "I ain't heard that since you were a little girl."

"How are you feeling? You look good." Daijah closed the distance, resting the card and balloon on the table next to his bed. She settled into the closest chair.

"Alive, baby girl. I'm alive."

"Praise the Lord, Saints as Ms. Mimi would say." Daijah chortled and Mack joined.

"I heard you braved the hospital for me." Mack reached for her hand.

She nodded.

"Thank you for being there for my boys. I'm sure Doni was ready to tear shit up." He chuckled.

"You already know. I made him buy lunch for the entire ER staff and sent flowers. He's lucky he didn't get arrested. But he was concerned, just like the rest of us."

Mack aimlessly nodded his head as he gazed out of the window.

"And what about Xander?" He inquired, still blankly staring. "Did he release any emotions?"

"In his Xander way. Yeah, I think so." Daijah softly laughed.

"My son is so much like me. All business, emotionless." He shook his head. "That's my fault. After his mother died, I raised him to be a man under any circumstance. Tears were for punks. But I'm older and wiser and have cried a few tears of my own."

Daijah intently listened. Mack's method of rearing was understandable. The drug king single father of four boys couldn't raise no punks. That could mean life or death in the streets. Face laced with regret, Mack noisily exhaled before focusing his attention back on Daijah.

"In other news, I hear you are out here living your best life, Daijah Blu." He sneeringly inquired and she was acutely aware of his reference.

"Oh really. Who told you that?" She smirked, rolling her eyes. "But if you must know, life is pretty good."

"Mmm hmm. And what about my son?" Mack lifted a brow.

Oh damn. He's cutting right to the chase.

"What about your son? He seems to be living his best life too." She countered.

"With Aleah?" He growled. "That ain't shit but a band-aid. Just like Roman Strong is a temporary fix for you."

Daijah was silent.

"Does he know you came to the hospital? Sure, it was for me and your brother but your real concern was Xander. Does Roman know you spent the night on that couch with Xander after my surgery?"

Still nothing. She was voiceless.

"I didn't think so." Mack smirked, then took a sip of water. "I don't want to get in grown folks' business but y'all need to stop fucking around and just be in love. X needs you, girl. He's more strung out on you than those crackheads on the street. You're the cause and the cure, babygirl." Mack grunted in pain as he shifted in the bed.

"Don't get yourself all worked up old man. Your son made his choice clear. I've been here the whole time - through it all, Mack. There are only so many ways you can tell a person you love them just to keep enduring rejection. He knows where to find me when and if he needs me. Let's just leave it at that, ok Mack?" She lifted a brow silently begging him to change the subject.

"Now, what's the problem here? Why aren't you eating?" Daijah pointed to his untouched dinner tray.

"I don't want that shit." He barked.

"You want to get out of here, right? Then you need to eat this shit." She teased.

"Do you want me to call the nurse?" Daijah threatened with a smile.

"Yeah, if it's that lil chocolate nurse with the big ass. I'll eat my food for her pretty ass all day." Mack heartily laughed until he grimaced again in pain.

"Come on, Mack. Let me help you finish." Daijah assisted him until he cleaned the plate.

A deliciously roaring bass-filled voice disrupted their conversation.

"I've been begging you to eat all day and Daij is here for a few minutes and you're about to digest the damn plate." Xander shook his head with a slight smirk.

"You know she's got that voodoo, son." Mack laughed.

"Yeah. I know all too well." Xander sexily grinned.

"What's up Daij?"

"Hey Xan." She fought to suppress the blush coloring her cheeks.

"Knock, knock, Mr. Kindred." A pretty heavyset nurse with smooth mocha skin and an abnormally huge butt sang. "Good job. You ate all of your dinner. That's a great sign. You'll be out of here in no time." She squealed then winked at Mack. "Now, family, I need about thirty minutes alone with the patient to check vitals and get him cleaned up for the night. Ok?"

Mack salaciously smiled, shooing them out of the room. Daijah and Xander simultaneously rolled their eyes in disgust.

"I gotta get out of here anyway. I'm so glad you are feeling better, Mack. Be good, ok?" She leaned in to kiss his cheek.

He winked. "I can't make no promises, baby girl. You be careful out there."

"I'll be back, Pops." Xander said. Mack nodded, now acting helpless for the nurse.

"Hey Daij. Wait up?" He lightly jogged to reach her. "Take a ride with me."

"I can't. My study group is at nine." She glanced at her phone.

He peered at his sparkling diamond encrusted watch. *7:14pm.* "More than enough time. It won't take long, I promise." Xander extended his hand to her. He lifted a brow encouraging her to come with him.

"You don't trust me anymore, babydoll?" His adoring umber orbs weakened her knees.

Shit, I don't trust me. She mused, gazing at his outstretched manly hand. Saying no to Xander was just always...a no-no. Daijah knew she was playing with fire.

"Yes, I trust you." They shared a familiar, soothing blush before she clasped his hand willingly following his lead.

Thirty minutes later, Xander pulled his white Land Rover into a parking space at Bayon Breeze Park. B-Breeze sat atop of a small hill overlooking the airport. Although the park was abandoned, people still frequented to watch the planes descend and ascend over the city. Xander parked and he and Daijah gazed at the flashing lights that illuminated the runway in silence. They heard the roar of the engines as a plane took off into the night. Appearing deep in thought, Xander's eyes were fixed on something other than the planes.

"LA." He blurted.

"Nah, short flight. Chicago." Daijah retorted.

They heartily laughed. Daijah and Xander visited B-Breeze often on those nights when they had trouble sleeping. Guessing the destination or arrival location of the airplanes was a game they would play to pass the time. Xander exited the truck and circled to the passenger side door, assisting Daijah to her feet.

"Come on. I have a surprise for you."

Xander opened the hatch of the SUV where they perched in the back to get a better view of the planes. He retrieved the plastic bag that she didn't notice when he stopped at the gas station. A Styrofoam cup filled with ice, a bottle of cheap Sutter Homes red wine, a Snicker, a Payday, and a bag of barbeque chips were displayed on the truck bed. Daijah guffawed, tossing her head back at the exquisite meal.

"Did we really eat this shit everyday back then? Awful." She shook her head.

"Yep. And I bet you're going to eat this shit tonight too."

"You damn right. Open that bottle and give me my Payday." She snatched the candy, pretending to hide it behind her back when he playfully reached for it.

Xander laughed - carefree and peaceful. He twisted the cap from the wine, bending to pour a portion on the ground.

"For the homies." They said in harmony. Taking a moment in remembrance of the friends and family they'd lost.

"Xan, are you ready to talk?" Daijah poured her wine over the ice before starting to pick off the peanuts from her candy bar one by one.

Xander audibly chuckled. "You still do that shit, huh?"

She furrowed her brow, confused by his comment. He motioned his head toward the candy. "Eating all the damn peanuts first before biting into the candy bar. That's the craziest shit I've ever seen."

"You've always been such a hater." She rolled her eyes, plucking another peanut from the nougat. "Now talk."

Xander stared far into the distance for a long minute. Accepting the wine bottle from Daijah, he took a few gulps.

"This shit with my Pops is fucking with me." He whispered.

"Is he ok? Is something else going on?" Concerned, Daijah moved a bit closer, crisscrossing her curvy legs in front of him.

"Nah, he's good. The doctor says he'll make a full recovery. But he has to make some changes to his lifestyle. Smoking, drinking, and eating a bunch of shit has to stop. He's hard-headed and Ricki's stupid ass is dumb as fuck, so who's going to make sure he stays on track? Me."

"First of all, maybe if y'all stop calling Ricki stupid, she'll be a little more motivated to demonstrate what she's capable of. She's rough around the edges but Ricki loves Mack, so she'll do what's best for him." Xander shrugged as she continued. "And make your brothers step up, Xan. They're not little boys anymore. Shit, Sim is standing taller than Mack. They can do more than what you think if you would allow them to leave the brotherly nest."

"Ok, Iyanla, damn." He teased, leaning back to gaze out of the panoramic sunroof.

The pair sat in silence watching the planes and the moon. Daijah felt his sexy umber eyes glaring at her. She didn't want to look but he was like a magnet, his energy always drawing her in. Vainly managing the tremble in her pussy, part of Daijah wanted to mount that big man dick and ride it until she howled at the moon. The other part of her wanted to slap the shit out of him for standing before her so manly, and vulnerable, and unattainably delicious exuding all that big dick energy.

Still looking up to the sky, he muttered. "Thank you, Daij. I know it was hard for you to be at the hospital, but you came anyway because we needed you. You are always there when we - I need you. And I'm sorry. That shit with Aleah. You know she's not my -"

"Nah, no worries. You don't owe me an explanation. You deserve some happiness in your life. If that's her..." Daijah shrugged, voice squealing cynically.

"Ha, you know better, babydoll. Real talk." He shifted his glance to her. "I'm sorry.... for everything."

Daijah blushed, then nodded. She understood Xander enough to know that this was his apology for all of the shit that had gone unspoken over the past several months. That desire to straddle him suddenly elevated well beyond the brilliant, tranquil moon.

Xander stroked the arc of her face. He wanted to kiss her so fucking bad. Lifting her hand to his lips, he planted soft tiny kisses causing her quivering flesh to swell.

The reflective glare of her phone on the truck's roof brought her to attention. *Roman.*

Still caressing her hand, Xander's face said, *I wish the fuck you would answer that shit right now.*

"That's your study group?" He questioned sarcastically.

"No, but I need to go. My group is meeting in twenty minutes." She recoiled from his grasp, ignoring Roman's call.

Daijah gathered the trash while Xander waited to help her out of the truck. Hand clasped in his, she slid out, directly into his mountainous body. His steely manhood pressed against her stomach. She swallowed hard. Xander instinctively caressed her scar as they locked eyes, her hands wearisomely fisting the hem of his shirt.

"Don't." She whimpered, shaking her head as his thumb stroked her lips.

"Don't what, babydoll?" He continued to caress, simmering breaths against her ear.

"Whatever you're thinking, Xan, just don't. Restraint is nonexistent when it comes to you." Daijah squirmed, her panties soaked and wet. "I have a boyfriend." Those words sounded foreign before they even left her mouth.

Xander eliminated the already miniscule space between them. He rested his temple to kiss hers, velvety lips so close, their breaths were no longer theirs to own.

"Does your boyfriend know that the mark on your hand is from falling out of the tree in my backyard? Or that you love cheap red wine over crushed ice? I'm sure he doesn't have a damn clue that you take out the vanilla portion of Neapolitan ice cream to mix only the strawberry and chocolate." He chuckled in his Xander way.

"Does that nigga have a clue that I was the first to invade your sweet pussy? That my voice rocks you to sleep at night when you have a nightmare?" Xander wantonly glided his lips to the scar below her ear. "Babydoll, did you share with your fucking boyfriend that I'm the *only* mutherfucka who can make your pussy climax by my touch alone?"

His imposing frame was salaciously suffocating. Daijah fought to swallow the lump in her throat. Oxygen depleted with every sporadic rise and fall of her chest.

"X, please. I need to go." She croaked.

He gazed down into her pleading misty eyes for a moment longer before ushering her to the passenger side. The ride back to her car was hushed. Xander was about to get out of the truck to assist her, but Daijah placed a hand on his shoulder, pausing his motion. Her eyes were affixed on nothing but intensely engrossed.

"You're right, Xan, he's not aware of any of those things. But what he does know is that he's not afraid to openly love me, hold me, kiss me...no matter who's watching. He doesn't conceal his feelings for me behind the guise of material things." Sodden quartz orbs landed on his stoic, awestruck face. "So yeah, he has a lot to learn about the intricacies of my life, but...at least he's willing."

Daijah exited the car and didn't look back. She managed to make it through her study group without wailing uncontrollably. Perched in her car hours later, she stared at the front door for at least ten minutes unable to process her next move. It was after midnight and she was physically and mentally exhausted. The blaring ring of the phone through the car's speaker caused a shocking shudder.

"Blu, baby, please come to me?" The strain in Roman's voice was evidence of his desire. She peered up towards the door of the industrial building that housed his condo. He sexily stood in the doorway shirtless, eager to receive her. Daijah digested the strength of his immense frame.

"Ok."

8

"**M**mmhhh, X... yes daddy."

Xander took a sip of the dark liquor while slumped against the plush tan couch in his media room as he watched Aleah digest all nine and a half inches of his immense girth. She was all too excited when he responded to her text, allowing her to come through today. He hadn't fucked with Aleah since she pulled that shit at the hospital and she was practically begging to get back into his good graces. Honestly, Xander hadn't actually fucked anybody since the last time he was with her.

A few weeks had passed since taking Daijah to their spot in the park and he missed her. He promised that he would never ghost Daijah like he'd done in the past so Xander didn't completely disappear. They stayed in contact about his father's health, he saw her at Adonis' birthday party, and Xander actually stopped by her job on campus a few times, claiming that he was in the neighborhood. But honestly, it just felt good to be in her presence; however he could have her. But the nights when they were both plagued by horrific dreams were the times they connected the most. While the nightmares were infrequent lately, he was grateful that his voice had been the soothing salve she needed to rest.

Daijah's words still circulated in Xander's psyche. *But what he does know is that he's not afraid to openly love me, hold me, kiss me. He doesn't conceal his feelings for me behind the guise of material things.* That shit stung, but she was right. Xander knew he didn't have to buy Daijah another thing to maintain her love. It was his for the taking if he wanted it.

Aleah was relentless as she continued to pleasure his manhood when his phone chimed. Xander took another sip, grunting as she hit a sensitive spot.

"Shit." He whimpered, gazing at his phone.

Babydoll: Hey big head. We good? Finals are FINALLY done and I'm exhausted. Am I crazy if I sleep for the rest of the week?

Babydoll: BTW. Mimi cooked for the whole block. LOL She has some food for Mack that he doesn't need.

He smiled, rereading her simplistic words while imagining the beautiful beam on her face. Xander accepted Daijah's words as an invitation.

"Stop." Xander whispered, but Aleah continued her pursuit.

"Stop!" He shouted, nudging Aleah's face, encouraging her to remove her mouth from his dick.

"X, baby. Let me take care of you. I've missed you." She moaned.

"Nah, I'm good. I gotta head out." Xander impassively gritted, tapping on his phone screen. "Get cleaned up. I'm leaving in ten minutes."

Aleah leered at him acrimoniously. She was in love with a man who was incapable of loving her because he was in love with his best friend.

"Is that your precious Daijah? Your babydoll?" She resentfully spewed, rising from her knees scantily dressed in a sheer bra, g-string and black stilettos.

He nonchalantly sauntered away adjusting his basketball shorts, ignoring her sarcasm.

"What is so special about that bitch anyway?" Aleah roared.

Xander paused, slowly turning to face her. He shifted his head to one side, wordlessly giving her an opportunity to reimagine her statement. Aleah was warned not to question Xander about Daijah. They leered hushly, the only sound whispering from the television.

Abruptly, Xander diminished the gap between them aggressively backing her into the wall. He firmly grabbed her neck with one hand. The horrified gasp struggled to escape her lungs.

"I see I'm going to have to do something about your damn mouth." He tightened his grip as Aleah began to cry. "What did you say about Daijah? Say it again? I dare you say that shit again."

Aleah frantically shook her head, muttering, "nothing, nothing" through muzzled lips.

"I'm only going to say this once. Keep Daijah's name out of your fucking mouth. Do you understand?"

She nodded, her face tightly locked between his powerful hands. "Get dressed. You now have eight minutes." Xander released her red and puffy cheeks. He glared a second longer before leisurely exiting the room.

It was unseasonably cool for late May as Daijah trekked into her grandma's house. Daijah completed her last final exam of the semester and in a few weeks, she would begin her internship in the legal office of a national non-profit organization headquartered downtown. Weary and tired couldn't describe Daijah's demeanor. In addition to classes and work, she'd been fighting sinus and allergy issues since April with no relief in sight.

Roman had been in Charlotte all week visiting family with his mother. He was returning on Memorial Day and made plans to see Daijah that night. She honestly wanted to just sleep after the stressful week of final exams, presentations, and her tutoring job. While she was excited to see Roman, she knew he would require more attention than she was able to offer.

He had profusely apologized to Daijah after their disagreement in his bathroom a few weeks ago. Her refusal to talk bothered him and he missed the shit out of her. When Daijah arrived at his house after midnight just sitting in her car, Roman saw the trepidation coating her face. He begged, pleaded, and unceasingly made love to her until she moaned her sentiments of trust and forgiveness for him.

Ms. Mimi's house was filled with friends and family for Memorial Day. She barbecued and cooked enough food for an army. After helping her grandma clean the house, prepare food, and entertain guests, she snuck away from the crowd to rest. Daijah laid across her bed, belly stuffed after an overloaded plate of ribs, spaghetti, potato salad, and pineapple cream pie for dessert.

"Daij, just tell him you're tired. Roman won't care. He just wants to be with his beautiful Blu." Zaria teased, playing on her phone while perched on the oversized bean bag in the corner of Daijah's bedroom.

"I know, but I think he's surprising me with tickets to the New Edition concert. I just pray it's not for tonight's show. I need sleep." She pouted.

"Have you seen X lately?" Zaria blurted.

"Um, that was random. But no, not in a couple weeks. We've text. Why? What's up?"

"Just curious if y'all are back to number one best friend status?" The coy look on her face was different.

"Nah, I wouldn't say all of that. We're cool." Daijah's brow furrowed in curiosity. "There's a reason you asked, Z. Spill it." She tossed a pillow at her friend.

"I don't know, Daij. Real talk. No bullshit." Zaria paused, lifting an eyebrow seeking permission to proceed. Daijah nodded.

"Honestly, I'm surprised X has let you be with Roman this long."

"Let me be with Roman?" It was more of a question than a

comment. "I don't need Xander's permission to do shit. I'm with Roman because I want to be with Roman."

"Daij, just let me finish. What I mean is, it's fucking with Xander to know that you're with Roman. The fact that you actually have a real boyfriend. His mind is blown. Everybody sees it and we're concerned. He hasn't been the same since his birthday and definitely not since Mack's heart attack. Sim said he's been a recluse. Not hanging with his brothers, staying to himself, and he kicked that bitch Aleah all the way to the curb." Daijah and Zaria shared a harmonious eye roll.

"We are all shocked that he hasn't stepped up to claim what he knows is his. Confessed his love for you because that nigga loves the shit out of you. We're just ready for y'all dumb asses to be together already."

"Who is we?" Daijah's eyes ballooned. "Who else has been talking about this?"

"The brothers, Mack, shit, even Ricki is sick of y'all. And Mimi."

"Mimi! Lord, y'all are doing the most. Me and Xander clearly weren't meant to be more than forever friends. So just let it go." She paused, biting her bottom lip. "I have."

Daijah turned over in the bed feeling the emotions bubbling in her belly.

"Bitch, don't say no tomfoolery shit like that. He loves you and you love him. That's it, that's all." Zaria irritably stood from the bean bag.

"You make it sound so simple, Z."

"Love is that simple, Daijah. It's us crazy humans that make it complicated." She shrugged, perching next to her friend on the bed.

"Daij, although I'm best friend number two, I know you...and well. There is no doubt that you care about Roman. Shit, may even have some love for him. And rightfully so because he's been a good man to you. But Xander is the love of your life. Part owner of your heart since we were kids. You only get one chance like that. Life is simply too short to waste time not doing what, or who, you absolutely love." Zaria pinched Daijah's cheek before standing to leave the room.

Adonis's blasting voice reverberated throughout the house as he greeted family and friends in the living room. Simeon's thunderous bass followed when both their monstrous frames appeared in the doorway.

"What's up, sis? You sleep." Adonis knocked against her door. "What's good, Z?" He greeted Zaria.

"Hey Doni." They sang in unison.

"I'm glad I ate already before y'all big asses got here." Zaria giggled. Simeon's head popped up behind Adonis, surveying Zaria from head to toe. He smiled then motioned his head for her to come to him.

"Hey, Z." Daijah called out. "Is it just that simple for you, or are you a crazy human too?" She teased, eyeing her friend's giddy disposition as she disappeared down the hallway with Simeon.

"Have they fucked? I need them to fuck already. That flirting bull-shit is getting old." Adonis yelped.

"Shut up, boy! Worry about your own love life." Daijah smacked his arm. Adonis sat in the bed leaning against the headboard.

"Nah. I'm good on love. A good fuck? Yes. Love? Hell no." He shook his head in disgust.

"Yeah, ok. When that right one comes along and bites you in your ass, we'll see if you're still talking that shit." Daijah laughed through a yawn.

"Bite me in the ass? I ain't into that kinky shit, sis." Adonis quipped, tickling his sister as they playfully fought.

"You know she bites when you start tickling her, D?" Xander bantered. He leaned against the doorway with his hands stuffed in his jeans. Damn he was fine in distressed denim, a black vintage Scarface branded t-shirt, and black and white Jordan's.

"Ouch! Shit Daij." Adonis jumped up from the bed. They all heartily laughed.

"That's what you get lil boy." Daijah chuckled, stretching as she comfortably adjusted her body in a fetal position.

Xander slightly smiled, moving further into her bedroom as Adonis exited, still cursing under his breath and rubbing his arm.

"What's up Daij? We good?" Xander squinted his umber eyes trying to access her demeanor. It wasn't normal for Daijah to be hiding in her room when there's a house full of family. This was usually her comfort zone.

"I'm good. Just tired and these people won't let me be great. I've been trying to take a nap for over an hour."

"You feel alright?"

She nodded, further burying her face in the pillow.

"Classes kicked my ass. My brain feels like it's about to ooze out of my ears. I just don't want to think for 24 hours."

"You're so damn dramatic, Daij." Xander shook his head, settling next to her, taking Adonis's place against the headboard. He brushed the loose curls back from her temple, pressing his hand against her forehead to assess her temperature.

"I'm not sick, Xan, unless exhaustion is an illness." She sighed, blinking for a long minute.

"How'd you do? In your classes."

"I won't know until next week, but I think I did pretty good. My team killed the presentation so I'm not too worried." Daijah's eyes were still closed while Xander flipped through the Equity and the Law book on her nightstand.

"So, what's next?" He inquired.

"Internship this summer, research class, and one elective in the fall, then graduation in December." She finally opened her eyes, flashing a gratified gleam.

"I'm so fucking proud of you, Daij. No bullshit. You killed it, when you could've easily said fuck school, fuck everything. But you kept pushing. My babydoll is a boss." He rubbed a finger down the bridge of her nose that made her belly jump.

Daijah noisily exhaled, closing her eyes. She despised the way her rebellious ass body responded to such an innocent, sinless touch.

"So, what's phase four?" His boisterous timber disrupted the throbbing between her thighs.

"Huh? Phase four?" Daijah bemusedly inquired.

"The night of your graduation party, you said that phase three of your plan was finishing law school. So, what's phase four?" He curiously probed.

"Um, get a job or start my business, I guess. Probably a job first to stack some money, then make another plan to execute my dream of entrepreneurship."

"Tell me what you see in your dream?" Her perfectly arched brows crunched. "Daij, close your eyes and tell me exactly what you see when you dream about your next step." He gently brushed his hand down her face, encouraging her eyes closed.

"I see...a building near the neighborhood with maybe two or three retail spaces. An office for me with the Duvall Group scripted on the window, a conference room where I can teach personal development classes. An incubator for future entrepreneurs to innovate. Something the neighborhood has never experienced." She opened her eyes, then shrugged. "Maybe one day."

"Why not now? The hood ain't the hood anymore. Things are changing and we...meaning Black people have to be a critical part of that change to maintain the integrity, shit, the history of our hood." Xander motioned a finger between the two of them.

She nodded, keenly considering his words.

"I hear you, Xan. One day." Daijah closed her eyes and Xander decided not to push the conversation.

With several moments of silence, she drifted asleep as Xander remained perched on the bed. The curves of her face were guarded in his memory as he retraced the familiar path with his eyes. Curly highlighted tresses sprawled across the pillow, diamond studs sparkled in her ears, her hand nestled against her cheek. He muzzled a laugh when Daijah lightly jerked, her pouty lips more defined. She was breathtaking.

The noise throughout the house began to calm as the night progressed. Xander was focused on his phone, still settled against the headboard as Daijah slept. Ms. Mimi's voice grew closer to the bedroom door.

"She was going to take a nap so she may still be asleep." Ms. Mimi tapped on the door. "Daijah Blu, baby girl, are you-" She paused.

"Oh! Xander. I didn't realize you were still here." Mimi's eyes bulged. She was nervous and Xander quickly understood why.

Roman's imposing frame stood several inches above Ms. Mimi in the doorway. He didn't externally flinch at the site of his girl sound asleep next to a nigga he knew was more than just her best friend. But internally, he was homicidal. Ms. Mimi's brown eyes traveled between the two fine specimens of God's glory vying for her grand-daughter as they exchanged scorching scowls. Continuing the unyielding stare down, Xander lovingly tapped her shoulder.

"Babydoll, you have company?"

Daijah stirred, a resounding squeal filled the room as she animatedly stretched. Opening her eyes, she slightly smiled seeing Xander still comfortably resting against her headboard. Slowly shifting, she breezed past her grandma's worrisome orbs to focus on Roman. His riled charcoal irises depicted wrath, offense, and fucking annoyance.

"Roman. What are you doing here? I mean...I thought your flight didn't arrive until after seven." Daijah sat up in the bed, still reeling from the depths of sleep.

Roman stepped around Ms. Mimi to enter the bedroom. His voice was placid yet impassioned.

"I took an earlier flight. I wanted to surprise you, but I guess I should've called..." His words trailed off, indignantly glaring between his girlfriend and her best friend.

Xander remained unphased. Sitting up from the headboard, he leaned into Daijah extending his hand to caress her nape. She silently prayed that her body didn't react to his now sinful touch.

Daijah please don't smile, please don't shudder, please don't show any damn emotion towards this man.

"I gotta head out, babydoll." He kissed against her temple for a minute longer than necessary. *Petty ass.* She mused, internally irritated and aroused by Xander's possessive behavior.

"We good, Daij?" Xander's ass didn't give two fucks about Roman's feelings. He was solidifying his position in her life with that simple question that's been the bedrock of their relationship since kids.

She nodded, standing from the bed as he stood. Daijah locked eyes with Roman, wordlessly pleading his forgiveness.

"Come on, Ms. Mimi. I promised my pops a plate of your fire ribs." Xander wrapped an arm around her shoulder, disregarding Roman's glare. Xander would never start shit in Daijah's home unless absolutely necessary. He knew Roman was a smart man and would think long and hard about popping off tonight. Roman was alone on enemy territory so he willingly retreated.

Daijah anxiously observed Roman as Roman watched Xander disappear down the hall. He rubbed a hand down his chiseled face before turning to gaze at her.

"Get your shit and let's go. We need to talk." He casually traipsed out of the room.

————————

DAIJAH HAD BEEN RUNNING errands all day for her grandma and went by the school to pick up some financial aid information for next semester. Roman was settled on the couch intently focused on a random golf match. He lifted his head when he heard the key in the front door.

A few weeks ago, Daijah had the unfortunate pleasure of experiencing the 'Rome' side of Roman. After seeing Xander cozily resting in her bed, Roman was irate. Part of him was ready to clear the fucking block, his life be damned. But that level of bloodshed would be unnecessary over some petty bullshit. The car ride to his condo was intense. Once they arrived, Roman was unmoved. He loved Daijah and that night he did not inarticulate his feelings.

"Blu, baby, I love you. I have never said that shit to a woman and I'm saying it to you. But I refuse to tolerate fucking disrespect. That nigga laying in your bed like you belong to him. Under other circumstances, I would've fucked all that shit up - no fucking concern for whose feelings were hurt. But I respect you and Ms. Mimi. Daijah, that shit was inappropriate and wrong. I understand that y'all share a bond and I'm not asking you to discontinue your friendship. But that shit I saw tonight was much more than just fucking friends. But honestly, I don't give a fuck how long y'all have been cool; you either make it plain as fucking toast for his muther-fucking ass that I am your man. Or, you tell me right the fuck now if this is no longer where you want to be."

Daijah's frame violently shuddered from the inside out. Over-whelmed by tears, she sobbed uncontrollably and apologetically. Mutedly apologizing to Roman because she admittedly knew that a portion of her being would always belong to Xander. The ambivalence and confusion were overwhelming - it took her breath away. Daijah heavily rasped, suffocating, drowning in her emotions. While Xander was unquestionably quintessential, Roman had become a pivotal part of her growth as a woman. Frankly, Daijah knew her reasoning was selfish as fuck, but it was her truth. She craved the immediacy and familiarity of Xander to feed her addiction while desiring Roman's steadfastness. He abruptly encircled her, massaging her back while laboring to kiss every tear away. Roman lifted her chin, forcing Daijah to really look at him. To visualize the love, adoration, and sincerity he carried for her.

"I love you, Daijah. I want this. I want us to work."

"Me too, Roman."

Daijah hadn't returned to her grandma's house to stay overnight since that day. They were practically living together - not desiring separation and his condo was closer to campus.

Daijah locked the door, placing her Louis Vuitton Neverful on the bench in the foyer. Slowly ambling into the living room, Daijah's face was flushed, ghostly.

"Hey beauty." Roman smiled. He always admired her natural and unassuming prettiness. Innocently dressed in a simple t-shirt dress, flip flops, and hair in a high curly ponytail. His mirth quickly dissipated when he noticed her demeanor.

"Uh, oh. Did you bomb one of your finals, baby?"

"No." She whimpered, eyes lifeless, standing in front of him like a kid about to be scolded.

"Then what's wrong? Why the long face?" He stood, looking deliciously magnificent in black basketball shorts and a white tank top. Roman cupped her cheeks, observing the disconcertment across her fresh face.

"Baby, talk to me. What's going on? Did something happen to Ms. Mimi, your brother?" Roman searched her face for answers.

Daijah swallowed hard, but she couldn't abolish the boulder lodged in her throat.

"I'm pregnant." Daijah murmured, her tone panicked, yet still.

Roman's eyes narrowed, perplexed.

"What? Pregnant. Wha - How?"

"I went to the campus clinic today to get my allergy medicine changed since I figured it was causing my exhaustion. The nurse practitioner wanted to do an x-ray since I've had this cough since April. The clinic automatically performs a pregnancy test before x-rays." Daijah blankly stared at the mahogany hardwood floors, noticing the dark grey veining for the first time. "Positive. About eight weeks."

Roman swiped a hand down his face. "But baby, how? I thought you were on birth control." Noticing the rage brewing in her dewy orbs, he corrected his line of questioning.

"Blu, baby, I'm not accusing you of anything, just trying to understand how this happened."

"This wasn't intentional, Roman. Trust me, I don't want to be pregnant right now." She barked.

"Baby, I'm sorry. I know." He took one step closer, she withdrew, stepping back.

"The nurse thinks it could've been the combination of the steroid and antibiotic they gave me for the sinus infection back in April. They can weaken the effects of birth control. A side effect I wasn't aware of."

"Damn. Your internship, fall classes. Shit, graduation." He enfolded his fingers at the base of his neck, audibly exhaling through puffed lips. "Baby, I'll follow your lead. You know I got you, but what do you want to do?"

Absently gazing out of the floor to ceiling window overlooking the bustling urban neighborhood, Daijah captured the lone tear before it fell.

"Maybe a twenty percent chance." Daijah blurted, still standing and now outlining the intricacies of the industrial buildings lining the streets.

"Twenty percent chance of what?" He inquired, but she remained aphonic.

"Daijah." Roman yelped.

"Of getting pregnant. A year after the attack, the doctor's told Mimi that I may never be able to have children. Although completely healed, the internal damage was so extensive, children could be impossible. I've lived my life feeling inadequate as a woman...until today." She paused, finally making eye contact with him.

"A twenty percent chance of getting pregnant and a fifty - fifty chance of sustaining the pregnancy full term."

"Damn" He quietly uttered.

Roman was unconsciously pacing the length of the floor. They processed the news independently for a lengthy moment. Daijah finally settled in front of him, placing a hand at the small of his back, halting his advance. The flood of tears dripped from her face. She gazed into his chocolate eyes.

"Roman, this may be my only chance. And I want it...with or without you." Daijah hushly cried.

"Then let's take a chance, baby. I promise I got you. Ok? Do you understand me, Daijah? I promise." Surprisingly, his Colgate smile was real, genuine. He caressed her face, kissing as he tasted the saltiness of the tears against her lips.

"A December baby...like me." He gloated.

Daijah audibly sighed a sense of relief before a slight smile adorned her beautifully flushed face.

"My grandma is going to kill me." Daijah nervously chuckled.

"Nah. We'll tell her together. Ok? I think she'll be happy." Roman exhaled, settling his chin on the crown of her head.

"Daijah, I am going to take care of you and our baby. Please rest assured of that fact. I promise."

Roman embraced her as she released the breath she'd been holding since she heard the words, *Ms. Duvall, you're pregnant.*

9

Everyday seemed to be the hottest day of the month that summer in July. Mack invited his sons to the house for a barbeque since he was feeling like a lonely empty nester. Simeon and Hiram rehabbed two loft apartments in one of Mack's buildings in the city with plans to flip the other four units and sell them for a ridiculous amount of money. Adonis had an apartment near the university with his friend Rel who was also a student.

It had been a little over three months since Mack's heart attack and he was progressing well. Twenty pounds lighter, stopped smoking cigarettes, and exercising three to four times a week. Ricki even lost a few pounds. She'd cooked a variety of healthy and not so healthy side dishes for tonight's dinner to accompany the chicken, salmon, and shrimp Mack grilled earlier.

"Is X coming?" Aleah asked, while watching Ricki pull the twice baked potatoes out of the oven.

"Who knows? X hasn't been himself lately. But usually when Mack calls, he comes running so it's likely he'll be here." Ricki moved about the kitchen before pausing. "Why? X made it very clear that he wasn't fucking with you. You betta be thankful he didn't slap the shit out of you. I told your hard headed ass not to question him about Daijah. She is some shit you needed to accept and move on, but now you fucked up."

"So, you would be cool if Mack catered to some other woman while y'all are together? That he openly loved another woman while you're trying to build a relationship - a future with him." Aleah irritably inquired.

Ricki paused her rapid movement throughout the kitchen, then sighed breathlessly.

"It's been the story of my life for the past fifteen years." Ricki matter-of-factly whimpered.

"What? The fuck does that mean?" Aleah closed the distance between them taking a sip of her brown liquor. "Bitch, is Mack's big ass cheating on you?"

"Sshh! Damn." Ricki peered out onto the deck where Mack and his three youngest sons sat.

"No, bitch. He's not cheating on me. I've been with Mack for almost fifteen years and for fifteen years, I've known that aside from his late wife, Daivaughna Duvall has always had his heart."

"Daijah's mother!" Aleah whisper-yelled.

"Yep. Daijah and Adonis's fucking mother." Ricki rolled her eyes. "Like Daijah, Vaughn was a beautiful woman and could've had any man in the neighborhood. While Daijah looks like her father, she has the physical attributes and personality of her mother. For some reason it's like moths to a flame with them. After Daijah's father Jabari moved overseas to play basketball and never looked back, Vaughn lost a bit of herself. Of course, Mack knew her from around the hood, but the way he tells the story, one day he gave her a ride home from the bus stop and they fell in love. They were inseparable, much like X and Daijah. Shit, he treated her like a queen - helping with Daijah, paying bills, buying her shit. Then she got pregnant and he was ready to marry her and even adopt Daijah. But Vaughn's addiction was stronger than his love for her." Ricki blankly glared at a spot on the wall.

"One night, Mack was having a set at the house on Cannon. I was young, maybe twenty years old but I was partying. Shit, I wanted Mack's big ass so wherever he was, I wanted to be. We were all on the front porch then suddenly, seven year old Daijah was walking down the street in her pajamas carrying a screaming six month old Adonis. Vaughn left them at home; said she was going to the store to get diapers and didn't come back. Adonis was a mess - shit everywhere and hungry. Mack was ready to kill Vaughn. Instinctively, I scooped that baby up and got him clean and fed. I think that was the first night Mack actually noticed me as a grown woman. A few years later, we started exclusively dating although I knew he was still in love with Vaughn. He paid hella money for rehab, pulling her ass out of dope houses, and off of niggas' dicks. It was crazy and he finally said fuck it. He got full custody of Adonis and raised his son. But I know she still resides in his heart." Ricki blinked back tears, coming back to the present.

"And you just accept that shit? Fifteen years, Ricki, and no ring, no marriage, and you practically raised Adonis's ungrateful ass. But you have to live with the fact that he'll never fully love you. That's crazy as hell." Aleah tsked, scowling as she tossed back the rest of her drink.

"Shut up. Just shut the fuck up. Nah, I don't have a ring or marriage but Mack has cared for me in ways that my damn momma and trifling ass daddy never could. I haven't wanted for shit. Look around Leah." She motioned around the beautiful 5,000 plus square feet house.

"I picked this shit. I decorated this mutherfucker. Go check my closet...Gucci, Louis, Prada, Chanel, and the fucking list goes on. That man gives me everything I want. I don't need a damn ring to know what I got. And that's exactly what I was trying to tell your dumb ass. Being with a Kindred man ain't easy, but if you respect his fucking hustle, be there to support him through whatever and shut the fuck up. Shit, those simple actions would afford you this type of luxury. Your own shit instead of living up in here with me and my man."

"Aye."

Ricki and Aleah shuddered at the sound of Xander's voice.

"They outside?" He asked and they nodded. Xander momentarily observed Ricki. Her eyes were red and she appeared angry.

"You alright Rick?" Xander inquired.

He was trying to take Daijah's advice and be a little nicer to Ricki. She did step up in a big way after Mack's illness.

She nodded, flashing a faux smile.

Xander completely ignored Aleah as he walked out onto the deck of his father's house overlooking the swimming pool. His brothers and father were gathered under the pergola at the table with drinks and cigars.

"What's good Kindreds?" Xander questioned, greeting each of his brothers and father with a dap.

"What's good, bro?" Simeon retorted. "Where you been hiding? I ain't seen your ass in a week."

"Nah, just chilling. You know me - staying focused. Taking care of business." Xander poured a drink from the Macallan bottle.

The Kindred men laughed and talked shit until Ricki summoned them to eat. Given the scorching heat outside, they opted to have dinner in the dining room. The twelve seat dining table was beautifully decorated with deep blue and ivory hues accented with gold place settings. Ricki wore a proud grin as she placed the last serving tray on the table. Although she sometimes felt like an outsider, this was her family and she loved the Kindred men.

Mack settled at the head of the table while Xander took his position at the opposite end. Hiram's friend, Khloe, arrived in time for dinner as did Ricki's sister and nephew who were visiting from Chicago. Mack bragged about his grilling skills while Ricki fixed his plate. Surprisingly, they ate, fellowship, and guffawed for a couple hours with no drama. They transitioned into the massive great room for dessert, banana pudding and apple cobbler. The women gathered on the oversized midnight blue sectional couch with dessert and drinks while the men played pool.

"Yo, D. Where's your fine ass sister? I ain't seen Daijah in years." Leon, Ricki's nephew, asked. "You think she's ready to give me a chance?"

Adonis laughed, shaking his head.

"Dawg, my sister is way out of your league. She's about to become a bomb ass lawyer and your ass is -" He paused, resting his fingers on his chin as if he was deep in thought.

"What exactly do you do Leon? Did you even graduate from high school?" The men heartily laughed.

"X, dawg, have you hit that yet? Y'all been tight for a long time. She would at least have to be my friend with benefits or some shit." Leon chortled. "I'm surprised you ain't wifed her pretty ass."

"Mind your business, Leon. X don't play when it comes to the sweet and pure Daijah." Aleah slurred jeeringly, as she sluggishly meandered from the kitchen with another glass of brown liquor. "No sir, don't mouth a word about his sweet babydoll."

Aleah's reddened eyes were shooting daggers in Xander's direction and she was fired up and ready to spew her drunken truth.

"Leah, shut up and bring your drunk ass over here." Ricki yelled from the couch.

"Nah, Rick, I'm tired of shutting up. Ain't nobody else good enough for his ass but his cherished Daijah. I've been here for months trying to be what he wanted, but he doesn't see me. All X ever sees is *her*. I'm good enough to fuck but nothing more." Aleah's blood shot eyes flooded with tears.

She drunkenly stumbled closer to Xander but Hiram quickly grabbed her by the waist to pause her pursuit. Everyone one in the room clearly understood that it would not be in her best interest to cross Xander.

"You think she's so special and pure and innocent. Huh, X? Well, I call bullshit. We'll see if you keep that same energy when your precious Daijah delivers that Strong family seed in a few months." Aleah spat.

A collective gasp circulated through the vaulted ceilings.

"You need to listen to your cousin lil girl and shut the fuck up with all that bullshit." Mack chided, standing to his full height. His imposing frame should've been warning enough but Aleah ignored him.

"No bullshit, Mack. I know what I saw. Y'all's adoring Daijah Blu is pregnant. And she and Roman looked really happy about it when they were leaving the doctor's office yesterday. It was actually cute how he kissed her little bulging belly before helping her in the car." Aleah mockingly snickered, glaring directly at Xander as she continued to sip.

All eyes nervously darted between Aleah and Xander. His nose flared while tightly gripping the pool stick, seriously contemplating knocking the shit out of her ass. His umber eyes flamed at the thought of Daijah being pregnant and that this bitch was delivering the blow.

"Leah, get your drunk, stupid ass over here." Ricki aggressively snatched a teary-eyed Aleah, pulling her into another room.

Xander clenched his jaw so hard, he's teeth loudly clinked together. He immediately leered at his brother Adonis.

"D, let me holla at you for a minute." He sharply requested as he walked towards the sliding patio doors. Adonis followed with Simeon close behind.

"What the fuck is she talking about? Is Daijah pregnant?"

Xander queasily swallowed hard. Adonis peered around, unable to make eye contact with his oldest brother.

"And you knew about his shit and didn't say a fucking thing to me?" Xander gritted, umber orbs menacingly searing.

"I'm sorry X, but it wasn't my story to tell. When Daijah told me and Mimi, she promised she was going to tell you so I left it at that." Adonis shrugged.

"Where is she?" Xander angrily inquired.

"What?" Adonis furrowed.

"Where the fuck is she right now?" He demanded again.

"Probably at Mimi's. Daijah was helping her pack for her trip to

Milwaukee today to see my Aunt Thomasina." Adonis said. "But X, man, don't be taking all that stress bullshit around my sister. Yeah, the situation fucked up, but her baby is still my family."

Xander stepped to Adonis chest to chest but neither backed down. Shaking his head, Xander speedily exited the deck, heavily trekking back into the house. Snatching his keys from the hook in the kitchen, he was halfway through the foyer when Mack's gruff baritone resounded, pausing his advance.

"Xander."

"Pop, don't." Xander was trembling as he kept his back to his father.

"Don't what, son?" Mack unhurriedly closed the space between them.

"Don't tell me I shouldn't go talk to her." His voice was below a whisper, yet stern.

"Nah, you definitely need to talk to her. But when you do, calm that shit down and think about what role you've played in all of this. Daijah ain't fuck up this shit alone." Mack crossed his arms as Xander turned to face him. Their mirrored imposing images stood strong.

"Man to man - this is all on you, son. Your ass rolled out the red carpet for that nigga. You created this mess. So, what the fuck are you going to do to fix it?"

The overwhelming sense of rage and desolation lived in the rapid rise and fall of his chest. But remorse and guilt feasted on his heart. Jaws tensed, Xander absently held his father's stare for a lasting moment.

"Ain't shit I can do. I'm too late."

XANDER PARKED his Land Rover on Cannon Street watching Daijah help her grandma into the van that her Uncle Bean was driving. He surveyed her from afar for any signs of pregnancy. Leaning back on the headrest, Xander ran a hand down his face, exhaling his frustrations. Mack's words circulated through his head. *This is all on you son.*

After Ms. Mimi departed, Xander parked in the driveway next to Daijah's BMW. He blankly stared at the house, weighing every sane and insane action he could take. Climbing the steps to the front door, Daijah unexpectedly opened the door before Xander could knock.

"Xan. What are you doing here?" Daijah was glowing in a yellow romper and jean shirt rolled up above her elbow.

Xander digested her pretty face before journeying his eyes over the rest of her body. He paused at her stomach, a slight swell protruded her belly. Breathless, his lungs succumbed to the reality, making it impossible for him to speak.

"Xan, we good?" Daijah curiously questioned, still positioned in the doorway with her purse slung over her shoulder.

"Nah, Daij. We're not good." The boulders that previously settled in his feet were diminished as he crossed the threshold into the house seeking no permission.

Daijah swallowed hard, pausing momentarily before she turned to face him. Daijah anxiously crossed her arms over her abdomen. At seventeen weeks pregnant, subtle transformations were evident like glowing skin, slight spread of the nose, and a scanty but noticeable bulge to her once taut waist. Xander narrowed his eyes, leaning against the foyer wall with his hands stuffed in his pocket.

"What's going on, Xan? How did you know I was here?" Daijah backed up to lean against the opposite wall.

"Is there something you need to tell me, Daij?" Xander's voice was grimly low.

"What do you mean? Tell you what?" She shuddered, no desire to have this conversation with him.

"I'll ask one more time. Do you have something you need to tell me, Daijah? And please don't play dumb. Some news you need to share?"

The expression on Daijah's face was vacant, but her heart fiercely pounded, its collapse was inevitable.

"Xan, I was going to tell you." She blurted.

"When? Hmm? When you were swollen and wobbling?"

"Of - of course not." Daijah stuttered, leg uncontrollably bouncing. "I just haven't had a chance to connect with you. I didn't- I wanted to tell you face to face."

Xander thrusted from the wall as he terminated their physical separation to stand directly in front of her. She damn near gnawed a hole in her bottom lip as her oxygen grew unreliable.

Firmly massaging her nape, he stroked his thumb across the scar. But this time his caress was different, unnerving.

"Ok. Here I am, Daij. We're face to face. I'm listening."

"Xan." Daijah whimpered, dropping her head with her hand laced over her stomach. "Um, I..."

Xander cupped her chin, lifting her head forcing eye contact. Her quartz orbs glistened with tears. It was impossible for her to say those words to him and he knew it.

"Daijah, look at me." Xander slowly uncrossed her arms, resting his hand on her stomach.

"Is it true?" Xander's nostrils flared, eyes misted.

Daijah rubbed both hands down her face trying to fight off the swell of tears invading the corners of her eyes. She nodded.

"Nah. Say that shit. Tell me." He urged.

"I'm pregnant, Xan." Daijah's voice was weak, trembling.

Xander deeply inhaled. His eyes clenched tight, coupling his temple to hers as his hands firmly clutched her waist. He thunderously gritted, "fuck, Daijah."

"Xan, I'm sorry-"

"Nah." He interrupted. "No need to apologize. I was going to find out sooner or later, right? Maybe at the baby shower, or maybe that dumb ass gender reveal shit. Or why not fucking wait until you were in labor to share your miracle with your best friend? Everybody knows except me. Why Daij?" Huh?" He paused. "Why?" Xander shouted.

"Xan, I didn't know how to tell you, okay? I didn't know what to say."

"Well let me see. You could have looked me in the eyes and said, 'Xan, my very best friend since I was twelve, I'm having a baby with fucking Roman Strong'."

Xander clinched his eyes tight, dizzied by reality.

"Do you love him? Is he the love of your life, Daijah?" He aggressively probed, dismantling the miniscule space between them.

Daijah blinked, unleashing a puddle of tears.

"Don't do this, Xander." She pleaded.

"Answer me, Daijah."

"I am having his baby, Xander, so I must have love for him."

Daijah could not speak Roman's name.

Xander hadn't released her. They were so intertwined that surviving separation would be hopeless.

"That's not what I asked you. Do you love him?"

"I want this baby, Xan, and -"

"And what?" He forcefully inquired, still cupping her face.

Breathily she uttered, "And... I love Roman."

Xander gazed at Daijah for what seemed like a lifetime. They shared labored breathing, glazed eyes, staring deeply trying to uncover a mystery as if they were waiting to be rescued, ready to be extricated from this new nightmare. Those words were like kryptonite, weakening his ability to even think clearly. He recoiled, feeling like he'd been shot in the gut. Daijah tightly fisted his shirt, refusing to disconnect from him.

"Xan, please. You know better than anybody that this may be my only chance at motherhood. If I can sustain this pregnancy, she will be my miracle. The bright light at the end of ten plus fucked up years of trauma."

"*She.*" He mouthed, flabbergasted by this whole scene.

His babydoll was having a baby girl.Xander was numb - no words, no feelings, no resolutions. Reconnecting their temples, Xander

melting into her embrace tightly cupping the arc of her tear dampened cheeks. His quivering lips gently grazing hers.

"I'm too late," languidly spilled from his mouth like the saddest
love song.

He decided to do the only thing he mastered when it came to
Daijah - support, protect, and love her - through whatever.

"I'm happy for you, babydoll. I know that you wanted this for a
long time." Xander croaked, voice anguished but sincere.

"Don't hesitate to let me know if you need anything. And I mean
anything Daijah. This doesn't change shit between me and you."
Xander continued to retreat, creating more distance between them.

Daijah remained muted, frantically grabbing his shirt, pants
packet, capturing his waist, anything to freeze the extended loving
embrace. For a moment, Xander hesitated but he knew that wouldn't
stop her pursuance. He understood that Daijah required his blessing,
she needed to believe, *even if it was a lie,* that he was going to be ok. To
say that Xander was crushed was an understatement. He was devas-
tated, heartbroken - grieving an emotional loss that he would never
recapture.

"Xan, talk to me. Say something." Daijah searched his feverish
umber eyes for something. What, she was uncertain.

"We good, Xan?" Her pleading iris penetrated his heart.

He nodded.

"Always Daij. We good."

DAIJAH HADN'T MOVED from her position on the couch in her grandma's living room since Xander left a couple hours ago. She vacantly
stared at a picture of her and Xander the night he basically
kidnapped her from prom. A slight smile momentarily lined her face
before the image of him a few hours ago resurfaced. Xander

appeared, hurt, disappointed, defeated. The faint whisper of his word, *'I'm too late'* sickened her.

Daijah scrambled to the restroom dry heaving as tears clouded her eyes. While she was heartbroken by Xander's disclosure, she was maddened that a pregnancy was his breaking point. The ringing of a phone blared from the living room. Daijah trekked down the hallway to see that Roman was video calling. She exhaled, stretching her eyes wide, striving to erase the glumness.

"Hey."

"Hey baby. How are you feeling?" Roman smiled, gazing directly into the camera.

"I'm ok. I was a little nauseous earlier but better now. How are you? You look tired." Daijah observed his unfamiliar surroundings.

"I'm good, Blu. Don't worry about me. Just finishing up some business with my brother, Roland."

"Roland? He's in town?" Roman's second oldest brother Roland lived in Charlotte where his family originated before moving to St. Louis when Roman was five. Roland was somewhat the black sheep of the family - or better yet, the fuck up. But Roman always gave him an opportunity to redeem himself. Daijah met him only once and he lived up to his reputation.

"Yeah. He's moving back so I'm trying to help him get settled in a place. Did you finish everything for Ms. Mimi?" Roman asked, quickly changing the subject. Daijah sensed that he was irritated.

"Yeah. She's on the road with Aunt Germaine and Uncle Bean. They'll be in Milwaukee visiting my Aunt Thomasina for a week."

"I don't want you staying there by yourself tonight, Daijah. I'll be late but I would feel much better if you were at my place."

"Nah, I'm going to Zaria's. We are long overdue for a girl's night. I'm about to set the house alarm and head out." Daijah heard Roland in the background.

"You sure you ok, Blu?" He curiously questioned. She unconvincingly nodded.

"Alright baby, let me see what this nigga wants. Have fun and try to get some rest. I'll call you later, ok." She smiled then nodded before they disconnected.

Daijah drove twenty minutes to Zaria's townhouse. It was a cute community that was recently rehabilitated and occupied by young professionals who wanted the convenience of being close to the city but the comforts of a homey neighborhood.

"Hey Mama!" Zaria squealed as she opened the front door. Her excitement quickly dissipated when she saw the expression on Daijah's face.

"Daij, come in. What's wrong?" Zaria ushered Daijah to the crimson couch.

"Xander knows about the baby." Daijah expelled a roaring sob that she'd contained all afternoon.

She proceeded to tell Zaria everything about her encounter with Xander. The painstakingly heartbroken expression that laced his chiseled face. His admittance that he waited too long for them to try to be together.

"Daij, I'm sorry. I know that was tough for you - for the both of you. But what did Xander expect? For you to wait on him forever. Why do you think he kept saying he was too late? In Xander's mind, as long as he pampered you, you would never belong to anybody but him. Now he knows he lost and he can't do anything to fix this. Not his money, being a Kindred, shit, even y'all's crazily intimate history." Zaria settled next to Daijah with a box of tissue.

"Think about it, Daij. Xander has only lost one other time in his life, and that involved you too. His biggest regret in life was not protecting you. And now, you slipped through his grasp again." Zaria shrugged.

It was as if a lightbulb ignited in Daijah's head. Zaria was absolutely right. Xander's visage that afternoon was eerily similar to his demeanor that night of the attack and the countless moments in the hospital- anguished and hopeless. She massaged her growing belly, exhaling as she nestled into the corner of the couch, whimpering, "I guess he is too late."

10

Autumn in Missouri was the best time of the year. Earth tone leaves filled the streets, kids carefreely playing without the threat of the blazing summer sun. Sunny, yet a light cool breeze made for a perfect day. Xander was pulling into the circle driveway of his father's house when he received a notification from his assistant Nicole. He did a double take at the message that crawled across his screen. Not believing what he was seeing, he called Nicole to confirm.

"Hey boss." She eagerly answered.

"What's up Nic? Did he say what the fuck he wants to meet me about?" Xander questioned.

"No, sir. But he said it was urgent and needed to happen today. I told him your schedule was booked but he insisted that he only needs a few minutes. I can cancel it."

"Nah. Have him meet me at the Kindred building in two hours." Xander ended the call and immediately instructed the auto-dialer to call his brother.

"What's up, bro?" Simeon answered, gruffly chuckling.

"Sim, what are you laughing at? I ain't said shit funny."

"Nah, I was laughing at Zaria's silly ass. We just finished lunch. I'm about to drop her off." Xander heard Zaria in the background.

"*Hey X.*"

"What's up, Z? Aye, Sim, can you meet me at the Kindred building in an hour? It's important."

"I got you, bro. Zaria is about to get up with a friend so I'm pulling up to her crib now." Sim said, then whispered something to Zaria.

"Sim? Can you be there?" Xander anxiously confirmed.

Suddenly, the sweetest, most soothing angelic timbre sounded through the phone's speaker.

"Hey Sim. Long time no see." Daijah laughed as she leaned into the passenger side of Simeon's car where Zaria was seated. Her voice took his breath away but Xander remained silent, attentively listening. Simeon and Zaria tensely peered at each other, wondering if Daijah heard Xander through the car speaker.

"What's up, Daij? Um, damn, look at you. Progressing right along I see." Simeon muttered, hopelessly attempting to act normal.

"Yep, I guess progressing is what you can call it. Big as hell is what I call it. This is almost seven months of progression." She chuckled, rubbing her belly while Zaria exited the car, ushering Daijah away.

"Bye Sim. Tell everybody I said hello."

Simeon nodded, watching Zaria and Daijah until they disappeared into the house.

"X." Simeon said, wondering if his brother disconnected.

"Yeah, I'm here. A friend, huh. You full of shit, Sim. One hour, nigga." Xander's tone was strained as he disconnected the call.

He hadn't heard Daijah's voice since the day he found out she was pregnant. They sporadically text, but no substantial communication. Xander exited his truck as his father appeared in the doorway to greet him.

"Hey son. You look like you got a lot of shit on your mind." Mack embraced him before stepping aside to allow him in the house.

"I can't stay as long as planned. Some shit just popped up."

Xander said, ambling through the massive two story foyer. They settled in Mack's home office to privately discuss the matter.

"You think he's on some bullshit? Don't go without protection." Mack said, still viewing the meeting request on Xander's phone.

"Nah, never that. He'll be on my turf. I scheduled the meeting in two hours in your office. Simeon is joining me there. But I honestly don't think he's stupid enough to step to me on some bullshit."

"You may be right, but niggas never cease to amaze me." Mack chortled. "Speaking of amazing, guess who I had lunch with last week?"

"Pops, no guessing game, please. I have enough shit on my mind." Xander rolled his eyes.

"Daijah Blu." Mack sang.

"Daijah? When?"

"Last Thursday after my doctor's appointment. I saw her walking into the bakery next door to the medical building when I was coming out. We ate lunch and talked for a couple hours." Mack nonchalantly rested in his recliner.

"That's what's up. I'm glad she's doing well." Xander's sentiment was genuine but he really preferred not to engage in this conversation.

"And she's looking well too. Daijah's always been a beautiful girl like her mother, but pregnant - she's absolutely stunning."

"I'm about to be out, Pops." He definitely had no desire to hear about Daijah's pregnancy glow. It was hard enough to hear the elation in her voice earlier.

"Nigga go talk to her. She's still family, Xander. Y'all have been friends too long and been through too much shit to just throw it away. When I talked to Daijah, she had the same dumbass, lovestruck smirk on her face that you are wearing right now. Both of y'all trying not to ask about the other. It's bullshit. She may be having a baby with somebody else, but her heart is still with you."

"I hear you, Pops. I just - I can't right now. I'm truly happy for Daij but I can't see her swole with that nigga's baby." Xander stood, dapping Mack, then headed out to take care of his business.

Thirty minutes later, Xander was perched in his father's office at the Kindred building. It was the headquarters for all businesses related to the family enterprise. Kindred & Sons occupied the top three floors of the ten story building. The other companies in the building rented space. Mack's office comprised the entire tenth floor complete with a private conference room, full bath, kitchen, and a few secret panels that were not visible to the naked eye. Simeon arrived on time as always.

"Hey X. What's going on, bro?" He dapped and hugged his brother.

"I received a request for an urgent meeting today." Xander slid his phone across the desk for Simeon to view the message.

"Yo, what the fuck, bro? You think he's on some bullshit?" Simeon questioned as he checked his gun.

"I guess we'll find out momentarily." Xander passively leaned back in the chair, clasping his hands over his abdomen, pondering the intent of this meeting.

About thirty minutes later, Nicole's voice piped through the phone intercom.

"Mr. Kindred, your guest has arrived. He has been cleared by security, sir."

"Thank you. Send him in." Xander was immobile as he stared at the entry door, hands leisurely folded across his abdomen. Simeon stood behind him leaning against the oversized window.

The door slowly crept open and the three men glared in silence for an extended pause.

"Close the door and feel free to take a seat." Xander instructed.

"I'd rather stand."

Simeon cautiously strolled across the room to pat down the guest for extra security.

"What can I do for you today, Mr. Roman Strong?" Xander's voice was pleasantly threatening.

"I'm not here on business, X. I came to talk about Daijah." Roman said.

"Then you are here about business because Daijah *is* my business. Always have been. Always will be." Xander candidly expressed, unflinched.

Roman annoyedly chuckled. "Well, let's get down to business then. Alone." He peered at Simeon, who didn't budge and wouldn't until his brother instructed.

"It's all good, bro." Xander consented but didn't release his eyes from Roman as Simeon departed.

"Now, what can I do for you?" Xander smirked.

"Daijah is a beautiful woman. Smart, confident, bold, and so in love with life. I honestly didn't believe such a woman existed. Not for a nigga like me at least. Shit, she's changed everything for my good. And now that she is full with my baby girl - oh, if you didn't know, Blu is blessing me with a little girl - my princess, Reign." Roman was attempting to taunt Xander, but he remained visually unbothered.

"Anyway, starting a family with Blu has required me to take some extra precautions to ensure my woman and my baby are safe, protected. And I believe that's one thing we have in common." Roman lifted an eyebrow seeking consensus.

"What do you believe you and I have in common?" Xander cocked his head to the side, eyes narrowed anticipating a bullshit response.

"Do you love Daijah?" Roman questioned.

"Yes."

"Are you *in* love with Daijah?" He probed further.

"Yes." Xander confidently retorted, his movements were fixed, unstirred.

"And you would do anything to keep her safe and protected?" Roman continued.

"Without question."

"Then, X, we have a lot more in common than you think." Roman decided to finally take a seat.

"You have sixty seconds to get to the fucking point of this meeting." Xander vexedly sat up, resting his elbows on the mahogany desk.

"Ok, let me cut to the chase then. The type of lifestyle you and I live, we always need a little extra protection, insurance. Would you agree?" Roman paused.

Xander nodded.

Roman pulled out a manila folder that was tucked under his arm and slid it across the desk. Daijah Blu Duvall was written on the tab. Xander remained motionless, eyeing Roman, trying to decipher his motives.

Xander leaned his head down, placing his right ear closer to the folder.

"Should I listen for a ticking sound? You know niggas these days get creative with bombs and shit." He chortled but was dead ass serious.

"Nah, I'm not here for no shit like that. This is a peaceful encounter." Roman facetiously laughed.

Xander opened the folder, reading the contents for about a minute. He narrowly peered up at Roman, wordless.

"Can I count on you for that?" Roman rose from his seat and extended his hand to Xander.

Xander stood, accepting the handshake.

"You have my word."

———————

"IF MY ASS gets any bigger, I can be Santa Claus for Christmas." Daijah chuckled, standing in the full length mirror ridiculing her very pregnant frame. She was thirty six weeks pregnant and ready to pop.

"Z, can you help me with my shoes?" Daijah pouted.

"Daij, you look absolutely beautiful. It's your graduation

girl...from law school, bitch. Cheer up." They heartily giggled. "I'm so proud of you, Daijah."

"That makes two of us." Roman leaned against the doorway of his bedroom that had recently become their bedroom since he convinced her to move into his condo. He admired Daijah in a flowy black dress, her fresh braids pulled into a low ponytail, the diamond hoops he gifted her, and black peep toe booties.

"Blu, you look beautiful, baby. You ready?" Roman closed the distance between them, softly kissing her before bending to sweetly kiss her bulging belly.

She nodded.

They sauntered into the living room where Ms. Mimi, Aunt Germaine, and Uncle Bean were waiting for her. They all tearfully beamed with pride. Zaria unveiled Daijah's graduation regalia from the dry cleaner's bag. The brilliant blue robe with full belled sleeves, black velvet panels, and gold piping with the coordinating black velvet tam was regal. Daijah's robe was decorated with honors.

"Grandma, will you help me please?" Daijah's sparkling quartz eyes were already crowded with tears.

Ms. Mimi proudly draped her granddaughter in the robe and perfectly positioned the hat on her head before taking a step back to admire Daijah.

"Thank God." Mimi gratefully whispered.

The auditorium was packed with fellow graduates, professors, family, and friends. Daijah examined the crowd searching for her family. Her supporters were few, but they'd been her foundation from day one. Spotting her grandma and Roman, she waved and gleefully laughed when she noticed Adonis, Simeon, Hiram, Mack, and even Ricki waving oversized pictures of her a few rows back. Her elation momentarily wavered at the disappointment of not seeing Xander there. Shaking off the sadness, she involuntarily caressed her belly as she eagerly paced the floor awaiting the processional.

"Daij."

She swallowed hard. The sound of his pacifying bass-filled timber snatched her breath away. Daijah slowly shifted, eyeing Xander dressed in all black from head to toe with a hint of color from the woo camel-colored overcoat. He was so deliciously fine, the women, and a few men, were literally swooning. He quickly erased the distance between them standing directly in her face.

"We good, babydoll?" He sweetly blushed.

Daijah blinked back tears. Overwhelmed by the mere presence of *him*. She missed him terribly.

"We good, Xan." She adoringly smiled.

Xander hugged her tight for a long overdue, heartwarming embrace. He audibly exhaled because Daijah was his weakness and strength.

"Congratulations, Daij. I'm so fucking proud of you." Xander nestled against her ear and literally inhaled her heavenly fragrance. She squeezed him tighter.

"This is for you, Daij." He glided the small black box into her hand before withdrawing.

Daijah didn't want to let him go. Not again. She clutched his coat lapels, the rise and fall of her chest uncontrolled.

"Xan." She lovingly whined. "Thank you for coming."

"Where else in the world would I be?" He stroked a finger down the bridge of her nose then trailed his fingers to caress her nape. Instinctively, Daijah leaned her head to the side to kiss the palm of his hand. The intimate exchange lingered a moment too long, allowing memories of their lost love to ceaselessly invade their subconscious. Xander wanted to kiss her terribly. A jolt against his stomach distracted their gaze. Daijah glanced down to her very pregnant belly as the baby animatedly stirred.

"She likes you." Daijah whispered with a miniscule smile.

Xander digested her beautiful eyes for a moment longer before vanishing into the crowd.

Daijah proudly processed into the auditorium taking her seat. She opened the box revealing two platinum diamond encrusted bracelets with, "*I see the moon and moon sees me,*" on one, and the other continued, "*God bless the moon and God bless me.*" Daijah smiled coyly, noticing the inner inscription that read, "*To Mommy.*"

Two more identical bracelets slid from the other side of the box into Daijah's lap but much smaller in wrist size. She closely examined them, confirming they were definitely too small for her, then she read the inscription, "*To Reign.*" The flood of tears unleashed.

———————————

REIGN IMANI DUVALL STRONG was born happy and healthy on Christmas Day, just eleven days after Daijah graduated magna cum laude with her juris doctorate degree. While her doctor hoped Daijah would be able to deliver vaginally, she had to endure a cesarean to safely bring Reign into the world. Roman was closely by her side throughout the almost 24 hour labor and delivery. Reign was the mirror image of her mother, only carrying Roman's mocha skin and almond eyes. She was a beautiful baby.

Daijah and Roman were getting accustomed to being new parents. Late nights, early mornings, breast feeding, diapers - it was a whirlwind. They blinked and it was already Valentine's Day. Roman snuck away to prepare a surprise for Daijah. It was one of the few times either of them left the house since the baby was born. Seven week old Reign rested in the bath sling watching her mommy relax in the tub. Candles, sparkling cider, and soft music pacified mommy while a full belly and fresh diaper nurtured baby.

"Blu, baby, wake up." Roman stroked her brow.

"I'm awake. Just resting my eyes while she's asleep."

"I guess this bathtub holder thing was money well spent. Reignbow loves it." He kissed Reign's tiny toes, causing her to smile in her sleep. Daijah smiled, loving when he called Reign by her newly minted nickname.

"Baby, get dressed. I have something for you. I'll get Reign settled for the night." Roman leaned down to kiss the top of her head.

Daijah hurriedly discontinued her bath, lathering her smooth skin with lavender-vanilla lotion. A black spaghetti strapped casual cotton dress fit her new mom curves perfectly. Braids freely swinging over her shoulders. Fresh faced, she sauntered down the dim hallway peeking into Reign's room before she entered the living room. Candles delivered a luminous glow throughout the space, two dozen red roses sat on the cocktail table, a plush red blanket was spread across the floor in front of the fireplace, and two dinner place settings. The perfect indoor picnic.

"Happy Valentine's Day, baby." Roman whispered, snuggling behind her as they enfolded into a loving embrace.

"Aww, Roman. Thank you. I completely forgot that it was Valentine's Day. I didn't get you anything." Daijah pouted.

"Yes, you did, Blu. You gave me Reign. My gift is you and my Reign-bow." He sexily smiled before gently kissing her lips.

Caressing through her chocolate curls, Roman deliciously crowded her mouth with his tongue. Kissing down her chin to her neck, steering clear of the scar, he tenderly nibbled and licked and sucked repeatedly.

"Roman. You know we can't. The doctor said two more weeks -"

He firmly clutched a handful of her ass, dispensing a guttural moan from her mouth. "Ahhh, Roman."

"I know, baby. But the doctor didn't say I couldn't please you in other ways."

Roman ushered Daijah towards the fireplace. They slowly danced and lustfully kissed to the sounds of Brian McKnight. He delicately settled her on the plush blanket, journeying his hand up the length of her curvaceous thighs to rid her of soaked panties. Roman cuddled her full pillowy breasts, admiring their beautiful ability to nourish his seed, while bringing him so much pleasure. He carefully navigated the surgical scar, cupping the arc of her pussy, massaging her swollen clit at a dallying, leisurely pace. Daijah knew they were on borrowed time given Reign's sleeping habits, but the shit felt so good, she welcomed the sluggish tempo.

The crackle of the fire coupled with the symphonic melodies offered the perfect backdrop. Roman disrobed her from the dress, her brown sugar skin shimmered against the sepia flames. He digested the fullness of her beautiful frame, painting his eyes over every inch of her body like it was a fine work of art. Hypnotized by the swell of her plump breast, rotund ass, and the redolence of her dripping arousal, Roman's dick was painfully primed.

He whispered, "Fuck Daijah. You are absolutely exquisite."

The strength of his ever-present erection pressed against her stomach, continuing to render Daijah breathless.

"Roman." She whimpered.

"I got you, baby. Pleasing you pleases me. Let me make you feel good, Daijah."

Roman stealthily traversed the length of her body, inhaling the sweet smelling nectar before licking her puss from the bottom to the top. Resting at her clit, he tenderly sucked, tugged, and kissed. Daijah fondled her fingers through his soft coils, massaging his scalp to the rhythm of his magnificent tongue. Roman plunged one finger, then two into her throbbing jewel, relentless, unceasing until Daijah trembled. Anticipating a reverberating moan that was certain to awaken Reign, Roman swallowed the satisfying tone in his mouth. Slowly circling his tongue, her flavor making the kiss that much sweeter.

Reign decided to be a good girl for mommy and daddy, allowing them another hour of intimacy, then dinner before she wailed.

The next morning, Daijah awakened with a smile - completely sated, yet exhausted. She stretched, extending her hand searching the bed for his sizable frame. It was empty. She paused momentarily because the house was unusually hushed. Daijah jolted, wondering if Roman had to leave and she'd slept through Reign's cries. Peering around the room, her eyes landed on the most heartwarming sight. Reign's tiny frame snuggled into the curve of Roman's massive chest took her breath away. Daijah quietly retrieved her phone from the nightstand to capture the moment. Gazing for a moment longer to file away the memory, Daijah tip-toed out of the bed to start breakfast.

"Hey sleeping beauties." Daijah teased as Roman entered the kitchen with Reign laying on his shoulder. "Let me finish cooking before you get too close. You know she can smell her milk from a mile away."

Daijah cooked scrambled eggs, potatoes, sausage, biscuits, and mixed fruit. Roman ambled into the kitchen planting a kiss against her forehead before grabbing her ass. Reign's little head bobbled, searching for her nourishment. While Daijah fed the baby, Roman stuffed his face. They enjoyed a collective moment of silence while Daijah lovingly stroked Reign's cheeks as she fed.

"Blu?" Roman's deep morning timbre shifted her attention. She lifted a brow acknowledging him.

"I need to go to Charlotte next week." He blurted.

Daijah's tranquil demeanor quickly flustered. The growing crease in her brow was a key indicator.

"Go to Charlotte for what Roman?" Irritation invaded her tone.

"Roland needs me to look at this property down there." He leaned back in the chair preparing for her wrath. Roman knew that this was not the time to take a trip but he needed to settle shit with his brother once and for all.

"Now? You need to do this now? What about Raymond? He's the oldest. Why is it always Roman to the rescue?" Daijah heatedly questioned, adjusting Reign to the other breast.

"Because he's my fucking brother and he's trying to find his way, so I'm going to help him." Roman deeply exhaled. "I'm sorry. I didn't mean to yell. But I'll only be gone a few days. Baby, I promise."

"Your promise doesn't make it better, Roman. We have an almost eight week old baby who requires around the clock attention. And not to mention, the mother of your child is not fully healed. This is not a good time for out of town business." She yelped, trying to keep her voice calm.

"I can ask Ms. Mimi to stay with you. I think she'll love that. And I'm sure Zaria will be willing to help for a few days." Roman's smile would usually soften the blow, but not this time.

"Sounds like your mind's made up and you have it all figured out." Daijah's tone was direfully flat. She stood, resting the baby against the burp cloth on her shoulder. Her sparkling quartz orbs, now fiery red.

"Baby. Come here -"

"No, Roman. Enjoy your trip." She angrily stormed down the hallway into Reign's room.

———————————

XANDER WAS sound asleep when the deafening ring of his phone agitated him from his slumber. Peering around, he eyed a lump on the opposite side of his king size mattress. *Shit!* He forgot he allowed his latest piece of ass, Tamia, to spend the night. She shuffled against the satin sheets, exposing her naked plump ass. Tamia worked in the Kindred building and had been a consistent presence in his world over the past month. Unlike Aleah, she didn't press him for his time and was cool with being available at his leisure.

2:58am. Xander squinted, the bright illumination reflected against the navy blue wall.

"What the fuck is wrong?" Xander angrily questioned.

"X. We need to roll out." Hiram's voice was calm but the background noise was chaotic.

"Ram, what's going on?" He bucked up, leaning against the headboard still reeling from sleepiness.

"Not over the phone. But we need to go get Daijah. Now." Hiram calmly instructed, understanding that anything pertaining to Daijah would cause his brother to violently stir.

"Fuck! Where?" Xander abruptly jolted from the bed, intently listening to Hiram's instructions. He pulled on boxers and black sweat-pants. Standing at the edge of his bed, he aggressively shook Tamia awake. She roused, stretching as her brow creased in confusion.

"Xan, what time is it?" Tamia gruffly questioned.

"What did I tell you about calling me that?" He cocked his head to the side, seeking her understanding. "Get dressed. I have an emergency."

"It's three o'clock in the morning. Why can't I just stay here?" Tamia remained snuggled in the sheets to his dismay.

"Because you are not staying up in my shit when I'm not here. Come on. And I need you to move quickly and please don't ask me any more questions." He demanded.

She nodded, hurriedly searching the room for her clothes as he finished dressing.

Thirty minutes later Xander pulled his truck behind Hiram's black Escalade at the location they discussed. He exited his truck to sit in the back of his brother's SUV. Simeon was in the front seat and Adonis was seated next to him.

"D, call to see if she'll answer?" Xander instructed.

Adonis called once, no answer. He waited a few minutes and called a second time, she answered on the third ring.

"Doni, what's wrong?" Exhaustion evident in her exasperated tone.

"Daij, I need you to turn off the alarm and open the door. Don't ask me any questions." Xander's commanding voice sounded, shocking Daijah as she intently listened.

Daijah had just awakened to feed Reign. She followed Xander's instructions and waited to turn off the alarm and open the door once she confirmed it was him on the other side. With Reign strapped to her body in the baby sling, Daijah's heart brutally pounded as she bounced the baby to keep her calm. Opening the door, she gasped at the site of all four gigantic brothers dressed in all black.

"What happened?" Daijah cried.

Adonis didn't speak. He glided past her to go retrieve Mimi from the guest room. Simeon stood watch outside while Hiram was posted at the front door. Xander momentarily ceased his pursuit. The visual of Daijah with this gorgeous curly-hair, chocolate baby girl strapped to her bosom, imitating every one of her mother's features, rendered him temporarily breathless.

"Xan, please tell me." Sleeplessness reddened her eyes but they were wide with fear.

"Daijah, what did I tell you to do if either me or my brothers suddenly came for you?" Xander firmly cupped her face.

"Trust you. Move quickly and don't ask questions because it's for my protection."

He nodded and Daijah expeditiously began to gather everything she needed for her and Reign.

She found a suitcase and packed bottles, a handful of clothes, diapers, toiletries, and her breast pump with no understanding of how long she would be gone. Hiram grabbed Reign's bassinet and bouncer seat from the living room while Simeon secured the carseat in Xander's truck. She could hear her grandma's terrified voice asking all of the questions she was seeking answers to but received only silence from the brothers.

"Daijah Blu, what is going on?" Frightened, Ms. Mimi sobbed silent tears.

"Grandma, calm down. It's ok. You're ok." Both Daijah and Adonis endeavored to soothe her.

Xander settled at the doorway ensuring that everyone was out of the house when he entered the code to arm the alarm.

"How do you know her code?" Simeon curiously crumpled his forehead.

"A combination of her birthday and mine." Xander nonchalantly responded as if that was normal behavior.

"Damn, y'all got it bad." Simeon whispered, shaking his head as he ambled to the driver's side of Daijah's BMW.

Adonis and Hiram helped Ms. Mimi into his truck while Daijah rode in the backseat of Xander's truck with Reign.

An eerie hush overwhelmed the truck as Xander and Daijah rode in silence. She absently gazed at her beautiful baby girl peacefully sleeping as streams of tears drowned her cheeks. Less than an hour later, all three vehicles pulled up to the secured gate at Xander's home as the sun began to play peek-a-boo with the dissipating moon.

Adonis helped his grandma get settled in the guest room while Simeon arranged the baby's things in the smaller of the two master suites on the main floor of the house. Daijah washed and fed Reign before resting her in the bassinet next to the king size bed. Xander leaned against the door jam, arms and feet crossed as he silently admired Daijah carefully and patiently nurture her daughter. Once Reign was sound asleep, Daijah's zombiesque frame wandered across the stunningly decorated room to settle on the couch facing the lake behind the house. She could feel Xander's presence drawing closer to her positioned behind the couch.

Vacantly staring into the early morning light, Daijah whimpered, "tell me."

Xander stroked a hand down his face before rounding the couch to sit next to her. He coupled his hand with hers before uttering, "Roman is dead."

11

The glaring sun was completely disrespectful and unruly as it blazed through the patio door of Daijah's room. She leisurely staggered out of the bed ambling over to Reign's crib. It was almost ten o'clock in the morning and her baby girl hadn't made a sound. At six months old, she was finally sleeping most of the night but an early morning grand rising from Reign-bow was guaranteed. It was almost four months to the day that Daijah's world as she knew it changed forever. The night she discovered that the father of her then two month old baby was murdered. Shot in the back of the head execution style.

Roman called Daijah the day before she found out he was dead, informing her that he would be in Charlotte a couple more days. She'd tried video calling him several times that day but no answer. Daijah was so busy with Reign, she didn't consider that something was deathly wrong. Confusion and suspicion around Roman's murder were still prevalent months later. While he was supposed to be in Charlotte, his body was found in one of the abandoned buildings that his family owned on the north side of the city - in St. Louis.

Questioned numerous times by the police, Daijah's mind was

reeling trying to decipher his last few phone calls and text messages but she doesn't recall anything out of the ordinary. Roman's mother held a memorial service but took his body to Charlotte where she decided to relocate. Indigo Strong was a brave woman but the death of her most beloved son just a few years after her husband mentally crippled her. Daijah had only left the house for the memorial service and Reign's doctor's appointments. Otherwise, she spent her days in the massive bedroom suite at Xander's house.

After basically rescuing her from potential harm, Xander refused to allow Daijah to leave since they still didn't know if Roman's murder was random or targeted. But honestly, Daijah didn't have anywhere to go. Roman's condo was off limits due to the open murder investigation and too many memories, and her room at Ms. Mimi's house was simply too small for her and a growing baby.

Daijah was suffocating. Bemused and overwhelmed by Roman's death and powerless in her inability to find an iota of motivation. Bathe, dress, feed, and play with Reign, that's all she did - in that order. Her baby girl was her only source of inspiration to face each day.

Daijah peeked into the crib prepared for their morning game of peek-a-boo but the bed was empty. She loudly exhaled, then mouthed, 'Xander.' It was not unusual for him to creep into her bedroom to retrieve Reign. While Daijah vainly attempted to act irritated by his actions, she appreciated the few extra hours of sleep. Grabbing her robe, she covered her half naked body before meandering down the hall and into the kitchen. It was clear that Miriam, the housekeeper, had come and gone. Coffee was made and a delectable looking breakfast casserole was on the stove. Continuing her search, Daijah wandered into the media room where Xander and Reign were knocked out on the couch. Her miniature fingers sprawled across his hairy face. A random cartoon played in the background on the screen as they harmoniously snored. Daijah swallowed hard, a range of emotions inundated her body, recalling how Reign similarly cuddled with Roman.

Abruptly, Reign shuddered, sensing her mommy's presence. A head of big chocolate curls popped up from Xander's chest. The most deliciously cute gummy smile greeted Daijah.

"Hey Reign-bow bright! Good morning babygirl." Daijah scooped her up into the sweetest embrace. Reign's early morning beam made everything right with the world.

"It's like Kitten can smell you coming." Xander chortled, eyes still closed. His gritty resonance transported a tingle in her core.

"Yeah, I am her personal milkmaid. At her beck and call." Daijah positioned Reign under the nursing cover while perching at the opposite end of the sectional.

"Thanks Xan, but you can wake me up if she's fussing."

"She wasn't fussing, just up playing so I grabbed her." A shirtless Xander sat up on the couch gazing at her.

For the past four months Xander often found himself carefully surveying Daijah. He respected her need for space to grieve, but Xander was concerned that Daijah was falling into a depression. She only ate to maintain nourishment for Reign and he often heard her pacing the bedroom floor at night. Daijah and Reign's safety were his number one priority. The massive quiet house was now filled with the bustling activity of a baby. He'd fallen in love with the curly hair chocolate drop that he affectionately named *Kitten*. Now two Duvall women had stolen his heart. Xander knew he was in a world of trouble.

"So, what's on your mind, Daij?"

"What do you mean?" She shyly avoided his eyes.

"I heard you pacing last night. Talk." Xander commanded.

"I just have a lot to figure out. I need to find a job and get us a place to live so we can get out of your hair." She sweetly smiled.

"We've been over this, Daij. You know you can stay here for as long as you want. But you also know that I'm not comfortable with that until this shit is settled." His bullish tone frustrated her.

"Xan, I don't want to be your burden or your hostage." Daijah blurted, rolling her eyes.

"I need my own shit for a change. All of my life I've been dependent on something - my grandma, financial aid for school, food stamps to eat...you. I'm twenty-five years old and it's time for me to grow up and find my way." Her misty quartz eyes were transfixed on everything and nothing at all.

Xander leaned his head to the side, brow angrily creased.

"Is she sleeping?" He motioned at the baby hidden under the cover.

"What?" Daijah questioned, enthralled in her irritation.

"Is Reign asleep?" He sternly questioned.

Daijah peeked under the cover and her baby girl was in a milk induced coma.

She nodded, confused by his firm tone.

Xander abruptly rose from the couch, collecting Reign from Daijah's hold. He reticently sauntered out of the media room, returning a few minutes later.

"Xan, what are you doing? She was fine." Daijah shrugged.

"Nah, I put her in the crib. We need to talk." Xander returned to his previous position, wearing a pissed off scowl.

"Daijah, what's the real issue? You know damn well you are not a burden or a hostage. If I didn't want you here, you wouldn't be here. I could identify plenty of other options available for you. So, talk."

Legs nervously trembling, Daijah gnawed the inside of her cheek, quelling the bubbling inferno building behind her misty eyes. They settled in agonizing silence for an extended beat.

"I feel so fucking lost, Xan. I am a single mother because my daughter's father was murdered when she was just eight weeks old and I have no clue why or by who. I hate that our last conversation was an argument. I'm angry that Roman was clearly lying to me. I'm scared as shit that somebody is out there lurking in the darkness waiting to hurt me or harm Reign. I pace the floor, watching her for most of the night. Petrified." Daijah mightily closed her eyes, cradling her body as she rocked back and forth.

"You remember when I got out of the hospital? I didn't want to talk or move or breathe. That's how I feel sometimes, Xan. I am suffocating. Like I'm thirteen again... terrified that Mishawn is going to come and finish what he started. But that little girl in there is the only reason I drag my ass out of bed everyday. To nurture and protect her. But the longer I'm living here, the longer you cater to me, not forcing me to do more - to do something, the deeper into that same black hole I will fall. And I don't know if I'll make it out this time."

Xander hurriedly eradicated the space severing their connection. He lovingly embraced Daijah as the dam broke, flooding them both with tears.

"Daij, babydoll, I will never let anything happen to you or Reign. I will die before any mutherfucka considers laying a hand on either of you. Daijah look at me." She shook her head, still nestled in the folds of his neck. "Look at me." He urged and she acquiesced.

"You are not a single mother. Yeah, the circumstances are fucked up but you have a complete support system and we are going to love and nurture and support Reign. She won't ever have to want for anything. Not as long as I have breath in my body. She's mine. You're mine, Daijah. You always have been."

Xander softly kissed her forehead, her nose, cheeks, then lips.

"I'm thankful you recognize that you're falling but it's ok to break, shit, crumble if you need to, Daij. And I will be there to pick up every fragment. I know that you want your own shit and I wouldn't expect anything less, but a nigga is selfish, Daijah. I want you here. I want you and Reign right fucking here."

She attempted to speak, to oppose his stance, "Xan, you can't -" but Xander digested every potential word of opposition. Wantonly licking the seam of her lips before making love to her mouth with his tongue. His sweet, sensual kisses turned erotically violent and Daijah welcomed every blazoned tongue lashing. Xander effortlessly lifted her to straddle him and she shamelessly grinded against his swelling steely dick. Her robe unraveled without any persuasion. Xander ogled her motherly sexy ass body. Inflated blackberry nipples visible through the white tank top, her ass pleasantly settled into the fitted boy short. She was better than he remembered. Xander was practically drooling. No other woman had ever appeased his greed because Daijah was his hunger and his feast. Ready to bust in anticipation of having her delightful essence on his palate, Xander crowded his mouth with an abundance of her breasts. Licking, suckling, nibbling as he kneaded and massaged her ass.

"Ah, shit. Please, Xan." Daijah begged.

It had been too damn long since she'd had sex. Valentine's Day was the last time she felt the sensual touch of a man and her pussy was aching for a release.

"Please what, babydoll? Tell me what you want?"

"Xan, I need to cum... now!" She whisper-yelled, quickly approaching her pinnacle from the grind alone.

Xander ripped the fabric of the grey and white striped boy shorts from her flesh. Slightly lifting her frame, he swiped two meaty fingers down the mouth of her pussy before bringing them to his mouth, tasting her pleasure.

"Fuck, Daij. You still get this wet for me, baby?"

"Only you, Xan." Daijah deeply inhaled, smelling her candied, smoldering essence bubbling over like hot molasses.

Xander wasted no time invading her puss with two blunt fingers while gripping the curves of her ass, creating a pathway to sinfully fondle her private hole.

"X!" Daijah screamed, instantly releasing her gooey butter goodness.

Licking the evidence of her delight from his fingertips, Xander wiped his hands with the shredded fabric of her panties before tickling down her spine, causing a guttural chuckle to release from her. He was elated to see her smile. They both instinctively checked the baby monitor when they heard a slight stir. Reign was still comatose. Daijah slowly slid off of his lap into a squat coming face to face with that *hey big man* dick she loved. Xander was seriously working with a monster. She gently caressed the magnitude of his veiny, sleek, glorious erection. Licking her lips, craving his amplitude against her tongue.

"Daij, what are you doing?" Xander's umber eyes were lustfully heavy. He nibbled the corner of his lip, coupling his hand with hers, jointly massaging his manhood. That was the sexiest shit Daijah had ever encountered.

"You tasted me. So, I want to taste you too." She shyly blushed. "But, I've never done it, sooo.... I may be bad at it."

"Are you serious, babydoll? Why didn't you ever with -" His voice trailed off as his eyebrows raised.

"Real talk? No bullshit?" She asked.

He nodded.

"Because I wanted to give you all of my firsts." Daijah's tone was so sweet yet so seductive.

"*Fuck.*" Xander mouthed as she languidly licked from the base to the sprouting tip of his manliness.

Flirtatiously eyeing him, she peppered soft kisses before slowly, steadily, salaciously stroking up and down his shaft. Xander desperately desired to grab her head and guide her where he wanted, shit critically needed her to be. But Daijah wasn't a damn novice. She knew exactly what she was doing. Taking his shit like a boss, inch by inch, covering his entirety with her savory mouth.

"Shit, Daij. Goddamn, babydoll." Xander loudly moaned. "You're fucking savage." He snatched the throw pillow, muffling his pleasure with a nearby pillow.

Twisting, turning, sucking, licking, she suctioned his mass while caressing his balls. Xander was fucking down for count. Unable to contain his animalistic desire, he firmly grabbed her curly tresses encouraging the rhythm.

"Mmmhmmm." Daijah sang. She favored his amorous participation.

"Daij, babydoll. Shit. I'm cumming." He grunted. "Move Daij, for real."

Xander pointlessly struggled to escape her grasp. She incessantly proceeded with the gloriously debilitating dick lashing.

"Fuck! You keep doing this to me, Daijah." He gritted, seductively fondling through her wild hair. His grip grew tighter and harder until he exploded.

"Babydoll! Fuucckk."

Daijah savored his syrupy nectar, temporarily quenching her thirst for him. Xander possessively snatched her from the floor resting her on the couch. Labored breathing, they locked eyes, searching each other for comprehension, understanding...love.

A blaring cry shook them from their reverie. Reign's pouty tear-stained face filled the baby monitor screen. Taking a moment to gather themselves, Daijah and Xander hurried to caress her. Before they approached the baby's bedroom door, Daijah turned to him and whispered, "to be continued."

———————————

TWO WEEKS PASSED since Xander and Daijah's unexpected entanglement in the media room and there was no continuation in sight. They moseyed through the house as if they were co-parenting friends. Neither of them were willing to address what happened a couple weeks ago. Ironically, the sensual engagement sparked a modicum of motivation for Daijah. She started walking the neighborhood with Reign, visiting her grandma and Mack; she even invited Xander to Reign's first swimming lesson. They were a typical dysfunctional American family.

One Sunday evening, Adonis and Hiram came for dinner. They'd had a festive time feasting on Daijah's cooking. Baked chicken, macaroni, greens, green beans for Xander, and candied yams. Reign was exhausted after being tickled and tossed by her uncles all day. Once she was down for the night, Daijah heard the doorbell ring and then a woman's voice. Tip-toeing out of her bedroom, she leaned against the wall closest to the foyer.

"Tamia, what are you doing here? How did you get through the gate?" Xander leered, protectively surveying the surroundings.

"It didn't close after your brothers left." Tamia smirked.

"So, you basically are trespassing on my property. Should I call the police or just get my fucking gun?"

"X, I mean, what the fuck? I haven't seen you in months. I've been calling and texting. Baby, what's going on? One day we were chilling and the next you were ghosting me. We got beef I don't know about?" She stepped in closer but was blocked by his overwhelming frame.

"Like you said, you ain't seen me in months so that must mean that I don't want to see you. Leave Tamia. Now." His eyes narrowed, offering her only one warning.

"Really, X?"

A soft wail escaped from the hallway. Reign was crying.

"Xa, xa, xa." She balled. As of late, those incomprehensible words were directed at Xander only. For the past week, when he entered the room, she would drool *xa, xa, xa* and could not be consoled until he picked her up.

"Oh wait, do you have a baby now? Wow. So, you were fucking me and fucking some other bitch and got that skank pregnant."

Daijah was ready to buck up and beat Tamia's ass as if those comments were directed at her. Wisely deciding to mind her business, she ambled into her bedroom unsuccessfully attempting to comfort her baby girl. Reign stood on her chunky legs in the crib holding her favorite yellow and gray blanket covered with elephants.

"Xa, xa, xa." She whined.

"Xa, xa is busy, Reign-bow bright. Do you want your elephant or mousey?" Daijah picked her up only to be greeted by a screeching cry.

"Kitten. Why are you making all that noise, huh?" Xander's familiar baritone calmed her immediately. Reign almost jumped out of Daijah's arms, whispering, "xa, xa, xa." Daijah chuckled and rolled her eyes at her finicky child. Reign had the nerve to rest her head on Xander's shoulder and loudly sigh a sense of relief.

"I see how you do mommy, Reign. Don't be calling for me when you need some milk. Ok, lil girl." She playfully cooed.

"I'm going outside for a little bit. Are y'all good?" She avoided eye contact with him.

He nodded, sensing her annoyance.

Daijah suppressed her tears until she was tucked away in the corner of the patio facing the lake. This was one of her favorite places in his house. So quiet and peaceful. The perfect escape to meditate, pray, and cry. Daijah considered the area with the swing chair her cleansing corner. Pressing the button to call Zaria, she aggressively wiped her tears.

"Hey Daij. Did you save me some food? I'm sure those big ass niggas ate up all the greens." Zaria giggled.

"Z, I can't do this anymore. I can't be here anymore. Can me and Reign stay there for a little while? Until I figure this shit out." Daijah cried.

"Of course. I can be on my way now, Daij." Zaria was that kind of friend - loyal, ready to roll out at any moment.

"Nah, I need to get a few things taken care of, so probably tomorrow."

"What happened, Daij?"

Daijah told Zaria everything, including the woman named Tamia.

A few hours later, Daijah sauntered back into the house. Her eyes were burning from crying. She was so damn tired of shedding tears but found some clarity on her next moves. Closing and locking the patio door, she meandered through the darkened living room, Xander was perched in the wingback chair holding a beer.

"Daijah."

She paused, dropping her head then releasing a deep exhale. Daijah was tired of his fruitless promises and conversation. She was done. Her somber voice was but a whisper.

"Xander, so many times in this friendship, I set myself ablaze just to make sure you were warm and comfortable. But my sacrifices in this relationship were concealed by flashy gifts, diamonds, a car, and the attention of *the* Xander Kindred. The night we made love...relinquishing my virginity to you... I told you I wanted all of you, and that meant more than just your dick. You stole all of my firsts without any care for my feelings or my heart. So, you win, Xan - you were right. You said you would possess my soul and I would never be the same. Consider it gone - my entire soul snatched right from up under my nose and I haven't been the same - will never be the same. If you do this - if you desert me again, Xan. If you reject me again. I won't recover. We.... won't recover. I'm done."

"I can't make you understand how hard this is, Daij." Xander hung his head, resting his temple in the palm of his hands.

"It's not that hard. It's just us crazy humans who make it difficult." She uttered, recalling Zaria's words.

"What do you want me to do?" He rose from the chair but didn't move.

"Trust me. Trust us - to love each other through it all under any circumstances. Love me, Xander. Openly, freely, with no conditions." Daijah didn't wait for a response. She brokenly journeyed to her bedroom, locking the door behind her for the first time.

XANDER HAD a full day of meetings and needed to connect with his father on some new real estate opportunities. Last night, he was pissed that Tamia showed up at his house. And even more pissed that security didn't catch her pulling into his gate. His first order of business that morning was to regulate the security company for their mishap.

It took a couple hours before Reign finally fell asleep last night. He brought her to his room to give Daijah some time alone. She was pissed and that shit was written all over her face when she stepped outside. Xander didn't have the energy nor desire to explain anything about Tamia because she was a nonfactor. He hadn't laid eyes on her since the night he made her leave his house. Sitting in the living room waiting for Daijah, he intended to explain but she had other plans for the conversation. *Trust me. Trust us. Love me.*

Xander shook his head, dispelling the pondering from his mind. He lazily crawled out of the bed, pulling on black basketball shorts before going into the bathroom to relieve himself. His normal morning routine consisted of checking on Daijah and Reign before he showered and started his day.

It was 8:07am and Reign's bed was empty on the monitor he kept in his bedroom. At some point in the middle of the night, Daijah treaded into his room to put Reign in her crib. Trekking through the living room and kitchen to Daijah's room, the house was hushly still. Xander softly knocked on the door, not wanting to disturb them if they were asleep on the couch. The door slowly crept open - no Daijah, no Reign. His brow furrowed, checking his phone for messages. Nothing. Xander called down to the security guard on duty and was informed that Daijah left about an hour ago. He stood in the middle of the room dumbfounded, not recalling any doctor's appointments or other errands she had. Peering around the room, Xander noticed that several things were missing, including Daijah's breast pump and Reign's pack and play.

What the fuck? Xander mused, immediately dialing Zaria.

"Hello." Zaria sang.

"Where is she, Z?"

"Well good morning to you too, X." She teased.

"Z, don't fuck with me today. Where is Daijah?"

"She just put Reign to sleep and is trying to get some rest. But do not even think about coming here Xander. Nigga, I got a security gate too, so don't even try it unless she sends for you."

"Are y'all fucking serious right now? She just leaves with my daughter and doesn't say shit." Xander was pacing.

"Well, technically Reign is not-"

"I swear to god, Z. Don't ever fucking say that shit. Reign is *mine.*" Xander gritted.

"Well, think about what you're doing then, Xander. Daijah is serious because she's tired and hurting and broken." Zaria emotionally croaked.

"She's managing a new baby, this shit with Roman, and the emotional roller coaster known as *you*. My friend has loved you for as long as I can remember. She loved you even when you struggled with all of the various versions of Xander Malcolm Kindred. But what did you do? You showed her love through material things. But I guarantee you she would set all that shit on fire to simply have the fullness of your heart, X. Then you had a bitch show up at your house last night. Really, Xander? Your shit is usually tighter than that."

"Zaria, please put Daijah on the phone before I fucking explode." Xander gritted.

"Well, you gone have to blow the fuck up then, X, because I'm team Daijah. You are my boy and I love you, but I will fuck you up over this one. I believe this is the final straw for you, X, so gone and keep that emotionally obtuse energy going and you will find yourself... by yourself. If you truly love her, give her some time and then tell her the truth." Zaria hung up.

Xander was standing still but his head felt like it was circulating around the room. He cupped his head, endeavoring to stop the pounding. Deep inhales and exhales on repeat delivered a semblance of calm. His vision was slightly blurred when he viewed his phone to dial a number.

"Pops, I need your help."

12

Five days, one hundred - twenty hours, seven thousand - two hundred minutes painstakingly ticked away as Xander impatiently waited for her. After Zaria read him his entire life and threatened to fuck him up over her friend, Xander called the only person who could pull him out of the black hole he'd lived in for over ten years.

Mack immediately drove to his son's house to find him on the floor in the darkened media room holding Reign's babydoll that he found in the couch cushion. Xander blankly stared at the screen. *New Jack City* was playing but the room was mute. Mack didn't say a word, he simply perched on the couch next to Xander.

"Daijah left. Zaria cursed me out. And D won't answer my calls. I fucked up." He drank directly from the Hennessey White bottle.

"It's time, son. Time to tell her the truth. Reveal what you've been struggling with. Face your demons that are preventing you from having the love of your life."

"If I tell her, what if she rejects me? What if I become a character in her nightmares?" Xander's expression was empty.

"You won't. She won't. Daijah is the only one who can fill in the blanks for you. You've formulated this story in your head for so long, that you believe it. And I don't believe it's true." Mack rested a firm hand on Xander's shoulder.

"Did she agree to come?" Mack inquired.

Xander had Daijah's favorite flower, yellow roses and chocolate dipped strawberries and pineapples delivered to Zaria's house with a handwritten note asking her to have dinner with him on Friday night at his house - alone. Zaria agreed to keep Reign - in her words - *for as long as it takes to get y'all shit together.*

After a few painful hours of him pacing, she finally texted him accepting the invitation.

"Yeah. Tomorrow night."

"All you can do is make it make sense for her. Just tell her the truth." Mack and Xander sat in silence for hours.

DAIJAH WAS SOAKING in the bathtub at Zaria's house enjoying the chocolate covered goodies and inhaling the fragrancy of the flowers. She was resolute in her decision to leave Xander's house that morning. No plan and a little money in the bank, she was determined to figure things out. Daijah called her former law professor who had previously recommended that she consider teaching since she did so well as an assistant. Her internship manager also reached out to ask if she would consider doing some consulting for the non-profit agency since they couldn't afford to pay her an annual salary. It appeared that once she made her mind up to put Daijah first, the floodgates began to open.

For the first time in a week, Daijah genuinely smiled. She relaxed against the bath pillow when her cell phone rang. It was an unknown number.

"Hello."

"Yes, is this Ms. Daijah Duvall?"

"This is Daijah. Who's speaking?"

"The is Stephanie McCullen from Pioneer Bank and Trust. For security purposes, ma'am can you verify your birth date and social security number?"

"No. You are calling me, so can you verify my birthdate and social security number?" Daijah studied enough content about the legal mess of identity theft not to fall for a scam.

"Um, yes ma'am. I have a birthdate of eight, thirteen, 1995. SSN ending in 1198. Last known address 1420 Cannon Street."

"That is correct. What can I do for you, Ms. McCullen?"

"Ms. Duvall, I am the manager coordinating the estate of the deceased Roman Lamar Strong, Jr. We have an outstanding account that needs to be liquidated to fully settle the estate. You as well as a minor by the name of Reign Imani Duvall - Strong are listed as the beneficiaries; however, I have been unable to contact the primary overseer for the account. A Mr. Xander Kindred. Are you connected to Mr. Kindred?"

Daijah was speechless. She sprung forward in the bathtub inadvertently splashing water everywhere.

"Um, what? Xander Kindred? Um, yes, I - I know him." She stuttered.

"I've attempted to reach him by phone at his office at Kindred & Sons, as well as via email with no response. Ms. Duvall, we really need to settle an account of this substantial amount as soon as possible."

"Substantial. What does that mean?"

"Let me see. It's an immediate payout of fifty thousand dollars and then a monthly support payment of ten thousand dollars until the minor Reign Imani Duvall-Strong reaches the age of twenty-five."

Daijah's eyes bulged as she mouthed, 'What the fuck?'

"Ms. Duvall? Are you still with me?"

"Yes. Yes, I'm here."

"Given that Mr. Kindred is not a certified owner of the account, we do not need his permission to release the funds. All I would need from you as the adult beneficiary is two forms of identification, the minor's birth certificate, and your signature notarized in our office. Then we can initialize an immediate deposit into your account here at Pioneer."

"I don't have an account with your bank."

"Quite the contrary, ma'am. Mr. Strong opened a checking and savings account in your name on February 14th of this year."

Daijah's eyes flooded, tears stinging her eyes. She was overwhelmed by Roman's thoughtfulness - his love for her and Reign. In the same breath, she was angry and perplexed. Why would Xander be the overseer? And why wouldn't he tell her about the account?

"Ms. Duvall?"

"Yes, Ms. McCullen. I will gather those items and come by the bank on Monday."

"Perfect. I will send you a confirmation text message at this number and I look forward to seeing you on Monday." They disconnected the call.

"Holy Shit!" Daijah yelped.

DAIJAH PULLED up to Xander's house a little after seven o'clock Friday night. She sat for a brief moment, not certain of what she hoped the outcome of tonight would be. After the phone calls about two potential job opportunities and the news from the bank, Daijah was overloaded with information and decisions. Honestly, she wanted to just have an uneventful dinner with her friend and dismiss all of the other bullshit for now. She shuddered at the sound of Xander opening the monstrous ten foot entry door. Damn, she despised that his ass was always so fine. He stood in the middle of the doorway with his hands folded behind his back dressed in distressed jeans, black button down shirt with the sleeves rolled up, exposing his tattoos, and Ferragamo loafers.

He leisurely strolled to the driver's side opening her door. Since this was the first time Daijah had the opportunity to dress up a bit since Reign was born, she stepped that shit up all the way. The eggplant-toned strapless bodycon dress fit her curvy body like a glove. Her normal double D breasts were a bit fuller due to breast-feeding and her hips were more defined since being pregnant. Yves Saint Laurent sandals that Roman gifted her for Valentine's Day cladded her feet and gold chains of various lengths dressed her neck. Zaria silk pressed her hair into a straight long bob parted down the middle and light touches of makeup.

"Babydoll, you look magnificent."

"Thank you. You look nice too." Daijah blushed.

Xander ushered her into the house. The foyer was lined with luminaries casting an exotic glow throughout the two story entry. Entering the kitchen, her favorite pineapple rum and a bottle of wine rested on the counter. Daijah beamed, excited to partake in a little alcohol for the first time in a very long time. She ensured Reign had more than enough breast milk to last her through the night with Zaria.

"I remember you saying you could pump and dump since Reign is not taking as much milk. But there's plenty of ice tea and lemonade if you don't want to drink."

"Oh, I want to drink. Trust." Daijah's giggle gave him chills. He desperately missed the sound of her sweet timbre.

She opted for a glass of wine before they continued to follow the illuminated path onto the deck. The scenery was gorgeous. A table for two decorated with hints of crimson, ivory, and deep purple. More candles lined the deck, but the full moon stole the show. The glistening, luminous glow of the moon reflected white and silver rays against the rippling lake. Xander caught glimpses of her as the moon's bright gleam crystalized her beautiful eyes.

"Dinner is ready whenever you are, but no rush." Xander leaned his back against the deck rail shamelessly ogling her frame.

"It's beautiful out here, Xan. Really, you outdid yourself. Thank you." Daijah lazily stroked her lips across the rim of the wine glass before taking a sip.

"Don't thank me. Thank Miriam. This was her brainchild. I told her I was desperate and she came through for me." He sexily smirked then winked.

"Well, in that case, let's eat."

Daijah got her wish - a simple dinner with her friend was exactly what he delivered. They comfortably ate, drank, and laughed. Daijah caught him up on all things Reign that he'd missed over the past week.

"Reign-bow misses her, Xa Xa." Daijah teased.

"I miss her too. And I miss you, Daij." Xander's sexily narrowed eyes lovingly peered.

"Xan, I don't want to fight." She blurted.

"Neither do I. I just want to talk, that's all. Can we do that?"

She nodded.

They transitioned into the living room for dessert and more drinks. Daijah kicked off her shoes to get comfortable in the house she'd called her domicile for the past four plus months. The room was pleasantly hushed. Both of them relaxed from the numbing effects of the alcohol and each other's presence. Xander was seated in his normal place, the wingback chair, while Daijah settled on the ottoman across from him.

"Every time I opened my eyes, I prayed that you would open yours for just a second. When you didn't, I would place the one hand I could move over your heart to make sure you were still breathing." Xander's umber of orbs narrowed. He repeatedly circled his pointer finger around the rim of the cognac glass.

"I remember the demonous evil on Mishawn's face. He would touch you or hit you while you were unconscious just to get a reaction out of me. He taunted me. Kept asking if you were my girlfriend -

if I ever tasted your lips. So many things are still a blur from that night, while others, I've subconsciously blocked. But everytime I see your pretty face, I have to barricade the visuals of you being beaten, raped, and mutilated and there wasn't shit I could do about it. Daijah, that shit fucks me up every day." He cleared his throat.

Daijah recognized a familiar expression of uncertainty on his beautifully mocha face. She couldn't take it. Daijah could not tolerate any more rejection from Xander.

She aimlessly shook her head. "Xan, my heart is tired. Just tell me you don't want this - that you don't want me."

"Please Daijah, just listen to me, please. Never question if I want you, because all I've *ever* wanted was you." He gazed directly at her to ensure there was no uncertainty. "But...I have to protect you. Keep you safe."

"Protect me from what?!" She blurted. Daijah's deafening scream shocked them both.

"ME!" Xander's bass-filled shout widened her eyes. "I can't remember, Daijah. It'll kill me if I hurt you."

"What are you talking about, Xander?" Her brows furrowed in confusion.

"That night. I don't know if my nightmare is true. This horrific, recurring feeling that I hurt you, Daijah... physically. I can't remember if that crazy mutherfucka Mishawn forced me to do things to you-"

"No! Stop it, Xander! You didn't. You *never* touched me." Daijah was frantic.

"How could you know, Daijah? How can you be so certain?" Xander remained placid as if his body was bolted to the chair.

"Because I know!" She screamed.

"I remember every touch of their filthy, scaly hands, the sound of their voices, the smell of their cheap cologne. Those bastards beat me, mutilated me. Once they were done with me and put us in the room together, you *never* touched me... other than holding my hand. Xander, baby, you were my only comfort- my saving grace."

Daijah quickly diminished their separation. She knelt before him, cupping his chiseled face.

"Look at me Xander. You *did not* touch me. I promise you. Xan, you never hurt me." Daijah's eyes darted back and forth aligned with his.

Xander dropped his head into his palms. She could hear the strain, the relief of his labored breaths.

"My nightmares have always ended with me wandering through the hospital looking for you, Daijah, and I finally found you... but you scream for *help* when you see me - *terrified* of me. Then other nights, they end with you slipping further and further into a deep blackened hole. The only nights that I find any peace is when I recall the look on Mishawn Carr's face right before I put a bullet in his head." Xander's eyes were transfixed on the flickering flames in the fireplace.

Daijah's beautiful quartz eyes widened. Now she was fearful and awestruck. She couldn't breathe. All of the oxygen escaped her body. If she wanted to run, she was incapable because of the boulders lodged in her feet.

"What? Xander, what are you saying to me? *You* killed Mishawn? When?" Daijah apprehensively probed, unsure if she really wanted the answers.

"A year after the attack." He whispered.

"What! Xander, you were only sixteen. How? Why?"

"Because he's responsible for all of this shit, Daijah! Those other niggas were ready to walk away but Mishawn was the instigator. He did everything!" Xander shouted. "To you, to me - *everything!*"

"Wait, wait, wait." Daijah thrusted from her kneeling position, backing away from him. "What do you mean to you?" Her breathing was sporadic, eyes bulging.

Hushed, Xander absently stared.

"Xander!" She screamed. The rapid pace of her beating heart threatened an attack. Daijah was uncontrollably quivering.

"He did shit to me too, Daijah. Nobody but Pops knows. But what he did to me wasn't shit compared to what he did to you. After the other two were taken care of, Mack put the call out to the streets. He offered a hefty ransom for that nigga to be brought to him alive. Ironically, some of the Strongs' street boys found Mishawn hiding out in one of their crack houses. I remember that night like it was yesterday."

"As usual, I was up pacing in my room, actually about to hop out of the window to come to your crib when Pops knocked on the door. His face was cold, blank. He said, "*son, I found a way for you to sleep soundly again.*" I didn't think shit about it when he ushered me to a hidden section of the basement I had never seen before. Mishawn's naked body was beaten, bloody, and tied up. Shit, everything he did to us, they did to that nigga ten times over. I can still see the whites of his eyes bulging with the single light swinging above his head. When I walked in, I was immediately transported back to that dusty ass car wash. Pops placed the gun in the palm of my hand and didn't say a word. I eyeballed that nigga for a long minute, searching for any signs of remorse - he had none. Then images of your sweet face laughing and jumping on those cracks that afternoon flashed before me. Then I heard the resounding wail of your screams echoing, that's when I pulled the trigger. I dropped the gun and walked away before his body hit the concrete. I returned to my room and slept like a baby."

Daijah was immobile, eyes painfully swollen and fiery red. Her cry was cavernously deep, sobbing from her soul. It all made sense now. That was the day "Xander" died and the callous, cold, emotionless "X" was born. She painstakingly sobbed, mourning the loss of her best friend's innocence... for the second time.

"Daijah, please, say something. That look on your face is exactly why I never wanted to tell you. Your nightmares are treacherous enough, I don't want to create new terrors for you, baby. I don't want you to think I'm a monster. I won't survive if you fear me, Daijah." Xander hesitantly closed the recent distance she created, extending his hand, praying she would accept him. Unconditionally. She maintained the distance, but only for a moment.

Accepting his embrace, Daijah searched his saddened eyes,

cupping the curves of his face in the same way he'd captured hers for so many years.

"Xan, I am so sorry. I'm so sorry you've had to carry this burden alone. It breaks my heart that you were even put in that situation."

Xander released the breath he'd been holding, thankful for her consent to live in his truth. Conjoined tears engulfed their swollen, puffy faces. Tasting the salted corner of his mouth, she delicately kissed his lips.

"I love you, Xan. Your secret is always safe with me. I promise." She whispered.

"Daijah, I fucking love you and I'm so damn sorry. I will never allow anything to keep you from me ever again. Forgive me, babydoll. Please come home." Xander lovingly commanded.

"Home?" Daijah's big doe-like quartz eyes blinked rapidly.

"This is your home, Daijah. You and Kitten." Xander nestled the folds of her neck, caressing his imposing hands against her nape.

———————————

"Still In Love" by New Edition piped through the surround sound speakers. A lustfully sexy smirk crossed Xander's face. Twirling loose curls of her hair around his finger, he smiled.

"Dance with me, babydoll." He bit his bottom lip, snaking his protective limbs around her waist then slowly slid his hands to cup her ass.

Daijah welcomed him, tightly clasping her arms around his neck. She tossed her head between her shoulder blades consuming every morsel of his glorious face. Xander gazed deeply, passionately, the chiseled arc of his face was coated with love, respect, honor, and adoration. He thumbed the lingering tears away before warmly kissing her lips, softly singing the lyrics through his sweet smooches. Making love to her mouth with a tongue so thick, warm and wet, goosebumps invaded her flesh. Moaning, their mouths unified in the most delightful caper. Tongues harmoniously dancing to the rhythmic melodies.

Xander spun Daijah around, her plump ass snuggled against his brawny erection that he'd been suppressing since she stepped out of the car in that sexy ass dress. So close, he captured her every exhale to supply his inhale. They were positioned directly in front of the oversized twelve foot antique mirror leaning against the wall flanking the fireplace. Exchanging affectionate, impassioned reflective stares, they ogled each other like the moon, grateful for another night. Xander maneuvered his giant hands up the curves of her hips, then across her taut waist.

The wanton smirk paired with the racy gleam of his beautiful umber orbs had the seat of Daijah's thong drenched. He continued his exploration, massaging her doughy ample breasts, rock hard nipples distended against the fabric. Daijah adjusted her head, offering her neck to him as he planted supple, arousing kisses before devouring the full of her lips. Daijah kissed him with her eyes closed so tight, filing this moment away for safekeeping. She was hopelessly devoted and enamored with the boy who was now the man of her dreams. Xander unzipped the dress, intently watching it ripple to the floor, eagerly anticipating the sight of his honey-hued goddess.

Stroking her inner thighs, Xander mouthed, 'open' as he nudged her weakened legs apart. Effortlessly, he moved the lacy material thong that temporarily prevented his entry - slipping one finger then two into her dripping treasure. Daijah raspily moaned, clenching her orbs tight.

"Open your eyes, babydoll. Look at how beautifully wet you are."

Daijah reveled in the sight of her perfectly imperfect body being ravished by this splendidly divine man. He glided those long, fat fingers slowly and gently - incessantly thrusting into her core, circling his thumb at the tip of her throbbing clit. Xander never disjointed his gaze from her the entire time. Firmly, yet gently holding Daijah's neck, encouraging her to partake in the deliciously erotic movie that was *her*.

"Ahhh, Xan."

"I missed you, baby. It's been too long." He gritted.

"I missed you, too." She whined.

Xander slowly withdrew his fingers from the depths of her essence. Daijah abruptly gasped, missing the steamy connection.

"Xan, don't stop. Please." She begged.

"Are you going to be a good girl and keep your damn eyes open?" His stern eyes glared at her in the mirror.

"Yes." She breathily whimpered.

"Show me what you want me to do to you, babydoll."

Daijah sexily leered at their reflection, resting her hand atop of his, guiding Xander back into her ocean. She directed his fingers to play at her clit before she continued her delegation, supervising the pressure and pace against her pussy. After an extended moment under her control, Xander regained conduction, plunging two fingers into her sex while fondling her ass. Guaranteed to produce a salacious scream. As if on cue, Daijah screeched.

"X!" She summoned.

The turbulence disturbing her core was overwhelming. That deliciously violent orgasm crippled her, legs trembling and weak. Xander picked her up, wedding style, carrying her across the house into the master bedroom. He wasted absolutely zero time, removing his clothes at warp speed. Daijah rested on the bed delightfully naked. She giggled, reminiscing on the last time Xander stripped in front of her.

"Say his name, babydoll." He sexily grinned, stroking the mass circumference of his magnificent dick. Yes, it was monstrous, but it was a beautiful beast. Carefully sculpted, perfectly patterned plump veins - in a word, immaculate.

Daijah licked her lips.

"Hey big man." She giggled, desperately wanting to taste the sweet and salty goodness against her palate. But Xander had other plans.

Tugging Daijah to the edge of the bed, his dick was perfectly angled to take immediate residency within her soaked treasure walls. Inch by inch, he filled her to capacity. Xander gradually procured her sensitive pussy in deliberate, purposeful strokes. After almost a year of unwelcomed celibacy, the pleasure outweighed the satisfying suffering as Daijah winced in pain, yet enthusiastically stretched to meet his girthy demand.

"Xan. I can't-" She mumbled breathlessly, arms flailing, reaching for nonexistent shit.

"You can't what, babydoll? You don't want your *hey big man* dick?" He teased, never ceasing the divine thrashing of her puss.

She audibly whined. A single tear slowly released.

"No bullshit, baby. Do you want me to stop? Talk to me Daijah."

"No. Xan, please don't stop. Fuck, I've missed you." Daijah fervently sobbed tears of joy and relief.

Xander's sluggish, yet expeditiously rhythmic pace felt like miracles and blessings from heaven. Hitting every corner and crevice of her pussy, he granted her his dick unselfishly. Gazing deeply into misty quartz orbs, whispering *I love you baby* as they admired each other's making love faces. Repeatedly and methodically thrusting at the most alluring cadence, torrent tears escaped as Daijah's climax peaked for the second time.

"Oh my God! Mmmhhh! Xander! X! Baby, I love you so much." She sang.

Xander pleasantly pounded into her, reaching a beautiful climax of his own.

"Daijah! Babydoll, I love you." Xander gritted, burying his face into the nook of her neck. Breathless, his body was motionless, sheltering in the comfort of her warm frame. Graciously accepting the weight of his body, Daijah joyfully entangled with Xander. His stately frame repeatedly shuddered as the sensation of hot tears seamlessly streamed from his face to hers. Daijah caressed up and down his spine, massaging fingers through his hair to comfort him through his muted sobs. She breathlessly whispered.

"I see the moon, and the moon sees me."

Xander's muffled timber continued.

"God bless the moon and God bless me. I love you, Daijah."

"I love you, Xander."

13

"Mmmhhh, Xan. Baby, what are you -" Daijah's impending inquiry was quickly discontinued when Xander settled his heated mouth against her smooth bud. He tongue-kissed the mouth of her pussy like it was the sweetest thing on earth. Twisting, turning, licking to the lyrical rhythm they produced with their melodious moans. Daijah propped up on her elbows, slightly arching her back to get a better view. She didn't know if he was spelling her name, singing a song, or reciting the Pledge of Allegiance in her pussy but the shit was lethal. Xander pushed her back onto the bed, lifting thickalicious thighs to rest on his shoulders. He delivered unyielding, sloppy kisses to her private lips, eliciting a guttural tremor in the pit of her belly. Daijah was convinced that Xander was on a rescue mission. He clearly lost something in her pussy last night that was buried in the cavernous depths of her ocean and he was refusing to relent until it was located.

"X. X. X!" She yelped, fisting the shits, clenching her thighs around his head.

Xander was smothering, but he cradled her clit in his mouth, retaining possession until her climax peaked then unhurriedly descended.

"Oh my God, Xander, I'm still cumming." She whined and squirmed uncontrollably. "Baby, what is that? Shit."

"Ecstasy." Xander hissed, lustfully licking his lips. "Good morning, babydoll."

Daijah was knocked out asleep before the word *baby* left his lips.

About an hour later, Daijah awakened to a mushy mess between her legs. She smiled, recalling the morning goodness Xander delivered. She heard his raspy baritone on the phone.

"So, you still gone fuck me up, Z?" Xander laughed. "Nah, she's asleep. I promise you Daij is good. Where's my Kitten?" He paused, seemingly receiving an answer to his question. "Tell her Mommy and Daddy will be there shortly."

Daijah remained hushed but she couldn't quell the smile on her face hearing him assign the title of *daddy*. Once he hung up, Daijah stretched her thick, curvy body to lay on his chest.

"Good morning, Xan."

"Good afternoon, Daij." Xander chuckled.

"Afternoon? Oh my God, what time is it? We gotta go get Reign." She jolted, naked frame minimally concealed by the silken white sheet.

"Calm down, I already talked to Zaria and Kitten is good. Her Uncle Sim fed her eggs and now they're playing. His big ass ain't nothing but a big kid."

Daijah nodded, still cuddling against his chest. She listened to the soothing pound of his heartbeat as they settled in comfortable silence for a long minute.

"Xan, can I ask you a question and you promise you will tell me the truth?"

"Yes." He confidently stated. No hesitation.

"Why are you listed on a bank account that Roman created for me and Reign?"

He paused, glancing down at her. Curiously nervous eyes greeted him.

"How do you know about that?" He asked.

"Nah, big head. I'm asking the questions. Xan, you promised the truth."

Xander tossed his hands up in surrender.

"Roman came to me a few months before Reign was born saying that men like me and him need extra protection and insurance for the people we love. He gave me a folder with the banking information and instructions on how to get the funds released if anything ever happened to him. He asked me if I would take care of you and Reign if shit popped off. I gave him my word."

"But you didn't have the money released. The bank called me yesterday to settle the account." Her brow furrowed.

"I gave him my word on taking care of you and Reign. I never said I was going to do that with his fucking money. I can take care of y'all with my own shit. I don't need help from no nigga. I never reviewed the contents of the folder again...even after I found out he was dead."

"Roman knew something was going on. He made all these plans as if he knew some shit wasn't right."

"Looks that way to me." Xander agreed.

"What should I do, Xan?" Her big eyes peered at him.

"Do whatever you think is right, Daijah. You know I got you. But if you want to get the money and stack it for Reign - do that. But I don't want nor need that shit to take care of my family."

Daijah's eyes filled with tears at the mention of his family. This was certainly not the way she desired to make a family with Xander, but she would make the best out of the situation. If she could snap and have Roman alive, she would for Reign's sake.

"What am I going to tell her, Xan. About her father? How do I tell her this tragic story?"

"Focus on the triumph and not the tragedy. Tell her that he loved her. Probably gave his life to protect her. She only had him for two months but do everything in your power to keep his memory alive within her, Daij." He shrugged.

"That is what I would want for my seed. But trust me when I say this, Reign is never going to want for a father. It may not be blood, but I'm her daddy as long as I have breath in my body." Xander firmly exclaimed.

Daijah nestled her face into his broad expanse.

"You are something special, Xander Kindred. Thank you."

THE ONLY WAY Daijah could describe the last month with Xander was blissful. He'd always been attentive and caring but his recent behavior had been utterly solicitous. Courting Daijah as if they were teenagers. Special flower deliveries, romantic dinners, jewelry, designer bags - it was a bit exorbitant, but she knew her complaining would be in vain because Xander was going to do whatever the hell he wanted. Daijah was the happiest she'd been in a very long time. She had a beautiful baby girl who was growing like a weed and she had her man. Xander was the manifestation of undreamt dreams. Everything that was righteous and good with the universe resided in the depths of his eyes. Loving moments when he didn't know she was watching, Daijah simply admired the beauty of him. Even his flaws and imperfections were magnificent. Loving Xander meant accepting him as was, so Daijah was receiving a crash course in navigating the intricacies of Xan versus X.

The August heat was sweltering, downright homicidal. The streets and parks were ghostly because it was simply too hot for outdoor activities. It was Daijah's twenty-sixth birthday and she was awakened by the cutest little fingers and toes cuddling her face.

"Ma-ma." Reign sang as she planted sloppy kisses on Daijah's cheeks.

"Good morning, Reign-bow bright. Are you giving mommy messy kisses?" She tickled her chubby thighs and Reign fell out on the bed in a fit of giggles.

"I see somebody is playing possum. Acting like she was asleep when I laid her in the bed. Kitten be phony." Xander guffawed, joining them on the bed.

"Good morning, babydoll. Happy birthday." He feverishly kissed her. Almost forgetting that the little one was watching until Reign wanted a kiss too.

"Thank you, love." Daijah blushed.

"Your bath water is hot and ready and I'll bring you coffee and breakfast. We need to leave no later than one o'clock. I'll get lil chunky mama over here dressed." He nibbled against Reign's toes, causing her to howl in laughter.

Daijah had no clue what was happening today but she was going with the flow. Xander bought her a sexy backless floral print sundress to wear and he'd packed a bag for yet another unknown destination for tonight. Stepping into the steamy hot water, Daijah audibly moaned. The past month had been a whirlwind. In addition to settling the account at the bank, Daijah was studying for the Missouri bar exam and she signed a consulting contract with the non-profit agency where she interned. She didn't realize how much she enjoyed employment and equity law until her internship so it became her niche. The agency recommended her for another consulting opportunity and now Daijah was on her way to securing three consulting contracts. The Duvall Group was coming to fruition faster than she anticipated.

Xander delivered her breakfast, resting the plate and coffee cup on the bath table positioned across the jetted tub. He perched on the bench next to the tub, lustfully smirking at her.

"What?" She coyly questioned, taking a bite of the bagel.

"Nothing, babydoll. I can't admire your beauty?"

She nodded, blushing.

"Can I give you a bath?" He nibbled the corner of those luscious ass lips.

"Bae, where is Reign?"

"Miriam is watching her. She's good." He paused, moving the bench closer to the tub. "Can I bathe you, babydoll?"

Xander rendered her breathless daily. All she could muster was a nod.

He retrieved the bath sponge from the ledge, soaking it with champagne-vanilla scented body wash. Xander cleansed Daijah from the crown of her head down to her pretty white painted toes. But not without making a pit stop at the apex of her curvy thighs. He massaged, tickled, fondled, and fingered her into joyful oblivion. If this was the start of her birthday celebration, then Daijah was confident twenty-six was going to be an amazing year.

A few hours later, they headed out of the house to the undisclosed location. Xander was practically drooling when Daijah ambled out of the bedroom wearing the dress he picked. The white backless halter dress with hints of light and charcoal grey flowers fit perfectly like a layer of skin. Her thick chocolate curls pulled up in a big puff and makeup flawlessly applied. Daijah beamed when she saw that Reign was wearing a sundress matching the floral pattern. Identical chocolate curls tamed by a matching bow. Reign was a gorgeous baby.

During the almost forty minute drive, Xander rested his hand on Daijah's thigh that played peek-a-boo through the deep split in her dress. They arrived in the Grover Heights area, a neighboring community to Pleasant Pines. Pulling up to an industrial building, Daijah was confused by their fancy attire. This place called for shorts, a t-shirt, and Jordan's. Reminding herself to go with the flow, Daijah remained hushed. Xander picked up a sleeping Reign from her car seat and settled her in the stroller before they meandered to the front door. There was no visibility inside because the doors and windows were covered with brown paper. Opening the door, Daijah was greeted with a collective yelp of "surprise." Family, neighborhood friends, and former classmates gathered at cocktail and dinner tables draped with lavender satin cloth with grey and silver accents. Waiters dressed in black and white held silver trays lined with champagne flutes, wine glasses, and hor d'oeuvres. Food stations were spread throughout the space and a full bar sat against the farthest wall. The space looked like a refurbished office building that was beautifully decorated for the party.

Daijah swiftly turned to Xander with dewy eyes. This man never ceased to amaze her.

"Happy birthday, babydoll." He kissed her temple.

"I love you, Xan." She blushed, swiping her thumb across his lips to remove the Fenty gloss.

"I love you more."

The party was spectacular. Outstanding food, delicious drinks, and the neighborhood DJ never disappointed. Daijah danced herself right out of her four inch Christian Louboutin heels.

"Aye. Aye. Can I have everyone's attention please?" Xander's sexy voice reverberated through the microphone.

Daijah was across the room laughing with Zaria.

"Uh oh, bitch. This might be it." Zaria squealed.

"What?" Daijah's brows furrowed.

"A proposal, dummy." Zaria scowled. "Here, put on some lipstick. You can't be looking bogus when that big ass rock hits your finger."

"Girl, shut up. That is not about to happen -"

"Birthday girl. Can you join me over here?" Xander crooked his finger, beaconing her to come closer.

Oh, shit. Daijah nervously mused. Zaria gave her a little nudge to loosen the shackles that momentarily restrained her feet. Swallowing hard, she sauntered in his direction. Xander kissed her neck before he spoke.

"Babydoll, we have shared our hopes and dreams with each other since we were kids. You have persevered through unthinkable trials. Undergraduate degree with honors, law degree with honors, and let's not forget the fact that she crossed the stage eleven days before giving birth to that beautiful little girl over there." He adoringly motioned to Reign. "For as long as I can remember, my goal has been to erase your nightmares and make your dreams come true. So..." His voice trailed off, handing her an envelope. "Here's to phase four of your new beginnings."

Daijah's eyes darted from Xander to the envelope sporadically. Hands trembling, she pulled the prongs to unseal the package. She nervously revealed a document, frantically roving her eyes over the words, *"Property Deed declaring legal ownership of commercial property at 102 - 106 Forest Park Place to Daijah Blu Duvall."*

"What the fu -" She paused. "I mean, what in the world? Xan, bae, are you serious?"

He nodded.

"This?" Daijah circled her finger in the air. "This building is mine?"

"Yeah, babydoll. You own this shit. Come on so you can do the honors." Xander grasped her hand, ushering her to the window to remove the paper. Daijah ripped through the heavy brown material, revealing a logo imprinted on the window, *The Duvall Group*. She collapsed her face into the palms of her hands, blissfully wailing. The crowd cheered and celebrated as Xander cradled her.

"Xander Kindred, you are something special, baby." Daijah firmly, lovingly cupped his face, passionately kissing him as if no one was watching. Xander's steely erection was becoming ever present.

'Shit, Daij.' He mouthed.

"Aye! Y'all ain't gotta go home, but we're about to get the hell up outta here." Xander guffawed.

Even Reign clapped and cheered with laughter. After gathering Reign's things for her to spend the night with Ms. Mimi and Aunt Germaine, Xander walked them to the chauffeured car he'd arranged to drive them back to Ms. Mimi's house. Daijah gawked in awe of the crescent moon shaped logo branding her company - her dream. Xander leaned against the door admiring her astonishment.

"We'll take a tour of the other spaces in a few days once the painting is done." Xander said, drawing Daijah from her haze.

"I can't believe you did this. That you even remembered the conversations. Thank you, Xan. Truly, from the bottom of my heart, I appreciate the way you love me."

Xander swallowed hard.

"We good, Daij."

"We good, Xan."

14

Xander and Daijah spent a euphoric evening at the Four Seasons Hotel. They rapturously assaulted each other from the moment they crossed the threshold of the presidential suite overlooking the city. Making passionate, ravishing, mind-altering love repeatedly with the incandescent lights of the cityscape as their backdrop. Daijah demonstrated her gratitude for her man in the car, the kitchen, the shower, while Xander delivered her birthday licks against a few walls, on the balcony, in the lounge chair - exploring every square inch of the hotel suite.

"Good morning, babydoll." Xander's morning timbre was deep and glazed with satisfied haziness after he awakened to Daijah's glorious lips, sprinkling kisses against his morning manhood.

"Good morning, love." Daijah slyly blushed. "You hungry?"

"Mmmhhh, I could eat."

"I ordered room service, so we should get showered." That lustful sneaky grin returned. Daijah was insatiable. Unable to get enough of his lasciviously tasty *hey big man* dick.

"Daij." He grunted. "Baby, I need to take care of some business today and you need to pick up Reign."

She pouted.

"To be continued. I promise." Xander kissed her temple. They showered and dressed before the room service arrived. Simeon was on his way to pick up Xander so Daijah could take his truck to get Reign.

"I should be no later than five. I'll bring dinner, ok?" Xander leaned into the driver side of his Range Rover to kiss her. She nodded as they exchanged endearments.

Daijah ran a few errands before picking up Reign, including Ms. Mimi's request for Chinese food. "Daijah Blu, please don't forget your uncle's shrimp St. Paul and peach Vess." Mimi's loud voice boomed through the car speakers.

"I know Mimi. I've only been ordering y'all Chinese food since grade school." Daijah rolled her eyes.

A couple hours later she pulled into the driveway at her grandma's house a little after three o'clock. Gathering up the grease-stained food bags and a few grocery bags, Daijah trekked to the front door. Unable to reach her key, she rang the doorbell but no answer. After a few attempts, she rested the bags on the patio to retrieve her key. Daijah unlocked the door then scooped up the bags to enter the unusually quiet house. Closing the door with her foot, she peered around, yelling.

"Hey, where is everybody? Grandma? Aunt Germaine? Uncle Bean, can you help me with the bags please?" No response.

Daijah advanced further into the dim house when she felt a rugged, scaly, overpowering hand around her neck, choking her from behind. She screamed, fighting, and scratching - flailing her body, causing the bags to fly from her grasp, spilling food throughout the foyer.

"Shut the fuck up or I swear I will kill you, Daijah." The glisten of the large silver knife ceased the struggle. The strained voice was eerily familiar.

Daijah glanced around looking for signs of life but she couldn't see past the entryway. The attacker forced her further into the living where she eyed her Uncle Bean bound by the hands and feet with tape over his mouth. He muffled obscenities, vainly attempting to break free from the restraints. Ms. Mimi and Aunt Germaine were perched on the couch struggling against the hand restraints with tears and fear invading every inch of their faces.

"Where is Reign? Where is my baby?" Daijah immediately questioned. "Reign. Baby girl?" She shouted.

The attacker cupped his filthy, trembling hands over her mouth. The knife was threateningly close to her face.

"That fucking baby of yours is sleep. Shut the fuck up and she won't get hurt."

Daijah continued to process the tenor of the voice. The slight southern twang played like scary music in her ear. *Roland Strong.*

Pushing her across the room onto the couch, Daijah assessed her grandma and aunt to ensure they were not injured. She mouthed, *"are you ok? Is Reign, ok?"* They nervously nodded in unison.

Roland's menacing frame hysterically paced the length of the floor. His solid athletic build and chocolate eyes were ghostly familiar, mirroring Roman's. His eyes were bloodshot red and bulged as he mumbled incomprehensibly to himself. Daijah spotted a gun strapped on his hip as he fisted the knife handle in his hand. So many things were circulating through her head. She'd just talked to Mimi and everything was fine. How long had he been there? What did Roland want? Why her family?

Daijah met Roman's second oldest brother, Roland, once at their mother's house for dinner and then a second time when he picked up Roman to leave for Charlotte in February. To her knowledge, Roland was the last person to see Roman alive. Known to be a troublemaker, Roland was a manipulator and drug addict. It was clear that he was high off of something at the moment. Daijah couldn't remember if she put her phone in her back pocket so she slowly shifted in her seat attempting to reach for her pocket.

"Don't fucking move, Daijah." Roland abruptly closed the distance, waving the knife in her face.

"Can I please check on my baby?" Daijah assessed the space to find an escape.

"No."

"What do you want, Roland?" She indignantly questioned.

"You remember me, huh?" Roland had the nerve to smile as if it was an honor.

"How could I forget? You and Roman could be twins."

Roland paused, eyes affixed on nothing, but saddened. "Don't talk about my brother to me."

"Well, what do you want to talk about, Roland?" Daijah surveyed the room, devising a plan of attack. She was ready to die to protect her daughter.

"Where's the money, Daijah?"

"What money, Roland?"

"I know Roman left you a lump sum of money. And don't fucking lie to me."

"You're wrong. He didn't leave me any money. Roman started a trust for Reign but I don't control it and can't access it in a lump sum."

"How much?" Daijah didn't respond, carefully contemplating her response.

"Like $5000." She lied, testing to determine what he knew. Roland was an addict so this was likely about getting access to more drugs.

"Fuck! If he would've just given me the money, I wouldn't have had to do any of this shit." Roland returned to pacing the floor, frantically banging a fist to his head.

Daijah's eyes widened. Did he just admit to killing his own brother?

———————

Xander and Simeon ambled into his house a little after six o'clock with barbeque and fried chicken. Daijah's car wasn't in the driveway so he assumed she parked in the garage. Entering the kitchen, the house was hushed.

"Daij. I'm sorry I'm late, babydoll. I brought dinner." He announced, placing the food on the oversized marble kitchen island.

No response.

Xander walked into the living room and it was undisturbed, no evidence of Reign's toys. He journeyed across the house to the master bedroom thinking they were napping. Nothing.

He retrieved the phone from his pocket and auto-dialed her number. The call went straight to voicemail. He called again and again. No answer.

"Yo, bro. Call Ms. Mimi's house. She's probably still there. You know they get to talking and Mimi probably cooked some shit better than this barbeque." Simeon chortled.

Xander was listening but something in his gut didn't feel right. He dialed Ms. Mimi's cell phone and house phone and they both rang unanswered. After trying Aunt Germaine and Uncle Bean's numbers, Xander called his brother Adonis.

"What's up, X?"

"Aye, are you on Cannon?" Xander's hardened tone concerned Adonis.

"Nah, I'm downtown. What's up?"

"Have you talked to Daijah?"

"Not since earlier after y'all left the hotel. X, bro, what's up? What's going on?"

"I don't know. She's not answering her phone and neither is Mimi, Aunt G, or Bean. My instincts are telling me something is wrong."

There was an extended moment of silence on the call.

"You still got somebody watching Mimi's house?" Adonis nervously asked.

"Yeah, I text that nigga Jah, but he ain't hit me back yet." Xander paused. "Some shit ain't right. Meet us at Cannon." He ordered.

. . .

REIGN'S ringing cries jolted everyone in the house from the reverie. No words had been spoken for over an hour. Roland transitioned from frantically pacing to frightening immobile. He glared down the hall towards Daijah's old bedroom where Reign was sleeping.

"I don't want no bullshit out of you or I swear you will watch every one of them die. Do you understand?" Roland threatened with the knife in Daijah's face. She swallowed hard, then nodded.

He harshly guided Daijah to the back of the house. Entering the bedroom, Reign was standing up in her crib, anticipating a familiar face to appear and retrieve her.

"Ma-ma. Ma-ma." Reign bounced with excitement. Daijah's heart fiercely pounded from panic and relief. She smiled, tightly embracing her baby girl, surveying her body.

"I didn't do shit to her. Come on. Hurry up and grab her lil ass." Roland commanded. He suddenly paused his pursuit, gazing at Reign. Daijah enfolded her tighter, unsure of his next move.

"She smiles just like RJ." Roland practically whispered.

"Yeah, she does. Their dimples are identical." Daijah kissed Reign's cheek. "Roland, can I change her diaper first?"

He nodded, blankly staring.

Returning to the living with Reign closely in tow, Daijah repositioned on the couch. The Chinese food and groceries remained sprawled on the floor. She was becoming restless with the whole situation. Daijah felt trapped, the dusky, filthy abandoned car washed flashed before her like lightning. She shuddered, ready to relent, to throw in the towel. Peering at her family, Reign was oblivious but clutching her tight; Ms. Mimi was weak and needed to eat so she could take her medicine; Aunt Germaine looked like she was ready to fight and risk it all; and Uncle Bean's fiery orbs were murderous. Daijah deeply inhaled, rejecting any moments of fragility or angst determined to protect her family. This was not going to end well because Daijah Duvall was not going down without a fight.

"Roland, what is your plan? Please, just tell us what you want so we can figure this out." Daijah pleaded.

"I need that money. If I don't get that money, I'm dead. If RJ would've just given me the money, signed over the properties, I wouldn't -" His voice trailed off.

"You wouldn't what, Roland?" She paused, tears welling in her eyes. "Did you kill Roman?" Daijah's voice cracked, but she remained strong.

Roland angrily glared at her for at least five minutes and she returned the fiery leer. His demonous glare became misty, expression momentarily laced with remorse.

"I had no other choice." Roland confessed whisperingly.

"He wouldn't give me the money. I owe these niggas two hundred and fifty g's. I thought Roman was going to sign over the building my family still owns in Charlotte so I could sell it. But he changed his mind. Told me I needed to work just like everybody else in the family and he couldn't save me anymore. Gave me some bullshit about needing to be there for his family. He fucking left me in Charlotte to be killed. Like he didn't give a fuck about me. But I followed him back to give him one more chance. That nigga looked at me like I was pathetic, like I was fucking simple. I didn't want to shoot him. But he gave me no other choice." Roland's eyes were terrifyingly devilish, inhumane.

"So, the way I see it, this shit is your fault, Daijah. If it wasn't for him falling in love with your ass and having that damn baby, he would be alive today." He callously spewed.

Muted tears burned through Daijah's crystalized orbs. She recalled arguing with Roman about his brother. Angrily rejecting his attempts for love and intimacy before he left for Charlotte. Constantly burdened by the regret she carried, Daijah's heart wrenched to discover that he was ready to prioritize his family over his brother.

"He was your little brother. Roman took up for you when you didn't deserve it. He was willing to do anything to support you,

Roland. And *you killed him* - in cold blood! You left him to rot in an abandoned building like he was *nothing* - like a fucking animal!" Daijah screamed violently, unphased by Reign's cries.

"But he *was* something, Roland, and he deserved better than what you gave him. Roman was your mother's son, my friend, and this little girl's daddy. Reign will never understand how much her daddy loved her. She was his Reign-bow, his princess. Roman was ecstatic the day she was born. She will never understand how he laid awake at night just admiring what he created. How he kissed her a thousand times before he left that day with you. Roland, *you* stole the possibility of more memories from her. And now you're ready to have more blood on your hands." Daijah shook her head, disgusted as she sighed in disbelief.

"Shut up! Just shut the fuck up!" He shouted, with his hand on his gun.

Reign shuddered, immediately bursting into tears as she clutched Daijah's neck tighter.

It was almost nine o'clock. Daijah, Ms. Mimi, and her aunt silently prayed that they would be safely delivered from this ordeal. Roland was becoming more and more unraveled as time ticked by and the drugs began to wear thin. He allowed restroom visits and Daijah picked up the snacks from the floor so her family could have something to eat. Reign cried for Xander.

"Xa-xa. Xa-xa." She was inconsolable. Daijah cradled her, crying because she wanted Xander too. They all just literally sat in agonizing silence, keeping a keen eye on Roland.

A soft knock sounded from the back of the house, seemingly from Daijah's room. Roland roused, demanding that everyone shut up when nobody was talking. The faint knock sounded again. Daijah and Ms. Mimi instantly locked eyes, recalling the familiar sound when Xander would knock on the bedroom window. Daijah audibly exhaled, closing her eyes, praying Xander figured out her location.

"Yo, X. I'm sorry man. My girl was tripping and I had to handle that. I'm at y'all old house now." Jah, one of Xander's lookouts, explained. He'd always had someone watching Daijah and Mimi's house, even when she no longer lived there.

"What was happening at Mimi's before you left?" Xander asked from the passenger seat as Simeon sped down the expressway to get to Cannon Street.

"Ms. Mimi and her sister were sitting on the porch with baby girl for a little while. They went into the house after their brother arrived. Daijah showed up about two hours later and her car is still in the driveway. I'm walking that way now." Jah was quiet for a second as he walked down the street. "Somebody else is in the house. He's too tall to be her uncle, but the nigga is just pacing back and forth in front of the living room window. You want me to check it out?"

"Nah, sit tight and watch the house. Don't let them leave. I'm pulling up in ten minutes." Xander instructed.

"Who the fuck could that be? We ain't beefing with nobody." Simeon inquired.

"I told y'all that Roman Strong shit wasn't over." Xander aggressively balled his fists. "Whoever the fuck it is...I swear to God. If he hurts anybody in that house, I'm fucking burning this city down until I find every mutherfucka responsible."

"We got you bro. What's the plan?" Simeon questioned.

Xander and Simeon arrived at their house on Cannon Street right when Adonis pulled up. Jah was parked on the street across from Ms. Mimi's house. The brothers casually strolled into their childhood home like they normally would, trying not to look suspicious just in case somebody else was surveilling the area. Xander called Jah to get an update.

"Yo, X. You ain't gone believe this shit." Jah muttered.

"What's up Jah? What happened?" Xander anxiously probed.

"That nigga finally opened the curtain to look out of the window.

It's Roland Strong, dawg. Roman's older brother. My girl gets her hair done at their sister's shop *Gemini* and I've seen him over there begging a few times. He's a feign, dawg, but is into some gambling shit too. Looks like he has a weapon but I couldn't tell if it was a gun."

"Fuck!" Xander bellowed.

"I did see Mimi and Daijah but couldn't see anyone else." Jah said. "What do you need me to do?"

"Alright. Me and Sim are going to go through the back from the alley. D is going to use his key to open the front door once we give the signal that Roland's punk ass is out of the living room. Him and Ram are going to get everybody out of the house. Jah, call the clean-up crew because I need this nigga to disappear when I'm done with his ass."

"WHAT THE FUCK IS THAT? Is somebody coming over here?" Roland whisper-yelled. "Who the fuck is at the back door?"

"It could be my neighbor coming to pick up her cake." Mimi lied.

The knocking continued as Roland started to move towards the hallway leading to the back of the house.

"If anybody fucking moves, I will kill you." He threatened. Roland held the knife in one hand while holding the gun in the other.

Once Roland was out of sight, Uncle Bean signaled for Daijah to try to untie him. She gently and quietly laid Reign in Ms. Mimi's arms. Hands trembling, she nervously untied the rope at his hands and feet while she continually peered over her shoulder. Suddenly, the front door slowly creaked. Daijah heavily gasped, quickly covering her mouth. Everyone's eyes widened anticipating who was entering the house. The oxygen was snatched from her body when Daijah saw her brother and Hiram come around the corner with their guns drawn. Adonis held a finger up to his mouth demanding that they keep quiet. Daijah grabbed a sleeping Reign then helped her grandma and aunt to their feet.

Pow! Pow! Pow! Three shots were fired and then a loud violent commotion ensued. Mimi and Aunt Germaine screamed as Uncle Bean practically pushed them out of the house.

"Move, move, move." Hiram ordered. Jah was outside with the truck running ready to help the two older women into the car. Adonis grabbed Reign from Daijah and quickly steered her to Xander's truck.

"Daijah, where are your keys?" Adonis sternly questioned.

"On the table in the living room." She cried. "Doni, where's Xander?" Daijah trembled at the realization that Xander could be shot.

"Daijah, no questions. Go with Ram." Adonis said as he strapped Reign into her carseat.

"But what about you? What about Xan? Simeon?" She sobbed as Hiram shoved her into the back seat of the truck.

"Daij! We don't have time for this shit. It's being handled. We gotta get the fuck outta here. Let's go!" Hiram shouted. He protectively eyed Adonis before bumping fists.

Daijah noiselessly cried as she observed her beautiful baby girl peacefully sleep through the explosive ruckus. The car ride felt bizarrely similar to the night she was ushered from Roman's condo to learn he'd been killed. Sickened by the thought of losing Xander, she wildly searched for the window controls, requiring air immediately.

"Daij, he's gone be good. X just got you back in his life, he ain't leaving you this soon. Not like that." Hiram's soothing timbre offered minimal ease but calmed the queasiness, nonetheless.

Hiram entered the code to enter the gate at Xander's home. It was after midnight and Daijah was an exhausted nervous wreck. Ambling into the house, she peered around, thankful that she and her daughter were unharmed but terrified that Xander's stately, loving presence would no longer fill this space.

"Daij, Jah took Mimi and your uncle to Aunt Germaine's house. I'm gonna head back to Cannon. You sure you're good?" She slowly nodded. Eyes affixed on nothing but heavy laden.

"We'll call you as soon as we can. I promise." Hiram kissed her forehead and then his niece.

· · ·

As soon as Hiram left, Reign howled to the top of her lungs for Xander. Refusing a bottle, she wanted to breastfeed. Daijah meandered into the master bedroom, immediately immersed in his sweet and spicy sandalwood fragrance that circulated the room. Reign was even familiar with his scent. Her big bright eyes peered around in search of her *Xa Xa*. Daijah decided to take a shower to calm her and babygirl. After undressing them both, Daijah and Reign perched on the built-in shower bench while breastfeeding. They inhaled the soothing lavender aroma from the shower tablet, momentarily calming Reign.

Daijah lotioned and dressed her daughter before dressing herself. Reign was still a little fussy nibbling on Cheerios while cuddling with her elephant. Daijah checked her phone every other second, praying Xander or somebody would call with an update.

2:07am. Daijah roused, she'd fallen asleep snuggled next to Reign. Peering throughout the familiar earth-tones hued bedroom, she lengthened her arm, hopeful to feel Xander occupying the king sized bed. But his space was empty. She perched on the edge of the bed eyeing the couch in front of the patio doors where they'd spent sleepless nights talking, cuddling, and making love. It was vacant. Daijah quietly traipsed out of bed, careful not to disturb Reign. The full moon lured through the window, summoning her to diminish the air between them. Pressing her forehead against the glass door, Daijah mutedly prayed, "please God. Let him be ok." In a daze, she settled there for countless minutes beholding the solitude and tranquility the moon gifted her for the past several years.

"I see the moon and the moon sees me. God bless the moon and God bless me."

Daijah's thirst was quenched by the sultry nurture of his resonant husky vocals.

"Daijah." Xander breathily bayed her name as if it was oxygen. He practically sprinted to her, wasting not another second.

She was speechless, exhaling the terror wedged in her core while inhaling *him*. Tears suffocated her rosy face, quartz orbs swollen from hours of intense wailing.

"Babydoll, are you ok?" Xander caressed the arc of her face, rubbing his thumb across her lips as she desperately kissed his flesh. Daijah rested her head in the nook of his chest, muting the deafening shriek that tormented her body.

Xander picked up Reign from the bed and cuddled her for an extended heartbeat. Surprisingly, she didn't stir as he rested her in the portable crib. Although Daijah already showered, she didn't hesitate when Xander asked her to join him. She bathed his Herculean frame from head to toe. Cleansing his hair, scrubbing his back, washing his feet - thoroughly purifying every gallant portion.

Xander nestled behind her, his magnificently elongated erection pressed against her ass. Both hands vainly gripping the shower wall, Daijah arched her back readying herself to enthusiastically receive the full measure of him. Eagerly, yet carefully, Xander slid the head of his titanic dick up and down and up and down the mouth of her saturated puss before resting on her clit.

"Xan, please. I need to feel you."

Xander didn't need an invitation, he drove knee deep into the depths of her womb. Stroking, pounding, thrashing, he rested his massive hands on the small of her back controlling the rhythm as her bodacious ass plunged into him. They harmoniously hummed, drinking the sounds of their unified satisfaction. The delicious ache residing between their legs was exquisitely torturous. His dick fervently feasted on her pussy until their uninhibited hunger was fulfilled.

Xander was restless as he gazed down at Daijah and Reign nestled in the comforts of his chest. He released the breath that was rooted in his throat all night. Avenging Daijah was his life's work, mercilessly willing to eliminate anything and anyone who sought to harm her. He meditated on the melodious hum of his two heart beats tranquil breaths. Just like the night he crawled from the basement on Cannon

Street, a murderous calm coated his psyche and Xander drifted to sleep, like a baby.

DAIJAH GIDDILY STRETCHED, receptive to the luminant sun, she smiled as she repositioned to embrace her two loves. But the bed was extremely lonely. She peered across the room to the couch, but no Xander or Reign. Grabbing her phone from the nightstand, Daijah noticed a note that read, "follow the Reign drops." She creased her brow, glancing down at the floor to see a trail of Reign's toys leading out of the bedroom. Daijah giggled, curious about what Xander was up to. She quickly washed her face and brushed her teeth before following the pathway that landed her at the threshold of her original bedroom in Xander's home. Daijah and Reign had been camping out in Xander's room since the night they officially rekindled their life-long flame.

Slowly opening the door, she was greeted by the most beautiful dreamsicle-toned bedroom with etchings of elephants and unicorns dressing the walls. A white four poster canopy bed, matching dresser and nightstands settled in the space where Daijah's bed used to be. A life size doll house complete with steps and a slide sat against the wall near the patio doors filling the glorious space. The words *Reign Imani* were scripted on the wall above the crib. The room was absolutely stunning.

"Xan, baby, what is all of this?" Daijah curiously questioned.

Reign was attentively following the train that circled the middle of her new play area. She gazed up at Daijah and immediately beamed with a glowing smile.

"This is Kitten's new room." He uttered, playfully tickling Reign's feet as she crawled by.

"What? Why?" Daijah stuttered, joining them on the floor. Xander parted his legs, encouraging her to sit with him.

"It was another part of your birthday gift. I had it decorated that day since we were spending the night at the hotel. The plan was to surprise you and Reign when we got home, but...change of plans." He lifted an eyebrow.

"Daijah, I wasn't bullshittin' when I said this is your home. You and Reign are my family. And I wanted her to have a space that she could grow into. A room fit for a princess." Xander wrapped his arms around Daijah, kissing against her neck.

"It's beautiful, Xan. And Reign-bow clearly loves it because she is not fooling with me this morning." Daijah chuckled, squeezing Xander tighter.

"Daijah, look at me." Xander's voice was suddenly laced with seriousness. She adjusted her position to face him, crisscrossing her thick legs.

"Our lives haven't been perfect and I've done some foul shit. But the one and only thing I've ever gotten right in my life is you. And three times now, I thought I lost you forever. Life is too damn short to waste time not doing what you love - and babydoll, I absolutely love you. Daijah, I want you *now*, not later when we think we've figured out what this could be. Life may not gift us the space or time to figure it out so I want you to be a partner in my trials, and triumphs - my complications and resolutions."

Daijah quivered through a sigh, pointlessly endeavoring to silence the cry that was brewing in her gut.

"That night at my birthday party. The night you met Roman. You said that you were not a fucking Kindred. But baby, you were wrong. You've always been kindred to me. We've shared an unbreakable bond, a heart connection that will never be severed. Daijah, I've loved you since the day your pretty ass beat me climbing the tree and the shit ain't going away. I can't live another day watching you not be mine. Babydoll, will you be willing to become a fucking Kindred?" He giddily teased. "Will you marry me, Daij?"

Daijah was hushed, faint, as the train sounded, continuously circling around. A small velvet box sat on the train car. Reign snagged it and immediately guided the box to her watery mouth.

"No, Kitten. Give it to mommy. Come here Reign. Give mommy her present." Xander chortled, wrestling the box from her firm grasp.

Reign cooed and babbled with spit bubbles drooling from her pursed little lips.

"Ma-ma," she sang, reluctantly handing Daijah the box.

Still silent, Daijah opened her gift, revealing a four carat cushion halo diamond engagement ring. Her tears of joy, redemption, liberation, and peace came flooding from her beautiful irises.

"Is mommy good, Kitten?" Xander snuggled Reign as he lifted Daijah's chin to scrutinize her gorgeous sparkling eyes.

"Are we good, Daij? Is that a yes?" His gorgeous umber eyes pleaded.

"Yeah, Xan. We are so good, baby. And yes, I wanna be a fucking Kindred."

Daijah released a boisterous laugh embracing her entire world into the expanse of her arms.

EPILOGUE
A YEAR LATER, CHRISTMAS EVE

T was the night before Christmas and Reign's second birthday. Daijah showered before taking her nightly stroll through the house admiring how her life had changed in the past year. She ambled into the living room lovingly ogling Xander who was perched on the floor assembling yet another train set for him and Reign to obsess over. The child had a variety of trains through her bedroom and didn't need another. Daijah peeked into Reign's room. Ms. Mimi was sound asleep in the queen sized poster bed, while Reign slumbered in her crib across the room. Ms. Mimi wouldn't miss her great granddaughter's birthday and Christmas so she spent the night. After the situation with Roland, Daijah unsuccessfully attempted to encourage her grandmother to move from Cannon Street. Mimi refused. In her words, *'that crackhead ass nigga ain't running me away from my damn house.'* As a compromise, Mimi allowed Xander to have the entire house reconstructed before she returned, leaving no signs of the horrific night. The house was like new, including a redecorated second floor space for Uncle Bean.

Reign was soundly sleeping in the cutest Rudolph the Rednosed Reindeer pajamas. She was growing so fast - walking, talking, a few teeth, and her chocolate curls now brushed her shoulders. Daijah glanced at the picture on the nightstand that she took of Roman snuggled with Reign at only a few weeks old and smiled. Photos of the two of them were sprinkled throughout Reign's bedroom. She and Xander were committed to keeping the promise, upholding his word.

Walking back into the living room, Daijah shook her head at her husband. Xander and Daijah were married shortly after he proposed in a small, intimate ceremony on the rooftop of the Four Seasons Hotel. But not before he solidified the adoption paperwork making Reign a *fucking Kindred* too.

"Really Xan, a Christmas tree and a birthday tree? You stay doing the most." Daijah giggled.

"You're lucky you talked me out of that damn pony. Kitten would've believed it was a reindeer or even a unicorn." His expression was serious.

"You say some silly shit, Xander Kindred."

"And you love my silly shit, Daijah Kindred." Sexily blushing, she couldn't deny that he was right.

Daijah joined him on the plush rug in front of the fireplace, handing him a cup of spiked hot cocoa. Dressed in their pajamas to match Reign's, Daijah snuggled against his firm chest admiring the beautiful Christmas tree and birthday tree. Xander had Miriam decorate a small yellow artificial tree with balloons, ribbons, party favors, gifts, and a happy birthday topper. Xander was adamant about Reign having birthday parties separate from their Christmas celebrations. There was no such thing as excessive when it came to his Kitten.

"Baby, this cocoa is weak as shit. You want another shot of whiskey." He asked.

"Nah, I'm good." Daijah leaned back on the oversized pillow.

Xander poured another shot into his cup of cocoa. They rested in blissful silence for a long moment.

"Xan, can I give you one of your gifts tonight?" Daijah blurted.

"Absolutely. Especially if I can lick right where Rudolph's nose shines bright on those pajamas." He bit his lip through a lustful beam.

"Shut up, big head. Here." Daijah handed him a silver-foiled box with a red bow. He lightly shook it with a sneaky expression on his face.

Daijah was absolutely enamored with this version of Xander. She never questioned him about what happened that night because she knew Roland was dead. But something in him transformed. Consistent glimpses of the carefree, vibrant Xan she loved. Since that night, their nightmares vanished, bestowing only traces of peaceful dreams.

Xander opened the box, pulling back tissue paper, uncovering a beautiful framed photo of him, Daijah, and Reign a few months ago. He furrowed his brow, confused as to why she would gift him the same family picture that sat on their mantle. Then he took a closer look.

"What does it say, love?" Daijah sweetly inquired, sipping her cocoa.

The top of the portrait read, *Kindred Family of Four*, and on the bottom, *Baby Kindred coming June 2021.* His umber eyes glistened with joy and pride.

Xander was settled with the possibility that Daijah may not be able to get pregnant again. Reign was truly her miracle - their miracle and he wore his *girldad* honor proudly. He gazed at her for what felt like an eternity.

"Are you fucking serious, Daij?" He nervously smiled, gently resting his hand on her stomach. "Are you carrying my seed?"

"Merry Christmas, Xan." She sweetly sang.

"You good, Daddy?" Daijah was trying to read the expression painting his face.

"Hell yeah! *We* good, babydoll."

THE END.

LOVE NOTE TO MY READERS

Hey Loves! Thank you so much for reading KINDRED ~ Xander's Story. This book did not exist on my lists of book ideas. But this story came to me in a dream and from that moment on, it flowed seamlessly.

The trauma, heartbreak, love, and the power of speaking your truth are at the foundation of this sexy, passionate, urban love story. The various versions of Xander were complicated to write, but Daijah - I felt every bump and bruise on the emotional roller coaster she endured with her love triangle. Tears, pain, joy, happiness, screams, and laughter. I absolutely love the way Daijah loved Xander - unconditionally!

Let me and the world know what you think by leaving a review on Amazon or Goodreads.

Who knows when inspiration will hit me, but I foresee another Kindred brother in the future. Who's next in the KINDRED series?

The Robbi Renee Collection

- French Kiss Christmas
- Pretty Shattered Soul
- Pretty Shattered Heart
- The Love Notes Journal

Join my private ladies only Facebook Group - Love Notes.

Follow me: Facebook, Instagram, Twitter

www.lovenotesbyrobbirenee.com

MEET ROBBI RENEE

Hey Loves! I grew up in St. Louis, Missouri (in the words of Nelly, "I'm from the Lou and I'm proud!) with two incredible parents and two amazing older sisters. Being the baby of the bunch, I always had a vivid imagination and was wise beyond my years - *too grown for my own good* if you ask my mother! My love for talking too much, journaling, various genres of movies, books, and all things Oprah led me to complete a journalism degree, doing everything but being a journalist. I dishonored my childhood dreams of being in some form of entertainment and pursued every career but anything related to reading, writing or journalism.

I rekindled my love for reading and writing during the 2020 pandemic where my alter ego, Robbi Renee was born, starting my publishing company, Love Notes by Robbi Renee.

Robbi Renee draws upon personal experiences with life and love. My written works are inspired by my adoration for Black love, and stories of romance, heartache, trauma, intuition and redemption.

Stacey/Robbi Renee enjoys her own Black love story with her husband and teenage son. Don't miss what's next for Robbi Renee at www.lovenotesbyrobbirenee.com.